TRACE THE FIFTH SEASON

BY

S.R. CHRISTIE

Contents

For everyone in the trace and those who pass by.

PART ONE

1 PALE CLOUDS, SWEET THOUGHTS

MORNING

Ashaft of light pierced the grey smudge of cloud on the horizon turning the sky lemon yellow in the nascent dawn. Sunshine flashed across the ocean, dancing over low waves until it reached Mayaro on the east coast; it skipped over sugar cane fields, bush, savannah and wetlands, lifting damp mists as it travelled, until daylight finally reached the Gulf of Paria in the far west.

In Ramdass Trace, a small community deep in the south west of the country, night sounds subsided, wild hog and raccoon retreated into the dense undergrowth next to Fyzabad Road, wood smoke from the embers of a fire in a teak forest drifted by on a zephyr. A hummingbird drank nectar from the flower of a heliconia bush until it was sated. Then it rose in flight, hovered, and hurried towards the salty air of the Gulf. An early rising red butterfly floated on to the timber balustrade of the front veranda at Mr. Dhanraj's house and stayed for a long time.

Mr. Dhanraj's house occupied the plot known as number twelve Ramdass Trace, a rectangular piece of land with a cleared rear garden adjoining untouched bush. There were no fenced off boundaries, no stakes or markers of any sort. The limits of each property in the trace were not a matter of contention.

In a similar haphazard and casual manner, the numbering of the houses in the trace was also not an issue. Number twelve used to be number six, but Mr. Dhanraj had changed it two years previously because his neighbour, the widow Dookie, had decided that number eleven was a luckier number for her than number five, according to the advice of a passing pundit, and Mr. Dhanraj wanted the numbers to be sequential.

"Can't have a eleven nex' to a six", he had told his wife as he hammered rough-hewn wooden numerals onto a porch post.

Mr. Dhanraj now sat alone on the veranda as the sun rose higher and the bush began to steam. The red butterfly stretched its wings twice, then relaxed; Mr. Dhanraj would normally have marvelled at this small demonstration of the natural world that surrounded him. The actions and antics of the non-human inhabitants could always attract his interest. But not today.

The hot pipes which ran parallel to the road in front of his house began to sing and hiss as the oil from a pumpjack on the Company Road was pushed via the trace through a circuitous route to the refinery in Santa Flora. Mr. Dhanraj's wife often used to walk across to the pipes at this time of day and place newly-washed clothes on them to dry. Not today.

There would also be no stroll for Mr. Dhanraj today to the end of the trace where it joined Erin Road, the main artery from San Fernando. Mr. Dhanraj often waited at the junction for the petrol tankers to pass by, driven by his former colleagues at the refinery. He would wave to the drivers and remember long hot days in the cab as he travelled the length of Trinidad delivering petrol.

Today he stayed in his chair on the porch, waiting, waiting for the morning to pass. If his normally straight back was slightly rounded and his shoulders stooped, it was hardly noticeable. He was smartly but casually dressed, his thick grey hair combed and parted, his shoes buffed to a shine. All around him, the earlier discordant music of the trace had settled into a rhythm – the hot pipes hissed, yellow corn birds chattered in their hanging nests, ragged-edge tarmac popped and bubbled in the early morning heat. The timber framed houses eased themselves on their foundations with clicks and moans. Mr. Dhanraj sighed and noticed nothing.

At the end of the trace, Jigs Boodoosingh stopped his polished Ford in a cloud of dust, waited while his sister got out, then drove off to business at Penal Junction. Girly Boodoosingh - tall, lithe and best-suited – walked towards number twelve with a swing of the hips and a half-smile on her lips until she caught sight of her uncle on his veranda. She rearranged her thoughts and her mouth, remembering where she was and what this day meant to him.

Girly carried a brown paper bag which she held aloft as she climbed the front steps of number twelve.

"Uncle, I have breakfast for you," she called. Mr. Dhanraj managed a smile for his favourite niece but it was soon drawn back and devoured by his heavy heart.

Girly sat down on the timber framed veranda close to her uncle. He began to chew on the breakfast '*doubles*' – bara bread with channa – but it was like dust in his mouth. Words of consolation and comfort choked in Girly's throat, were still-born and faded into embarrassment. There was no-one else in the house and she knew he felt the acute pain, the emptiness of bereavement.

A long silence was interrupted by a distraction – Devendra Roopnarine appeared, walking slowly along the trace supporting his aged father on his early morning exercise. Girly leaned forward. She remembered why she had been smiling earlier. She absorbed Devendra's appearance – tall with clear-skinned Indian features, pomaded hair swept back from a faintly lined forehead. Her wave was returned with a smile, a smile that faded into a respectful bow of the head when Devendra saw Mr. Dhanraj.

Devendra stopped his father in front of the veranda. There was silence as Mr. Dhanraj stood up on the desiccated, sun-punished floorboards. Old Mr. Roopnarine spoke but was not heard; a single tear streaked his dark cheek. His mind these days was uncluttered, like an empty room with curtains drawn, his thoughts grew in dusty corners and were soon extinguished by lack of light. But he dragged an image of Sumatee Dhanraj to the front of his memory from the abyss of dementia; before it faded, he felt sadness for her demise, more sadness than he could express. Old recollections of his youth, his glory days shared with Sumatee as children and young adults in this same trace were half-formed, then gone forever. He began to edge towards the front steps, to climb them once more and sit with an old friend but Devendra led him away along the trace, past the widow Dookie who was collecting low-hanging fruit from a satsuma tree, back to their house at number three. Which used to be number ten.

Girly watched Devendra's retreating figure. Of course, the rumour might not be true, but even so...It was said that he had bought a ticket from a rum shop kiosk at Palo Seco the previous year, and returned home to erect *jhandi,* prayer flags, to his favourite Hindu god on bamboo poles in the front yard of his house. It was also rumoured that when the lottery numbers were drawn in Port of Spain, the deity had smiled upon his devotee and made him a wealthy man.

There were no outward signs of Devendra's affluence, except that the bat shit had been removed from the rafters of number three and the galvanised iron roof covering was renewed. However, Girly had heard of an extravagance that interested her greatly. Her pulse quickened at the thought of a house in Penal Rock Road behind high walls and with heavy gates to keep out the passing riff raff who peddled their cheap wares. A house with gates! Girly was not avaricious – she ran a successful business with her brother Jigs at the Penal Funeral Parlour - but the image of her occupying such a house with Devendra Roopnarine had been growing in her mind for some time. Beginning as a black and white negative, the picture was now in bright, warm colours and enhanced every time she saw Devendra or passed the vacant house.

The house was close to the Penal Funeral Parlour so it would make sense for her to vacate the cramped apartment above the Room of Rest that she shared with her brother, but still be close to the business. Jigs and Girly had assumed control of Penal's only funeral service when their parents retired to Arima where Mr. Boodoosingh could indulge his equine interests at the local race track, and Mrs. Boodoosingh could make *roti* all day long in her new kitchen without the constant distraction of the scent of embalming fluids wafting up from the parlour.

There had been discussions between Girly and Jigs about expanding the service they offered to the people of south Trinidad - an extension to the parlour would provide a larger freezer room to accommodate more cadavers, a larger ante-room would contain a greater selection of caskets. And in view of the recent failure of Sadusingh's parlour in Santa Flora (the citizens of that town were annoyingly healthy), there was less competition to worry about. The mortality rate in Penal was not high but thankfully steady and Jigs could see that there was room for expansion.

Meanwhile, Girly kept her aspirations locked inside, her dreams swept into the far corners of her fertile mind. She looked at her uncle.

"Uncle, I have to see the widow. I'll be back soon."

Mr. Dhanraj waved a limp hand and continued to stare at the wild bush opposite the house.

Girly knocked on the door of number eleven. The widow Dookie - stick thin, shrivel-lipped and heart of gold - appeared holding a bunch of feathers.

"I'm cobwebbin'", she said, by way of explanation. Girly knew the house would be spotless.

"Mrs. Dookie, I want to ask you about what happened to aunty. Uncle says you were with her."

They stepped into the living room where Girly was unsurprised to see polished floor boards, dust-free surfaces, brightly painted walls. The house was typical of those in the trace – a timber frame with metal covered roof enclosing four rooms at road level, and there was a basement room for storage that sometimes flooded in heavy rainfall. A front porch or veranda looked out on to the road; there were other houses and wild bush opposite, Erin Road at one end and the Company Road at the other.

Girly marvelled at the neatness of the house where Indira Ramnath had been born many years before, the house where she grew up with a parsimonious mother and a feckless father. She had never left. In her twenties, she met her husband. Within one year, a daughter was born and Indira, who smiled little, smiled for three days until the joy was cruelly taken away when the baby developed breathing problems and died on the fourth day. Indira's husband had wanted a traditional name for the female child – Devi or Lakshmi – but she would not hear of it. Once, Indira had travelled to Port of Spain just to look at the big city and she heard an American voice in a crowded shop call to an acquaintance that was passing by: 'Caroline, Caroline Becker!' The name sounded just like that of a film star Indira had seen at the drive-in movie park at Palo Seco; the baby was named Caroline on the third and penultimate day of her life.

Indira buried her daughter one morning at Siparia Cemetery, where she maintained the best-kept grave. It was always neat and tidy – she took a taxi from the trace to the cemetery every Wednesday, the day on which Caroline had died, and often covered the small grave with red hibiscus or white frangipani flowers from her own garden. On returning home to Ramdass Trace after the funeral, she had walked into the bush at the back of the house, sat on a banana leaf and stayed until darkness fell. There, she went through a long agony of loss from which she never recovered. There were no more children; her husband spent a good part of the next twenty years in the rum shops of Penal until one day he just did not come home.

Indira heard later that he had died in Port of Spain. Indira Ramnath, who had married Anil Dookie, was now the widow Dookie.

She never cried for herself or her husband, but she cried for Caroline, the baby whose face she saw in all the children of the trace. She might have allowed the unfairness, the constant knifing pain to kill any kindness she had within, but she dragged a sliver of hope from her wrecked mother-soul and allowed it to grow in her acceptance of all babies and children. She never forgot the birthday of any child in the trace; they would all receive a present, often inappropriate: a new-born baby might be given a freshly baked coconut cake, a seven year old boy would be bewildered as a bowl of sweet rice was thrust into his hand as he walked to school. She never forgot.

Indira Dookie lived comfortably at number eleven for two reasons: her thrifty mother had never spent one dollar recklessly and, more to the point, she had owned a piece of land at the end of the trace upon which stood the pumpjack, the oil pump which now nodded rhythmically twenty four hours a day producing oil to be transferred by hot pipes to the Santa Flora storage tanks. The oil company paid a generous annual rent for this piece of land; Indira Dookie was the sole beneficiary.

"She got a flu'. Pump Man take us to doctor an' she come back dead!" said Indira.

Girly was aware that Indira would lapse into almost impenetrable dialect when excited or disturbed. She discerned that Mr. Sagar Narsingh, known as the Pump Man, had taken Sumatee Dhanraj and Indira to the doctor's surgery at the oil company's local base in Santa Flora. Mr. Narsingh's house and plot were opposite Indira Dookie's in the trace. He worked for the oil company travelling around south Trinidad to check gauges and dials on the oil pumps that were dotted around the countryside. He was always known as Pump Man.

Sumatee Dhanraj had been suffering from symptoms of influenza. Three days previously she had received an injection from a locum doctor who mistakenly believed she was diabetic. The insulin reduced her blood sugar level dramatically causing her to arrest and die on the surgery floor. Indira had returned to the trace in a state of shock, quite unable to coherently explain to Mr. Dhanraj the desperate attempts to revive his wife. Mr. Narsingh did his best to convey the brief facts, but was defeated. When the dreadful news was finally absorbed, Mr. Dhanraj was transported to the doctor's surgery where his late wife lay undisturbed on the painted concrete floor. A policeman took notes of the event from the devastated locum. Jigs Boodoosingh had been summoned to collect his aunt and take her to cold storage; an autopsy was swiftly arranged.

Girly probed Indira for further details, but the facts were simple, short and no-less shocking. There was nothing more and today was the funeral day. Jigs would bring the deceased to the trace at midday; the funeral procession would make its slow way to Mosquito Creek for the Hindu cremation. It was normal for such cremations to take place in the morning but the Creek was unaccountably busy and cremation pyres were limited.

Indira, lost in memories for some time, reached out and squeezed Girly's arm.

"Reach up," she said, pointing to a book on top of a teak wall cabinet, "I'm short of height."

Girly also lacked the necessary physique to gather the book. She climbed onto a stool and brought down a faded cream photograph album. There was no dust on its surface – Indira had clearly looked at it recently. Indira opened the pages, which were all blank apart from the first two, upon which she had long ago glued four photographs of her daughter.

"Caroline", she said simply, tilting the pages towards Girly, who looked at the images in their anaemic colours. Four pictures, almost identical, of mother and daughter. She touched Indira's arm which felt thin and bony beneath the black material of a house working, dust-seeking dress. Indira sat down on a plumped cushion – she held the album tightly and studied Girly closely. She remembered Girly's distress five months previously when she had staggered into Indira's garden without warning but with urgent need. Indira remembered the cry and appeal for help. Now, she noted the bright eyes, the healthy, sun-warmed complexion, and her smart attire. And her age...yes.

"Caroline", she repeated slowly, lost in a timeless, daughter-less pain.

***

At Penal Junction, Jagdeo Boodoosingh, known since birth as Jigs, emerged from the funeral parlour and wandered off towards Donna's bar on Clarke Road. Penal was bustling: street traders dispensed late breakfasts or early lunches to workers, travellers and loafers; traffic which should have been passing through either north to south along Erin Road, or vice versa, was held up by a lorry that had shed its load of sugar cane. Jigs shook his head at the chaos on the street.

He wore casual clothes – a yellow tee shirt and baggy brown trousers. There was an hour free before the time when he would have to assume his business attire and the saturnine expression that was not part of his usual demeanour. Death was his vocation but it did not dominate his whole life. He was bright-eyed like his sister, confident and fussy about his appearance. The neat, narrow moustache and trimmed eyebrows were evidence of an adequate amount of time spent in front of a mirror. Jigs was thirty, single and generally happy; if there was a vast world outside south Trinidad, he was not interested. The funeral parlour business afforded him little leisure time but when it did, he usually found his way to the

Quinam Road, driving past citrus groves to Quinam Beach where he would gaze at the coast of Venezuela in the distance, bathe in the warm sea or just look at the Hindu ceremonies on the brown sand. Prayer services were often held here before the acolytes would plunge into the water to wash away their sins, imagining this was the cleansing power of the Ganges giving them absolution in this remote place in the world where they practised a religion they barely understood, a faith born in a country they would never see.

Jigs was not a solitary soul. The frequent trips along Quinam Road usually included a stop at Angie's house, a single storey brick box which was plastered and pink colour-washed externally, sitting on a small clearing in a teak copse less than half a mile from the beach. Jigs and Angie had an understanding: it was understood that when Angie's husband was away in New York visiting a son and ex-wife, as he often did, Jigs was welcome to stop by the house as long as he never arrived in a hearse or parked at the front. The understanding went further on Angie's part. When her husband stopped returning to Trinidad, as she anticipated he eventually would because she had heard that the association with his first wife was being renewed due to his desire for American citizenship, then the arrangement with Jigs would naturally evolve into something more permanent. Jigs had not looked this far into the future.

Some aspects of his working life were kept at arm's length – a licensed embalmer travelled from San Fernando to provide that particular service. Jigs never touched a corpse if he could avoid it; his role was to provide coffins, drive the hearse and collect the fee.

Donna looked up as Jigs walked into the bar. She approved of Jigs but his profession made her nervous – she thought he had calculating eyes, which might have been acceptable and even attractive under different circumstances.

"Rum and *cutters*?" she asked. Jigs glanced at the glass cabinet on the counter. In a metal dish was a pair of chicken legs, feet still attached, marinating in a murky liquid. Donna followed his gaze: "No, no,' she said hurriedly, "Curried duck today". Clearly, the legs were yesterday's snack.

Jigs nodded and settled into a seat next to the window from where one could see the activities on the street. The bar afforded a clear view of the junction but Jigs saw nothing. He needed a small rum to calm his nerves. In the Room of Rest at the parlour he had left his dead aunt, returned from autopsy, with two sisters who would wash and dress the body, apply appropriate make-up and prepare for the final journey. It was a familiar procedure roughly in accordance with Hindu rites - Jigs had seen this many times but not involving close family. He had quaked at the sight of the cold figure on the slab and hurried out.

There was another reason for the disquiet Jigs felt as Donna bustled over with a small plate of cubed duck, sizzling hot, each cube pierced by a small wooden stick in place of cutlery. The glass of rum was larger than Jigs should have imbibed at that time of day but he accepted it without comment.

Donna cast a shadow in the room – she was large with corn-rowed hair, kind eyes and a propensity for wearing capacious, multi-coloured dresses. The bar was a conversion of an old storage building that at one time was used as a repository to keep sacks of rice dry before transportation to the north of the island. Donna and her husband had converted the rendered block work structure into a basic bar room with kitchen at the rear and other facilities in the back yard. The furniture was appropriate for the clientèle Donna usually attracted – basic and cheap. Jigs felt the hot stickiness of the plastic seat sucking at his thighs as he adjusted his position to listen to Donna's tart comments:

"Did you see that non-sense over there las' night?" she asked, nodding towards the junction whilst dropping into a seat opposite Jigs.

He was reminded of why he had been nursing an uncomfortable feeling all morning - it was not just the impending funeral. The previous evening, an election rally had been held at the junction, just a short distance from where Jigs now sat gazing through the heat haze outside. The hot vapours distorted the view of a small parade of low-rise shops, made them bend and warp like sugar cane in the fields of the eastern plains, teased by the Atlantic breeze. The junction was essentially the node at which four roads came together: Clarke Road, Rock Road and Lachos Road all meandered away from the main thoroughfare of Erin Road, although 'road' implies a certain capacity and capability to carry and transport traffic of various kinds. The roads of south Trinidad were a disaster of axle-breaking, bone-jarring, under-prepared tarmac which kept tyre replacement centres fully occupied.

A timber platform and stage had been erected the previous day in front of the shops – Mr. P.W. Ramday, Prime Minister of the Republic of Trinidad and Tobago, would be addressing the electorate of Penal Junction as part of his nationwide tour leading up to the general election which he himself had called in a moment of exasperation and annoyance. The coalition government with Michael Nelson's Unitary Party had fallen apart on disagreements over where budgets should be spent. Mr. P.W Ramday championed the south, which he felt had been neglected for too long. Michael Nelson, a pragmatic figure, promoted big business wherever it was located. Some thought the policies were also racially motivated on both sides but opinions were not voiced.

The stage from which Mr. P.W. Ramday would send out his message comprised timber boards, scaffold poles and galvanised sheeting. Portable floodlight pylons were stabilised at each end of the stage, a steel band had been engaged to entertain the populace before the prime minister arrived. Radio stations had sent emissaries from Port of Spain for the event. A large crowd, many hundreds of supporters, sceptics and curious bystanders, had gathered by the time Mr. P.W. Ramday arrived in his official car, one hour late, to be greeted with polite applause. The steel band thundered on as the prime minister mounted the steps at the side of the stage – his intention was to bounce onto the floorboards and rush to the lectern, centre stage, from where he would rouse every good citizen, back slider and double dealer with the power of his oratory. Everyone who was enfranchised.

It was at this time that the gods decided there would be an entertaining preliminary to the event; in his rush and enthusiasm to reach the stage, Mr. P.W. Ramday temporarily forgot that he was a middle-aged man whose feet were no longer as nimble, no longer as responsive as he would have liked for someone in his position. His sprightly skip up the steps came to an abrupt end as his foot caught the edge of a top step and he tumbled on to the stage on hands and knees. The steel band, until this point pitch and note perfect, lurched drunkenly into a new refrain; a burly assistant dragged the prime minister to his feet, gave him a gentle shove towards the lectern and all would have been saved if a handful of Unitary Party members had not witnessed the aberration. Hoots of derision rose above even the strenuous efforts of the steel band to lift the galvanised roof with the power of its decibel output. The band gave up and was silenced.

But then the republic's first minister stepped up to the challenge, ignoring the cat calls, launching immediately into a cutting diatribe which left nobody in any doubt that he, Mr. P.W. Ramday, blamed Michael Nelson for the political hostilities which reigned in Port of Spain.

"What was it you wanted, Michael?" he boomed, a look of incomprehension on his twisted, hurt features. Beads of perspiration tracked down his temples onto his immaculate white shirt.

"Was it power? If so, you should have come to me and I would have given you power", he argued, his face now a picture of all that is fair and reasonable. The crowd agreed with nods and folded arms.

"Or was it money, Michael? Was it money that you wanted? If so, you should have come to me and I would have given you money!" he shouted. Individuals now spread their arms in conciliatory gestures.

"Or was it something else, Michael?" He paused. "Was it woman that you wanted?" Mr. P.W. Ramday lifted both arms to the sky and stared at the Hindu heavens. He saw Michael Nelson's features in the milky smear of the stars; he beseeched, implored his political opponent to understand. The crowd held its communal breath.

"If so Michael, you should have come to me and I would have given you woman!"

A roar of male approval rose into the sultry night. Men slapped their thighs, sank to their haunches, laughing open-mouthed. Women sniffed, stiffened their lips and muttered behind their hands but their eyes sparkled, betraying humour. Mr. P.W. Ramday maintained his wide armed pose as if frozen, despite the warmth of the air, until every last guffaw had been drained from those who had votes. He continued with a promise to bring a water project to the south, irrigating parched areas away from the wetlands, and further extension of the San Fernando by-pass to link Erin Road. But it was all superfluous – Penal Junction would be his come election day.

As the rally wound down, the steel band continued its repertoire and the prime minister departed. Jigs turned to leave the vantage point he had occupied at the side of the stage when his attention was drawn to a woman who pushed through the crowd. She was overweight, bald and in a state of drunkenness.

"I vote Ramday", she shouted, "Because he like black people and the coolie." Jigs winced at the derogatory word sometimes used for Indians. The woman came to a sudden halt as she almost collided with a man, a white man in a white shirt standing in the penumbra of a shadow cast by a floodlight pylon. Jigs took an involuntary step backwards; there was a slight gasp in his breath as he recognised the figure.

"An' he like the white man!" bawled the woman as she staggered on, weaving her way past amused bystanders towards Krishna's Grill on Lachos Road.

Jigs stared at the white man; he was young, broad shouldered, wore a slight facial sun tan on even, clean-shaven features. He was in conversation with an older man, chatting easily while Jigs glanced towards the funeral parlour on the opposite side of the junction. A light shone in the apartment window behind a cane blind. Girly would be at home. David had returned to Penal Junction, not fifty metres from Girly, a small distance that formed a fragile buffer from anguish, sad memories and hopes destroyed.

***

Donna had decided that Jigs would not be easily shaken from his reverie, certainly not by light conversation. She was about to move off when there was a shout from the only other customers in the bar: Hari and Peaches, two sugar cane cutters who had finished their early morning labours at Rio Claro and were playing cards and drinking rum.

"Donna! Man here need a purge," shouted Hari. "Let him have somptin' fresh from your kitchen." The pair dissolved into wheezing laughter until Donna fixed them with a stiletto eye.

"I go settle with those two," she said menacingly. Jigs handed her two notes for payment which she smoothed lovingly between her fingers before sliding them into a recess of her dress.

Jigs stepped outside and was jolted by the ferocious heat. He screwed up his eyes against the glare; the platform used for the previous evening's rally had disappeared from in front of the permanent shops to be replaced by wooden stalls with awnings from where street vendors sold aloo pies, *doubles* and corn soup for those with hangovers. Pale clouds drifted down from the hills of the Northern Range, sealing the heat at ground level like a lid over the earth. Jigs looked at the sky and sighed. Truth or deception? How would Girly react if David appeared at the funeral? Was it now the moment to tell her the truth or allow fate to decide? Time snapped at his heels like an angry dog; he flicked a thirsty fly from his damp cheek and hurried back to the funeral parlour.

AFTERNOON

The Pump Man, Mr. Sagar Narsingh, stepped out of his house in Ramdass Trace onto a side staircase platform that trembled under his tread. Mr. Narsingh – forty years old, corpulent and satisfied with some aspects of his life - usually paused at this point, allowing the tremor in the staircase to subside before negotiating the rickety steps down to his garden. As with most properties in the trace, the garden and bush at the rear were below road level; it never occurred to Mr. Narsingh that the four screws securing the complete wooden staircase were insufficient, not to say negligently dangerous. The pause on the platform reassured him that the wood was sound, the steps negotiable. He could descend with confidence.

Today, Mr. Narsingh was perturbed. A letter had arrived from the oil company, Trinex Oil and Gas, not in connection with his role as an employee, but with regard to his status as owner of a substantial parcel of land between Ramdass Trace and the border of a stretch of Erin Road where it neared Santa Flora. He held the letter in one hand and the envelope in the other; the red-ink stamp of the company's logo stood out starkly in the afternoon sun. He walked off slowly into the bush which was not merely a mass of barely accessible vegetation, it was also a delight of citrus trees, banana, coffee, cacao and coconut palms; there was a sweetness to the air yet, here and there, a contradiction of sharp fragrances which confused the senses, sometimes caressing, sometimes striking until the mind could take no more of the lack of order, the insane mixture, and the body was forced to stop and take stock. There was also a dampness to the ground which never dried, a rustle of leaves and branches which were never quite still.

The boundaries of Mr. Narsingh's land were not staked or fenced in any way. At its furthest extents, one just simply walked out of the foliage onto the tarmac surface of Erin Road in one direction and the Company Road in another. Many years previously, before the Company Road had been constructed, oil tankers and sundry vehicles were obliged to traverse the narrow, rutted surface of Ramdass Trace in order to get to Santa Flora from Fyzabad, the two local hubs of the oil company's operations. The oil company eventually laid out and surfaced a new road, a Ramdass Trace by-pass, but never gave it a name; also, it appeared on very few maps of the area.

Although Mr. Narsingh had seen a site plan of his land many years ago when ownership passed to him and his sisters via inheritance (the plan and deeds of ownership were lodged with a lawyer in San Fernando), he had no idea that the asset amounted to approximately two hectares. Now the oil company, in written language that Mr. Narsingh found too strident for his taste, proposed to lease part of the land at a laughably low rent for the purposes of further oil extraction in the Santa Flora district. The key was the accessibility of the land from Erin Road and its close proximity to the refinery. Mr. Narsingh looked at the variation in textures and colours around him, the natural barrier surrounding his house. He imagined several oil pumps sitting on cleared patches of land, nodding day and night, spilling oil onto the green carpet. In a way, he could have foreseen this because he had noticed evidence of increased activity in oil extraction from the land during his work in south Trinidad; there had been more dials and gauges to check, more information concerning oil flow to record, more evidence of drilling rigs being erected in the most remote of locations. However, his complacency was understandable, given the type of land he owned. He remembered a conversation with the widow Dookie in which he remarked that the oil company might one day see fit to extend their operations near to the Company Road where she had already leased out a plot for one pump at the end of the trace.

"Your land safe" she had offered. "It full of bush".

Now, it seemed that the thickness of the vegetation would be no obstacle to the thirst for oil. The poor rent offered was immaterial - Mr. Narsingh would not have this development, this pillaging of his land that had been in his family's ownership for several generations. The language of the letter was a concern – there was an indirect reference to his position as an employee of the company. A veiled threat? Without realising his progress, Mr. Narsingh had walked quickly, his pace spurred by anger, now arriving at the oil pump that occupied the widow Dookie's plot next to the Company Road. He stared at the metal monster before him, an object so familiar to him during his working day but now a terror of steel, never still, never silent as it sucked oil from the earth. He had looked at it a thousand times in the past, read its dials, recorded the product of its thirst and never flinched. Now, it was a symbol of a power that sought to wreck his home, soil his land.

Mr. Narsingh was not prone to bouts of spontaneous anger. He lived a gentle, quiet life at number sixteen Ramdass Trace, all alone and at peace with his environment and neighbours. But there were occasional dark moments. He had no memory of when the sadness had started, the fleeting and prolonged anxiety mixed with low self-esteem, but he knew it was real. Sometimes, he would sit in his house and look at its semi-dilapidated condition and wonder where he should start. While he wondered, the roof leaked, taps dripped, cracked window glass permitted the ingress of wind-driven rain, the timber framing of the roof began to rot and distort. Mr. Narsingh's intentions were always honest and direct: he would make a start with the roof and work his way down. As he often explained to the widow Dookie:

"The house need fix. Building material come soon".

The house had been the first of its kind in the trace when constructed in the 1960's. Reinforced concrete columns supported the timber floors and roof, the walls were built of lightweight blocks as opposed to the normal timber frame and boarding. Mr. Narsingh's father had cement rendered the blocks externally and painted the finished surface a different colour every alternate year. On the demise of his parents, two sisters relocated to Tobago where they jointly bought a beach-side bar with living accommodation at Pigeon Point; responsibility for the upkeep of the house passed to Sagar Narsingh. Sadly, he was not up to it. Whenever he decided to commence the maintenance, a bout of inertia would afflict his whole being. Darkness invaded his night-time dreams and his daytime thoughts until he pushed it away but accepted its consequence: he could not lift a finger to repair the house. The anxiety, sadness and inertia did not affect his work with the oil company or relations with neighbours; it was a private burden of failure triggered by the house and surrounding land he loved so much.

Mr. Narsingh returned the letter to its envelope, sighed loudly at the oil pump and made his way along the trace, back to the house at number sixteen. There, he saw kitchen cupboard doors hanging at eccentric angles on their hinges, a sight that forced him onto his veranda from where he could see the water storage tank, high on its wooden podium at the side of the house. A continuous leak from the underside of the tank formed a muddy puddle on the soft earth below. The Pump Man had had enough. He sat down heavily onto a battered rattan chair and allowed the oil company's letter to slide to the floor. A wave of depression flooded his mind, pin pricks of pain tormented his well-being. His eyelids drooped, jowls sagged, a deep breath fought against the blackness. Before he could be overwhelmed, the sound of a car engine distracted the silent force, sending it into temporary retreat where it would hide until recalled by the voice of the house. Sagar Narsingh opened his eyes and focused on a black hearse entering Ramdass Trace from Erin Road. The funeral of Sumatee Dhanraj. Without the house to think about, he immediately felt better.

***

Jigs Boodoosingh drove the hearse carefully along Ramdass Trace and stopped outside Mr. Dhanraj's house at number twelve. A separate black funeral car slid quietly behind the hearse; the driver and additional pall-bearer, Rishi and Raj, emerged and stood respectfully next to the car. They were dressed soberly in white shirts with black ties and trousers. Jigs sported the same uniform but this was supplemented by a black jacket. When his father was the sole director of the funeral parlour, he had always worn a jacket with tails to burials and cremations, often complemented by grey striped trousers. He felt it imposed a certain ceremony, an authenticity to proceedings. Jigs thought it was an affectation, an unnecessary decoration to a sombre occasion. When his father had retired to Arima, Jigs handed the jacket one day to Ravi Bishoo who owned number fifteen Ramdass Trace and had often remarked on the fine quality of the jacket whenever he saw it worn by Mr. Boodoosingh senior. Ravi also cultivated the only lawn in Ramdass Trace; the jacket was last seen adorning the wooden frame of a scarecrow when the lawn was re-seeded.

The tail-less black jacket which almost fitted Jigs' angular frame was at the forefront of modern undertaking apparel in its cut and style; it was spoilt only by the white stains around the armpits. Jigs walked briskly to the front steps of number twelve; the house, which earlier had been empty except for Mr. Dhanraj and Girly, was now populated by friends, neighbours and relatives. The front veranda hosted only Mr. Dhanraj and his favourite niece. As soon as the hearse had arrived, Mr. Dhanraj stood motionless with eyes fixed on the white casket in the hearse. He had not visited his wife's remains at the funeral parlour – he dreaded the look, the arrangement of death features imposed by the embalmer. A cooling breeze ruffled his iron-grey hair; outside, a parrot ate mangoes noisily from a tree in the widow Dookie's garden; grey-headed kites circled and trembled in the sky above.

The arrival of the cars had provoked a silence in the trace. Those inside number twelve stood with hands clasped, avoiding eye contact; ten mourners, recently arrived. Mr. Dhanraj had forbidden visitors the previous evening when it would have been traditional for a Hindu wake to have taken place inside and around the house; he required no consolation from others, he had no belief that the ghost of his wife would haunt the house until she was put to rest. His only concession to tradition was to turn pictures and mirrors to the walls, take down curtains and thoroughly clean the house that would be considered defiled, despite the fact that the death had occurred elsewhere.

Jigs slowed his pace and stepped solemnly down the front concrete staircase, across the yard and up the steps to the veranda.

"How she look now?" asked Mr. Dhanraj, placing a hand on his nephew's arm.

Jigs glanced back at the hearse. "She looks fine, uncle. Very peaceful". He had virtually no local accent, his English was as precise and correct as he could make it without appearing or sounding false but no-one had ever heard Jigs speaking differently. When responding to a question or comment in dialect, Jigs would never lapse but would respond correctly; his language would never, however, intimidate or offend friends, relatives or strangers. Locals might have a vague idea that his spoken word related somehow to his profession, others might have considered that he had spent time in England and had assumed the accent up there. In fact, Jigs had never ventured past Port of Spain; the shaping and refinement of his language was almost entirely the result of many hours listening to BBC World Service radio and a feeling that his professional position demanded clarity of communication at difficult times. Girly found her brother's unbending correctness occasionally infuriating, especially during a dispute or argument, but she also had developed a 'business tongue' that steered her accent and speech away from the local dialect.

Rishi and Raj, at a signal from Jigs, slid the open coffin from the hearse and conveyed it slowly into the silent house. The local pundit, in white robes, performed a brief prayer service which was observed by Hindus and Presbyterians alike in the living room; a section of the fifteenth chapter of the *Bhagavad Gita* was included. Mr. Dhanraj placed flowers in the coffin whilst still unable to look directly at his wife. The mourners included the parents of Jigs and Girly, recently arrived from Arima, Sumatee's other sisters and assorted cousins and neighbours. The widow Dookie would not attend. She did not agree with cremation as part of a final journey. Her weekly visits to Caroline's grave not only gave her a purpose and comfort, they also reincarnated her daughter in mind and body – the remains were still there after all these years, in the same place she was laid to rest. Ashes were no comfort to anyone.

One of Sumatee's sisters had brought her husband unwillingly to the house. Lal looked at the fine coffin on trestles and wondered at the obvious expense. It was a premier range casket, pure white inlaid with gold features, from the Boodoosingh parlour collection, donated by Jigs and Girly to their aunt.

"No point burnin' good money", was Lal's response. Sumatee's sister drew a sharp breath and hoped no-one had heard. Everyone had heard and Lal was shunned for the remainder of the day.

At a signal from the pundit, and following some encouraging words to Mr. Dhanraj, the pall-bearers returned the coffin to the hearse. Sanctifying water was sprinkled by the pundit in front of the hearse; two white *jhandi* were affixed and the procession of hearse, funeral car and sundry other vehicles made slow progress out of the trace onto Erin Road and embarked on the journey to Mosquito Creek. The widow Dookie, Pump Man and Ravi Bishoo stood next to the hot pipes at the side of the rutted road surface of Ramdass Trace until the cortège had passed.

Mr. Dhanraj began to feel ill. He was a shrunken figure in a rear seat of the funeral car; the loss of his wife had slowly woven a pattern of grief inside his mind that drifted down inexorably and formed a weight in his heart. There, it divided, gnawed at him and settled as sorrow and sadness deep in his soul.

The convoy of vehicles passed through Siparia and turned onto the road to Teak Village where it met forests, bamboo groves and teak plantations along the way. All cars stopped five times before the journey ended to represent the five elements, including space, and to serve notice that the deceased was on its way to returning to its composite parts. At each stop the male mourners got out of the cars and conversed lightly on matters unrelated to the funeral. Damp foreheads were wiped, eyes surveyed the pale clouds above that bore no promise of rain. Mosquito Creek, just south of San Fernando, was reached after what seemed like an eternity. It was the only cremation site in the south and comprised a flat, open paved area containing two separate enclosures for pyres. The enclosures were marked by low, boundary bricks. A car park bordered the viewing space for mourners and on the opposite side of the site was the Southern Main Road next to the Gulf of Paria. A temporary awning was erected daily to shelter mourners from the sun and at the same time afforded a clear view of the pyre sites, one of which contained the smouldering embers from a morning cremation.

The pyre for Sumatee Dhanraj was typical: a pile of timber off-cuts donated by the Fyzabad Sawmills, approximately two metres high and incorporating a clear central tunnel for the casket. Jigs and the pall-bearers conveyed the casket to the entrance of the pyre and set it down on the floor. Girly supported Mr. Dhanraj as he placed further flowers around the exposed head and shoulders. He touched his wife's smooth, warm skin for the last time, finally steeling himself to look at her death visage. But this was not what he feared most: he would have to light the pyre in a certain way, the detail of which had been confirmed by Jigs as the correct and only way to start the cremation.

As the casket was placed into the pyre, five male relatives, some of whom had not been at Mr. Dhanraj's house but travelled separately to the Creek, began to walk around the pyre clockwise holding long, burning tapers. After five circuits they left the site without looking back. The remaining mourners looked at Mr. Dhanraj. Jigs knew he would need help; the body had been liberally sprinkled with camphor, sugar and *ghee* which would assist combustion. A camphor taper had been inserted into the mouth of the deceased; as Mr. Dhanraj had no children, he would have to perform the ritual that was normally the burden of an eldest son. He edged forward under Jigs' guidance.

"I can't do this, boy," gasped Mr. Dhanraj, longing to escape to the Southern Main Road he could see opposite and catch a taxi home. But Jigs helped him forward, steadying his hand while the camphor taper was ignited along with the remainder of the pyre; Mr. Dhanraj backed away unsteadily, stifling sobs as the pyre suddenly emitted a small explosion and burst into orange flames, the sacred flames which would take the body to reincarnation.

In a few seconds, the heat from the pyre drove all those nearby back to the awning. Girly was making her way to stand next to her uncle when she felt a slight tug on her sleeve. While preparations for lighting of the pyre were in progress, Devendra Roopnarine had arrived; his father had been safely entrusted to the care of the widow Dookie for the afternoon so that Devendra could attend the cremation and, following a morning spent dragging a modicum of courage from his heart to his head, instigate a serious discussion with Girly about his intentions. It occurred to him that although there had been something of an attraction between them for some time, evident in their greetings and in seeking out each other's company, no formal liaison had been agreed. It was Devendra's opinion that this should be corrected. He was now a man of substance, quite able to look this perfect woman in the eye without fear of rejection. As they stood facing each other between the pyre and the awning some twenty metres away, he believed it was high time he asserted himself to stand tall in her eyes and esteem. Standing tall in her heart would come later. It did not occur to him that this occasion might not be appropriate; seeing Girly that morning on the veranda of Mr. Dhanraj's house had made his spirits soar, his heart race. It had to be now.

Devendra had seen little of Girly in their formative years. While she attended the prestigious Naparima High School in San Fernando, he had been apprenticed to the Trinex Oil & Gas Company. They met periodically in Ramdass Trace and were courteous and friendly, but Devendra spent years away on offshore oil rigs, years that slipped away quickly until they almost became strangers before his final return. Whilst caring for his aged father, Devendra had decided to embark on a part–time occupation, initially buying a lorry and transporting water in large tanks to the rural far south of the country where there were often shortages. The lorry lasted until the Trinidad road surfaces exerted too much of a strain on axles and wheels. He then decided to buy a second-hand taxi, which he expected would eventually become a fleet of taxis, at about the same time that Trinex decided to cut down on production at the Point Fortin refinery and lay off workers, many of whom with redundancy pay in hand also purchased taxis and patrolled the same southern roads.

Devendra's taxi spent much time on a platform of wooden boards and scaffold poles at the front of his house in the trace. One day, when reversing off the platform, he noticed a substantial covering of rust flakes on the boards. After a moment of reflection, Devendra got out of the car and administered sharp kicks to three separate areas of bodywork, all of which revealed further evidence of corrosion. There were also now three holes in the faded paintwork. The taxi was taken to Bobby at Duncan Village, an acknowledged expert on all matters pertaining to auto-mobiles. Bobby sucked his teeth, listened to the grating pistons, looked at the oil bubbling from the side of the engine block and kicked further damage into the bodywork.

"Best leave it here for scrap", he opined.

Devendra now despaired of ever facing Girly as a man of means, an economic equal, when his God decided to intervene and make his pecuniary disadvantage a thing of the past with a winning ticket. Still Devendra procrastinated. He decided to buy the house with gates in Penal and repair his father's house in Ramdass Trace before setting out an action plan, a courting contract, before Girly. Today was the day – he would not be deterred by the solemnity of a funeral.

As Devendra began to frame his opening words in his mind, he saw the polite smile on Girly's lips and found it encouraging. The cremation fire crackled in the background, minor explosions from the dry wood sent yellow sparks into the air to be lifted by the sea breeze from the Gulf, scattering them to the east where they died on parched earth. Acrid smoke from burning wood, hair and flesh rose and drifted, assaulting the bystanders who gagged and cried.

Devendra regarded the magnificent Girly, business woman, heartbeat of the Boodoosingh monopoly in body disposal in south

Trinidad. He loved her grey business suit and even the necklace of perspiration beads, just visible through the open collar of her white shirt.

"In Penal, it have a house with gates..." he began but stopped. This would not do. Girly required correct speech and phrasing. He looked at the blazing body of Sumatee Dhanraj, collected his thoughts then turned to Girly again. There was a puzzled look in her eyes. The smile had half-closed on the full lips of the achingly beautiful Girly, with her smooth skin that could make him weep, deep brown eyes which settled comfortably on his, never demanding or accusing, her lustrous hair tumbling past her collar. The fabulous Girly, graceful, confident and kind, undoubtedly fecund.... Devendra was about to muse on Girly's further attributes and rephrase his opening remarks when he noticed that he had lost her attention. She stared somewhere over his right shoulder, her half smile had disappeared, her jaw had acquired a slightly thrusting set. Surely he had made a mistake, too hesitant or too forward? Her soft eyes had hardened, piercing the smoke just as the pyre imploded with the top section falling onto the human remains. Murmurs and gasps lifted from the mourners – some felt the comfort of a religious process being enacted before them, others were temporarily disabled by the horror. Devendra saw the change in her immediately – the welcome in her eyes had gone, they were initially almost devoid of expression but then there was a pain he could discern, mixed with something he had not seen before. At the point when he realised that this complete change in her was not directed at him, he turned to see David standing alone at the side of the awning and his confidence evaporated like ice in the Trinidad sun. Devendra realised he was still holding onto Girly's sleeve. Broken, he released her, for the other emotion he had also seen in her eyes became clear and it left him bereft. It was the understanding that along with pain and anger, there was a visceral attraction with which he could not compete.

Girly regained her composure and escorted Devendra back to the awning from where she turned to look at the pyre, still burning fiercely but reduced by half in height. Devendra melded into the small crowd sheltering from the sun and the effects of the fire.

***

David wished to avoid Jigs if possible. He surveyed the funeral gathering from a point outside the awning. Fifteen to twenty people under cover, now including Girly, two pall-bearers with Jigs standing as close as possible to the cremation. They would wait until the pyre was reduced further and the human form substantially consumed. David had never been to Mosquito Creek before, not in all his early life spent in south Trinidad had he been near to this place, so tranquil and beautifully located. He glanced at the neatly trimmed perimeter hedges of Ixora and the yellow flowered Poui trees. He walked inside the awning to stand at Girly's side; his eyes focused on the pyre.

Girly felt his presence but did not look at him or acknowledge it; she looked for Devendra amongst the small gathering but he had gone. What was it he had started to ask her? She was suddenly nervous and tense – David had been next to her for several seconds before he moved to stand in front of her, now separated by a barrier without shape or form, without colour. It was wafer thin but built on perceived deceit.

Finally, Girly snapped into a controlled fury.

"When do you go back up?" she asked, nodding vaguely in the direction of London. "Jigs will take you to Piarco now." There was another nod towards the airport in the north of the island.

"I came only for the funeral, nothing else," he replied.

Girly saw the lie as it left his lips, the words curling like black smoke across the space between them. She looked into his green eyes for confirmation of the lie but they were half closed against the smoke. She immediately thought back to the day he had left; the disappointment made her feel foolish. She had withdrawn into her culture which she suddenly felt he could not share, sheltered in the safety of her race, not wishing to ponder on the lost possibilities, the leap into the future and the now dead promises. He left without a word three months ago, vanished one day leaving her to face the false and real sympathy, the knowing looks of her friends. It was the real sympathy which hurt her most.

"I waited at Piarco. You never came," David continued. "I spent three months wondering why."

Girly had heard enough. The anger sang a mad melody in her head as she began to walk away from him. But she could not let it go. She turned on her heel and strode back, stopping short of the now clear green eyes which focused intently on her lips.

"You came here as a boy, given a life of privilege by your parents, never doubting you would be accepted. Did you walk back into that compound whenever you were tired of us?"

She referred to the oil company's estate for expatriate managers and operatives located some distance from Ramdass Trace along the Fyzabad Road. David had spent his formative years enclosed on the estate until as a teenager and young man he had discovered a new world beyond its fences and gates. The estate was effectively a village unlike anything outside its boundaries. Neat, comfortable bungalows served by smooth roads ringed a central core of medical and leisure centres, a school and two shops. David's desire to wander beyond the estate's perimeter had taken him to Ramdass Trace one hot afternoon where, aged seventeen, he first saw Girly entering her aunt and uncle's house. After a brief glance she had ignored him, certain that he had ventured along a wrong path and would find his way back to the estate from where he clearly came. She had seen Europeans only in Fyzabad before, all connected with the oil industry. It was only when sometime later she saw David in conversation with her uncle at the front of the house that she began to think about why he should have stumbled upon Ramdass Trace in particular, a good distance from the oil company's estate.

After David and Mr. Dhanraj had moved onto the front veranda, Girly heard her uncle relating a story about the estate.

"You know David, I went to the social club only two, three times. It was too formal for me although I was entitled." As a former Trinex employee Mr. Dhanraj could make use of all facilities on the estate despite not being a resident. He did not tell David about his discomfort at being amongst a European dominated community, but he remembered his first visit. At the entrance gate to the site, as he was showing his pass, a local middle aged man in tennis clothes walked up to the security officer, practised a few imaginary shots with a worn, half-strung racquet and asked if a game was booked for him that day.

"No game today," replied the security officer.

The man, still swinging his racquet, had turned without a word and wandered away. They watched him return along the road to an isolated wooden shack with his dreams of social acceptance undaunted and expectation of a tennis match that would never be played. Mr. Dhanraj noted his flapping shoe soles and grubby, off-white shirt. The security officer had shaken his head at the retreating figure. "He come every day expectin' to play."

"You see, that man come to the estate to mix with the people but they never let him in," Mr. Dhanraj shook his head and explained to David. "He was never a employee but it did not stop him from hopin' to play. They never let him in but he never got out of the habit of goin' and believin' he could join that club."

Girly had listened to this anecdote from within the living room that had an open door onto the veranda. She could just see the boy through a flimsy door curtain rippling slightly on an occasional breeze. How did her uncle know this boy? Know his name?

A few days later, Girly was sitting outside the Fyzabad Coffee House pecking at a pastry. Her father was inside discussing the recent demise of a mutual friend with the proprietor. David appeared next to Girly and sat down. He looked at the small flake of pastry at the side of her mouth; she immediately flicked it away. She intended to stare at him until he moved on. But he did not move. His eyes held her gaze as he appeared to consider whether he should speak or wait for her to remark on his presence. Girly knew instinctively there was nothing sinister in his eye contact or demeanour; at first, she thought he had something to tell her, maybe some communication from her uncle. But then she realised he was waiting.

"How do you know my uncle?" she asked quietly.

David immediately relaxed. She saw it in his sun-tanned features, in the way he leaned forward and spoke, almost conspiratorially as though he had a secret to share.

"A few weeks ago, I decided to explore outside the oil company estate. I knew there were back traces in the area and I wanted to see them." He paused. Girly noted that he alternated between looking directly at her and losing focus in trying to remember details. "I was about to turn back along the Company Road", he continued, "when I found Ramdass Trace. I wasn't lost, just a long way from home, but your uncle saw me and invited me to his house as I was walking by. I've been back several times – he tells me stories of the people he's known at the oil company. I saw you at the house on my last visit, and here again today. I had to stop."

David sat back in his chair as if that were the whole story of his presence at the Fyzabad Coffee House that day; if further information was required, Girly should draw her own conclusions. She was stunned into silence, not by the obvious nature of his explanation because she had assumed he had been lost or driven by curiosity, but by the way he had spoken to her, like an old friend, a contemporary and equal, with the assumption that she would not mind if he shared her table. There was no hint of conceit that she could discern, just a boy passing time with a friend.

How to respond? The awning over the external café tables did not quite keep the whole area in shade. Girly moved both feet out of the high sunshine; David saw the movement and immediately stood up, assuming she was about to get up and leave. Girly remained in the chair. She looked at the half finished pastry on a brown plastic plate next to a glass of water in which two black specks moved slowly across the surface in a desperate attempt at survival.

"I'm invited for tea tomorrow afternoon at Ramdass Trace," David offered. Girly rose as she saw her father emerging from the coffee house. She smiled inwardly at the English formality of the invitation. Her uncle would not have put it in those words.

"I won't be there tomorrow," she said evenly. Then she was gone. David looked across the busy street of central Fyzabad where a bank was closing its doors for a lunch time break and people queued outside the Caribbean Bakery to purchase the product of the second bake of the day. She would not be at Ramdass Trace tomorrow.

***

The funeral pyre was reduced to a pile of blackened burning embers with no discernible human form within, but the process would not be complete for many hours; tomorrow, Mr. Dhanraj would collect the cooled ashes, cross the Southern Main Road to the beach and cast them into the sea. Sumatee would be gone forever.

David felt he should have been stung by Girly's remark but he almost laughed. A life of privilege? She knew nothing of the claustrophobic, stifling effect of separation within the estate, the minimal contact with the world outside the fence, a small piece of

England in the sunshine. She would not know how much he had hated that part of his life until he discovered the world beyond. Then, the possibilities were endless.

Girly misinterpreted the faint smile she saw. There was no point in continuing to harangue him in public – the last connection with David had surely been severed, not three months before when he had left, but that night in Ramdass Trace two months ago. It had been a day of intermittent pain and discomfort. She had arrived in Ramdass Trace just before nightfall to visit her aunt and uncle and knew something was seriously wrong as soon as she stepped out of her car. Almost without knowing how it had happened, she found herself passing number twelve and staggering into the widow Dookie's garden, racked with abdominal pains that brought her to her knees on the damp soil. A full moon edged small clouds in white, the taste of the bush was carried into the garden on the soft peppery air. The pains made her moan out loud in the darkness, the dampness of the soil became wet beneath her and she knew it was over.

Indira Dookie appeared silently in front of Girly, lifting her to her feet with surprisingly strong hands, recognizing what had happened.

"Child gone now," was all she said.

They walked together slowly into the house, into the room that would always be Caroline's room and there Girly stayed until morning when Indira found suitable clothes in a tall cupboard. Girly knew the story of Indira's loss many years before but did not ask where the replacement clothes had come from or why they were hanging in a cupboard, almost new and untouched. Early the next morning, Indira stood outside her house ensuring no-one saw Girly leave. Girly emerged from the side door, furtively, into a morning mist, thick and warm; blue flowered jacaranda shrubs lined her path to the road, nodding as she shuffled past. She briefly touched hands with Indira to seal a shared secret; the clothes would be returned the following day.

Girly made her way home. The mental turmoil had caused a restless night in Ramdass Trace. It now gave way to a sad resignation as though a significant part of her life was complete; several wasted years had slipped away. She changed into a business suit in the apartment above the funeral parlour, spent the whole day at a desk arranging funerals and purchasing a selection of caskets from a joinery works in Port of Spain, then retired to her tiny room upstairs. Throughout the evening, amongst the spikes of hurt that stung her sharply, small ecstasies of memory emerged to ensure that no bitterness would remain. Memories of golden days with David impinged on the sadness, suppressed her anger, left her bemused but able to fight off a crushing depression. What remained was a spark of hope which fed on her innate goodness and special character to become a weapon to beat down the unfairness and start again.

Two days later, Girly had crossed Penal Junction to Doctor Naidu's surgery. He occupied two rooms on the ground floor of a modern building at the end of a parade of shops. His surgery walls were bare apart from his certificates of professional competence; his waiting room was rarely full due to his reputation as a man who despised malingerers and lead swingers. In the quiet, plain room, Doctor Naidu – horn rimmed, hard hearted and no sufferer of fools – listened to Girly. He decided this girl was different from his usual patients. He spent time with her, giving certain reassurances and the benefit of his long experience before sending her back across the Junction in better heart until, as she crossed the busy road to the funeral parlour, she remembered the widow Dookie's words, harsh and stark – "Child gone now." Except there had been nothing recognizable as life. The loss nevertheless felt the same. Finally, her own loud sobs eliminated the traffic sounds in her ears.

***

The halcyon days had begun inauspiciously, not with the meeting at the Fyzabad Coffee House but two years later when they were both nineteen. They had seen each other intermittently during the preceding two years, always at Ramdass Trace but neither had made any attempt to make contact outside this familiar venue. Then one day, Girly was entering the funeral parlour where she had joined Jigs and her father in business, when a small red sports car with open top pulled up at the low kerb and stopped. David levered himself over the driver's door without opening it and hurried over to her before she disappeared into the parlour.

"I wanted to see you before I leave the island," he said in that manner she had noted before, almost a presumption that she would be interested and as though they were very close and conversed regularly.

"Why?" she asked bluntly, to project a lack of curiosity.

He seemed momentarily surprised but regained his purpose.

"I have one week before I go to England. To university..," he prompted, in case she misunderstood. "I was hoping you would show me parts of the island I haven't seen." He waved a hand in the direction of the car.

"In that?" she asked. "How far you think you're going on these roads with a toy like that?" She watched him calculate whether it could be done or if she was correct and the thing should be abandoned.

"I'd like to start tomorrow morning. Will you come?"

Girly looked at the boy for a long time as he waited. She wanted to feel affronted at his approach, to tell him she was a business woman now who had no time for frivolous activities or being his tour guide. But he had a quiet charm which was almost soothing so that she could not summon up any animosity. Also, it was a slow period at the parlour – a day away would suit her fine. The only other consideration was whether she could safely spend a whole day with this boy who seemed attracted to her but whom she hardly knew except as a young acquaintance of her uncle.

"Don't come here," she said. "Wait outside Donna's in Clarke Road. Ten o'clock."

***

As Jigs Boodoosingh lovingly drove his polished Ford out of the Penal Funeral Parlour's yard the next day, he passed by Clarke Road at precisely ten fifteen in the morning; he saw Girly, who had requested a day off to visit a friend in San Francique, saunter towards a dusty red sports car where the young man he knew only as David was waiting. Jigs drove on and was not seen. He arrived a short while later at the house of a widower in Quarry to discuss a funeral arrangement; he was more than a little troubled by what he had seen at Clarke Road.

***

Girly had made no special effort for David. She arrived at the car late wearing a cerise shirt, a size too large, with sleeves rolled up above her wrists, and white shorts which were half a size too small. David immediately presented her with a white flower, plucked that morning from a frangipani bush outside his parents' bungalow, and a brown paper bag containing two chocolate muffins, purchased that morning from the Caribbean Bakery in Fyzabad. Girly accepted the gifts whilst examining the sports car more closely than the previous day: the red paintwork had faded and a thickness of dust had accumulated; the roof, constructed of dark brown fabric, was folded back in a concertina but still there was evidence of disrepair.

Girly thought she could see strips of brown tape over several seams in the fabric.

"The hood doesn't close now," David explained.

"And if it rains today?"

"I have a sheet in the back."

Girly exhaled with just enough volume so that he would hear. She approached the passenger door, waiting for him to open it.

"You have to climb over the door to get in," David explained. "The locks are broken."

She stepped over the low door to find herself with both feet on a worn leather seat, holding the gifts, one in each hand, and feeling faintly ridiculous. She sat down quickly, staring straight ahead. They drove off in silence.

They had set off slowly with Girly feeling anxious about spending a whole day looking at scenery she already knew so well and in the discomfort of a vehicle which looked and felt as if it would fail at any moment. However, he drove carefully enough to avoid most of the potholes and sundry surface defects so that the slight jarring to her frame was tolerable. David appeared not to feel any discomfort; he explained to her how he had acquired the vehicle from his father. On the understanding that David would drive him to work, which often meant several days away from the oil company estate, his father had allowed him free use of the car; driving experience was gained on the long roads from Fyzabad to Galeota Point in the far south east corner of the island where the oil company maintained its helicopter and transport base, mainly for conveying staff to off-shore oil rigs. The condition and appearance of the car caused David no embarrassment, nor did he give any indication that he intended to improve either facet.

The morning had passed in an atmosphere of tension pierced by brief conversations. David drove initially north through back roads to St. Julien, then eastwards through a heat haze on the Mayaro

Road, slowing through Tableland, Poole and Rio Claro until the little car finally reached the beach at Mayaro Bay. Along the way, Girly had pointed out rough wooden breakfast sheds by the side of the road, sugar cane fields, citrus plantations along with farms still remaining here and there despite the decline of agriculture in the region due to more profitable employment in the oil industry. As she looked from side to side of the car, she stole glances at him to take in his appearance and manner. He appeared genuinely interested in her local knowledge, asking clarification of certain points in particular with regard to the effect of oil exploration on livelihoods and environment. Girly noted that he seemed untroubled by the heat: there was no perspiration around the line of his fair hair, no dampness to the white cotton shirt he wore loosely over wide shoulders.

They drove north along the eastern coast road close to beaches fringed by giant palm trees. Off shore in the shallows, mounds of black coral washed smooth by the surf broke the ocean's surface and provided landing platforms for the sea birds. In the distance towards Galeota Point, purple clouds accumulated high in the sky promising heavy rain; David and Girly decided to turn around and return to Penal Junction before the afternoon storm clouds arrived. On reaching Penal, David extracted an agreement to meet the following day at Clarke Road when they would set off on a new direction. Girly had considered the reaction at the funeral parlour to another absence, then decided to openly declare her desire for more time away. Her interest in this boy was growing but she also realised a trait within herself that made her uneasy: she wanted to find fault with him, an imperfection that would allow her to step away, back into the safety of the parlour and a familiar world. Girly loved honest and true things; she was aware of her own adolescent failings surfacing during teenage years, and now, near the end of that part of her life, she believed she had eradicated certain attitudes that caused her to cast off friends too easily, or lack tolerance for those who did not possess the same speed of thought. She sought honesty as a first requirement in David, would not stand for any perceived or obvious lack of candour. Was there a small devil deep within him? She had yet to tease it out.

The following morning she arrived late again, stepping over the car door and settling into the damaged passenger seat without a word. They drove north and then west as they had agreed the previous evening along the South Oropouche River. The river meandered slowly down from the central hills, passing through and supplementing wetlands, irrigating the edges of dry plains. It passed close to Barrackpore where cottage industries soiled its banks, hurried beneath small timber bridges linking its shores and where the land fell away in rocky undulations, the river gained speed to cascade into shallow side pools. Beyond Barrackpore, with tree crowns casting shadows on the surface, the South Oropouche straightened and widened before opening its banks and merging its waters with the deep saline sea.

The red car made slow progress across the western side of the island, never far from the river. David and Girly spoke of young things; they began to talk about future hopes and intentions, always keeping their worlds separate, never allowing their lives to collide in some imagined future scene, keeping to parallel paths. Girly's unease at her own motives for being with him was outweighed by a compulsion to test David in every way. He was unerringly polite, keenly attentive when she occasionally spoke about the funeral parlour and with no hint of condescension that she could discern.

She tried mild sarcasm. When he told her he would be at university in London for three years studying petroleum engineering, she said:

"Of course, you'll rush straight back here when you finish."

"Oh yes. I hope to join Trinex as soon as I return," he replied. She folded her arms and remained silent for ten minutes.

Then the mood changed. In the late morning, they stopped at a breakfast shed close to Oropouche Lagoon. The shed was the usual basic timber framing with rough vertical boarding on the outside beneath a roof covered with savannah palm thatch. It was small inside, just five tables and a low counter at the rear. They sat close to the entrance door; David ordered *roti* and seasoned, mashed avocado for both of them, with lime juice and a dash of *bitters* to drink. As they were eating in silence, a man stepped into the shed and stopped at their table. He wore a threadbare singlet exposing strong, dark arms; a perspiration sheen dampened his Indian features. He looked at them separately before mumbling something to Girly in a low menacing voice. David had been unable to catch the words as they were in dialect but he understood their intention and impact; he also saw Girly's hurt expression. He rose, standing in front of the man, barring his way into the shed. The man initially smiled then assumed an aggressive stance and expression which were supported by his appearance: damaged nose, scar tissue on the forehead, the face of a brawler. David said nothing. His unwavering jade-green eyes held the man for several tense seconds until the man loudly sniffed up mucous, turned, spat on the wooden floor and left.

David sat down. Girly saw no sign of tension in his face, shoulders or movement. He found no need to comment or ask what exactly the man had said. Girly was shaken; she stood quickly, walked outside and waited for him. David placed some dollars on the table and followed her across the adjacent road where they sat down in a bower just as the sun was reaching its zenith. The air was still and heavy but the sweet scent of wild orchids had filtered into the bower earlier and remained suspended above the ground. Quite suddenly, she said: "I don't want you to affect my life. I don't want to like your life. Or you."

David said quietly: "I don't know what that man said, but it's not difficult to guess. The thing is, he seemed to touch a fear that you have, just under the surface." He paused, searching for the correct tone to express a firm opinion kindly. He could not show surprise or displeasure, it was not in his nature to compound the distress visible in her eyes, but he was reluctant to leave it unsaid. "It's a fear you shouldn't deny. Maybe you should try to overcome it because it affects your independence".

For the first time, she sensed disappointment in him, disappointment with her. He looked away, as if suddenly interested in the breakfast shed across the road. Girly walked to the edge of the bower where, from David's position sitting on the uneven, tree-rooted ground, she stood in silhouette against the blue, cloudless sky. "We're different." she said. She walked back to the car.

Instead of taking a direct route back to Penal, David detoured via Fyzabad in order to visit his home – the Trinex Oil Company estate for retained employees. Although always referred to as "the estate" or "the compound", it was actually a self-contained, secure village with a security guard at the entrance who manned a barrier comprising a sentry box with adjacent, horizontal red and white pole.

The red car was waved through to a perfect stretch of tarmac road lined with mature, vermilion-flowered *flamboyant* trees leading to a central square. Three subsidiary roads gave access separately to a residential sector of pastel coloured bungalows, a leisure complex incorporating indoor sports' facilities and external tennis courts, a school building of eau de nil painted clap board beneath a white metal roof.

Girly hated it. Although David, in apparent innocence, only wanted to show her his normal environment, the place where he lived, she made him stop the car. She told herself that despite the snarling, hurtful language and intent of the man at the breakfast shed, she didn't give a damn about David's background, race, or religion, if he subscribed to one. But she could not tolerate a trip around this 'forbidden territory' as one of her friends had named it.

She sometimes met with friends, old school friends and casual acquaintances at a street-side café in Penal to spread news and discuss their busy lives. On many occasions, the subject of the European influence in south Trinidad had been mooted in low tones; the consensus was that the Europeans deserved to be shunned due to their lack of integration, their reluctance to leave the ivory tower of the Trinex compound. They were rarely seen on Penal's streets. Girly would never close her mind to any group of people; she did not subscribe to the theory that those living in a parallel world should be ostracised but she felt a deep dislike for the idea of the kind of separation she could see in front of her.

"This is why we're different," she explained to David. She spoke earnestly, without the taint of petulance she had displayed on occasions the previous day. It was as though she had to convey a series of basic facts to him that should have been self-evident but were escaping his attention. "It's nothing to do with who you are. Can you see how Trinex hands out privilege to foreign employees which is denied to Trinidad people working for the same company?" Her tone rose to emphasise her outrage.

Girly looked steadily into his eyes to see if he understood. There was a flicker of anger but no riposte. He was infuriatingly taciturn whenever she doubted or criticised him. His self-control was like an invisible cloak he drew around himself to keep in any outburst which might cause offence.

David had terminated the visit in sympathy with Girly's view that it had been a mistake, but without offering any explanation. On returning to Clarke Road at the end of the day, David said: "I'll be here tomorrow at the usual time."

Then she said the words he had heard before: "I won't be here tomorrow."

And she wasn't at Clarke Road at ten o'clock the following day. David waited until ten thirty; he could not see the small window above the funeral parlour from where Girly craned her neck to observe the meeting point. She saw him climb into the red car and drive away; there was no hint of annoyance or disappointment in his body language. She spent the day attending two funerals at Mosquito Creek; her sombre mood was not caused by the sadness and seriousness of the occasions. Even at nineteen she was becoming inured to the process, repetitive as it was, whilst exhibiting appropriate decorum. Her mood was darkened by the realisation that she might be making a mistake. During the previous evening all negative thoughts she had towards David had begun to melt away. The visit to the Trinex compound had briefly angered her but that aside, what had he done? That morning when she had watched him from her window driving away in the red car, there were pangs of regret and something else: a short but overwhelming sympathy and admiration for him which brought an involuntary strange sound to her throat. Everything she had told him about their different lives no longer seemed crucial. She wondered if, as an outsider, he saw Trinidad as a picture or a series of tableaux; although he had spent most of his life in the country, it was, she supposed, a sheltered, separate childhood and youth. But he gave no impression of shallow fascination with her race, no uninformed views of the country or its population. His interest was real. One thing troubled her and may have been the true cause for her previous disquiet: she admired the fact that he was able to stand his ground with the man in the breakfast shed, a man she considered dangerous, but she hated the notion it was on her behalf. It had not been a display of bravado to impress, rather an automatic, fearless response to an outrageous slur. She should have seen it as a welcome intervention, but it troubled her because momentarily she saw a danger in him equal to that of the other man.

The next morning she dared to hope he would be waiting for her again at Clarke Road. At ten o'clock she saw him arrive at his usual place; she found herself hurrying downstairs, stepping stealthily across the parlour lobby to avoid Jigs and her father. The back door to the yard was open as she brushed past Rishi and Raj who were loading an occupied coffin into a funeral car. A short walk to Clarke Road brought her face to face with David; there was no mention of the previous day.

"We're going north. I'll show you religion," she said cryptically, ignoring his smile and evident pleasure that she had returned. She directed him to turn the car towards San Fernando via Erin Road, but they avoided the town centre and skirted to the Southern Main Road which hugged the coast, passing the Point Lisas refinery next to the brown waters of the Gulf of Paria, stopping only when they arrived at Waterloo on the west coast. David gave a short laugh then stared in amazement as he saw an ornate building at the end of a causeway projecting into the sea. The Temple in the Sea with its white dome rose from a concrete platform surrounded by the Gulf in a scene that David thought might be typical of any Hindu place of worship in India, but he was amazed to see it in Trinidad.

They entered the temple after removing their shoes. Girly pointed out the stone gods; she gave a brief account of their roles in the Hindu religion in a detached way as if the knowledge had been fed into her in the past, possibly at an early age, but was of no deep interest. It was part of who she was rather than a constant devotion.

Sunlight pushed its way through the multi-coloured glass windows lending warm hues to the interior. Outside, many prayer flags fluttered in the sea air above the incense, oils and flowers, left behind from *pujas*, the prayer meetings in honour of the Hindu gods that were a regular feature of the temple complex.

As they stepped outside, David said: "Your family members are not all Hindu." It was not a question - he had heard this from Mr. Dhanraj during their long conversations at Ramdass Trace.

"No. Extended Indian families in Trinidad sometimes have different religions, even amongst brothers and sisters. Hindu, Presbyterian and maybe Sikh way back. You can't tell a person's religion from the surname. Also, Hindus do not always follow their beliefs strictly. We see that at funerals." She stopped. She wanted to keep away from the subject of the funeral business.

They sauntered away from the Temple in the Sea; Girly looked at the sun, still high above them. The walls and dome were in full white light – the building seemed to float on the calm waters. She wanted to travel further north to the Caroni Swamps so that he could see the early evening return of the scarlet ibis flocks. The birds flew in thousands each day to feed in Venezuela then returned to the Swamps each evening. But it would be dark before they returned to Penal. She decided against it. David suddenly stopped, as if remembering something important, and said seriously:

"There's a man who stands at the barrier outside the Trinex compound – you saw him the other day." He was not deterred by the immediate narrowing of her eyes. "When I spoke to him this morning, he mentioned you and said I had 'Gone sweat rice'. Do you know what he meant?"

Girly placed herself close to him and directly in front so that she could search his features for signs that the question was disingenuous. She found none. She decided that although he had no idea what the expression meant, she was compelled to test him again, look for a reaction. She could have denied any knowledge of the term and left it at that. But the small mischievous spirit inside which surfaced when she was with David would not allow her to wave the question away. She edged further away from the Temple as if what she was about to say would offend the aura of religion.

An intimidating statue of Hanuman the monkey god, over twenty metres high, looked down on her, directly into her eyes she thought, from a short distance away. She was not dissuaded.

"In the Caribbean, when a woman wants to keep a man, stop him straying away, she boils up some rice." She looked to see if he was following. His eyes had lost focus, looking somewhere over her shoulder, pondering the problem. "Then she squats over the steaming rice and the sweat from her....drips onto the rice. The man eats the rice and he is hers forever."

David suddenly refocused on Girly's neutral gaze. "Do you believe this?" he asked seriously.

A short pause. "I'm West Indian," she said simply.

They burst into spontaneous, white-toothed laughter and he touched her for the first time, a brief hold on her arm as the laughter subsided into mild embarrassment. It was nearly the end of their time. A small sadness stole into the space between them.

Girly decided they would not travel on to Caroni. They returned to Penal; David walked around the front of the car to where Girly stood. Then, with hands behind their backs, they leaned forward and touched foreheads, briefly and awkwardly. Girly walked away before he could see the smile she felt inside rise to her lips.

The following day David had left for London. Early in the morning, he posted a letter for her at the funeral parlour in which he promised to write regularly and return as often as possible over the next three years. He kept the promise; she looked forward to his letters and, during the following two years, treasured his occasional visits.

***

As the smoke from the funeral pyre dissipated and its irritating tang gave way to the pure sea air, Girly and David stood alone at

Mosquito Creek. She shouted at him: "You left me...", but then she hesitated and thought back to an earlier remark.

"What do you mean you waited at Piarco for me?" she demanded.

David spread his hands wide in exasperation. "I had to leave at short notice. I left a note with Jigs so that you could meet me at the airport. I wanted you to come with me."

They stared at each other for long moments before turning together to see Jigs driving the hearse out of the car park and back along the road towards Fyzabad.

EVENING

Ravi Bishoo sat in his off-white underwear on the front veranda of number fifteen Ramdass Trace. He sat in companionable silence with his young son who drank from a coconut. In an untypical burst of energy, Ravi had climbed a coconut palm at the side of the house and dislodged its fruit. Several would be sold to the travelling coconut man the following day; Ravi had sliced the top off one coconut with a cutlass, just enough to expose a hole in the centre, into which he inserted a straw and passed it to his son. The enervating warmth of early evening wrapped its arms around the veranda and squeezed. Ravi scratched the parting in his dark wavy hair.

Earlier in the day, the postman had tossed a white envelope onto Ravi's veranda with practised ease. It was still there. A fly had occupied it for several minutes until the radiated heat from the sun became uncomfortable. The fly then left a small mark next to the red logo of the Trinex Oil and Gas Company and disappeared into the bush.

Safina, Ravi's wife, had looked at the envelope several times that day, reminding him to open it. He eyed it now with suspicion – it appeared to be very official. Ravi did not like to be bothered by official matters because they could be guaranteed to upset the comfortable balance of his life. He was an affable character who took his domestic duties seriously. Most mornings, he escorted Safina to the end of the trace from where she boarded a taxi to Krishna's Grill on Lachos Road. There, she was cook and general factotum, working ten hours daily. Ravi would return to the house where he pottered and dozed or clipped his brownish lawn.

Ravi began to read the letter but after several minutes, during which his mild curiosity had not converted to wisdom, he decided to consult Mr. Sagar Narsingh about the contents. He slipped on a pair of open-toed sandals and padded along the trace, a crepuscular ghost in his off-whites.

"Pump Man! I have a letter!" Ravi shouted, standing on the road outside the front of Sagar Narsingh's house. The Pump Man's face appeared at a front window, his features diagonally split by a strip of brown paper stuck over a crack in the glass.

"Is you, Ravi? Come."

Ravi would not ascend the wooden staircase at the side of the house. He preferred to cross the front yard and enter via the veranda. The Pump Man had retaken a seat at a rickety table in the kitchen; he gave up on a half eaten baked fish with bread. He felt no regret at Ravi's interruption.

"That fish have plenty bone, you know", he said accusingly, as if Ravi were to blame. Ravi had no intention of discussing fish.

"I have a letter today from Trinex," he began.

"I have one same. Everyone on this side of the trace have a letter". Sagar Narsingh wiped his fingers on a damp cloth whilst looking around the chaos of the kitchen for his own version of the Trinex missive. During the afternoon, he had passed along Ramdass Trace to enquire of each householder whether they were also in receipt of such a letter. There was no confirmation from the opposite side with the exception of the widow Dookie; it transpired that she had been informed of a reduction in the rent payable for the oil pump on her land at the end of the trace next to the Company Road. The Pump Man was at first puzzled. He then remembered that the question of access determined the oil company's intentions – land adjoining Erin Road was easily accessible for machinery and the necessities for drilling while the land opposite was not. The reduction in Indira Dookie's income was an extraneous matter and, in the Pump Man's view, vindictive.

Ravi absorbed Sagar Narsingh's explanation that Trinex intended to revive onshore drilling and oil extraction, with full government backing, after decades of winding down such operations and concentrating on offshore exploration and production. There would be four plots affected. In addition to those present, Sunil and Amit Jaggernauth, first cousins, and their families owned the other two plots on the same side of the trace, numbers nineteen and twenty, but incorporating three houses to accommodate the ever expanding Jaggernauth clan. In total, they had a further two hectares that could be affected.

No one could recall when Indira Dookie's mother had leased her small plot at the end of the trace to the oil company. The pump had been there ever since anyone could remember and was not on land contiguous to any dwellings. This was the difference now with the Trinex scheme: noise and change in the immediate landscape would impinge upon the residents' quiet enjoyment of their own properties. The rents offered, even if they had been fair value, would not have compensated for the disruption caused to a way of life long established in Ramdass Trace.

Ravi waited for the Pump Man's thoughts on the matter.

"Is a difficult t'ing for me as a employee," he mused. He had been considering his position all afternoon. Both hands were clasped across his ample stomach as he sat back in his chair. He dislodged a small fish bone from between his teeth with a sucking motion and transferred it to his plate on the end of a damp finger. Ravi, whilst waiting for further clarification, allowed his eyes to wander around the room. There was an eerie desolation about the place, like a long-abandoned mine, with a palpable sense of a house dying through lack of care. Negligence had opened wounds that would prove fatal unless the Pump Man could gather a vestige of courage to confront the certain demise. Meanwhile, the house bled inevitably towards the end.

The living room and kitchen were effectively one room running from front to back of the house. Despite the desperate lack of maintenance, the house was relatively clean. The Pump Man had no problem with basic housework – it was only the repair and upkeep of the fabric and fittings that troubled him and reduced him to hopeless despair. Ravi saw wood panels lining the walls, a few of which had long since been turned to dust by insect attack. But then, incongruously, there were five snow-white, short sleeved shirts with pen pockets on the fronts, perfectly laundered and ironed, hanging on a picture rail. The Trinex Oil and Gas Company logo was embroidered in red above the left hand pockets. Ravi knew of the Pump Man's anxiety relating to the house. He would not let his neighbour see him examining its worn surfaces. His eyes darted back to the table.

Sagar Narsingh stood up and collected a glass jug of juice from a larder cupboard. Earlier he had squeezed grapefruits from his own garden, mixed the juice with water, sugar and a touch of vanilla. He poured two glasses.

"What it need," Ravi offered, "is letter from all on this side of the trace to say 'no' to Trinex. Refuse rent. Trinex can take offer to other trace."

Sagar Narsingh thought for a moment, then said: "What it need is a representative, someone to take our views to Trinex." He raised his chin and regarded Ravi with half-closed eyes; Ravi took this as a challenge to contradict and also as an opinion that he was not the person the Pump Man had in mind.

"Jaggernauth cousins?" Ravi asked.

"No!" the Pump Man cut the air with the edge of his hand, dismissing the notion. "They don't have the words. But Jigs have the words and the way of sayin' them."

He thought about the effects of drilling he had witnessed at first hand as an employee: surface contamination by spilt oil being the most visible scar. The Pump Man always struggled with the dilemma of his employment. He hated the idea of potential damage to land, along with water contamination, but he recognised an economic need for the wealth beneath his feet. He shuddered mentally at the possible damage to his land, raising the spectre of Ranji Village. He would not discuss this with Ravi. Ranji Village...the Pump Man closed his mind.

They talked around the problem for several minutes before Ravi left with a mission for the following morning. He would accompany Safina to Penal, kiss her goodbye and wish her a happy ten hours of labour at Krishna's Grill, then call on Jigs at the Penal Funeral Parlour with a request from Sagar Narsingh, the Jaggernauth cousins and himself that Jigs should make an appointment with the writer of their letters, Mr. Wendell Soames of the Trinex Oil and Gas Company in Santa Flora, with the express instruction to nip this stupidness in the bud, as Ravi and the Pump Man had named it and agreed. The fact that the Jaggernauth cousins had not been consulted did not seem to be a concern.

Ravi walked back along the trace, past the widow Dookie's house on the opposite side where, in the neat and tidy living room, loneliness touched Indira on the shoulder and settled by her side on the sofa like an old friend. She was thinking of Anil, her dead husband, and mused on his careless, wasteful ways; she tried not to think of Caroline during sad times as if sad thoughts would taint her. The silence beat against Indira's ears, pushing at the delicate balance of her sanity, probing into her need to preserve at the forefront of her mind the only thing that had mattered in her life.

The potential loss of income from Trinex had occupied her for a long time that day; she walked into the smaller of two bedrooms where a tall cupboard stood in a recess. Inside were hanging rails with clothes of all sizes from child to adult; on the floor were piles of green cardboard boxes containing shoes. Nothing had ever been worn. Whenever Indira went to San Fernando to buy clothes or shoes, which she did occasionally, she always went to the same store where no questions were ever asked as to why she never tried on a shoe or a dress. Now, she feared she would have to stop. She preferred to stand at the entrance to the bedroom with no light except moonlight, especially at its zenith when it would cast a glow onto the pillow on the bed and she could picture the sleeping head of a child. Sweet thoughts would occupy her for a long time.

Ravi walked on, in no hurry. At number twelve he saw Mr. Dhanraj and David sitting together in front of the house, talking quietly. Ravi would not intrude. He went home.

***

David had accepted Mr. Dhanraj's invitation to spend the night at Ramdass Trace; he had nowhere else to go at short notice. He could arrange for a hotel room the following day, but that would mean a trip back to San Fernando where he had lodged on his return two days earlier. His parents had left their bungalow on the Trinex compound and rented a house near Galeota Point where he could stay, if he could find the house in that remote part of the country, but he did not want to see them yet. First, he needed to complete his reintroduction with Trinex.

He tried to turn his attention to Mr. Dhanraj and forget about the scene with Girly at the funeral that afternoon, but the depth of her anger had surprised him; it had circled round him then invaded his mind like a dull ache.

"Girly playin' the fool today?" Mr. Dhanraj asked. Despite the awful events at Mosquito Creek earlier in the day which had reduced him to despair, he could not have failed to notice the short meeting between David and his niece. He knew them both so well, especially Girly's occasional short fuse that had clearly received an incendiary touch that day.

David was nudged gently from his reverie by the low, avuncular tones of his friend. Palm fronds rattled in the bush at the rear of the house, easily audible from where they sat in front of the basement room; perfume from a sweet oleander invaded the area below road level. Dusk danced silently through the trace, deepening the shadows, stealing the remnants of daylight. It drew heat from the ground, scattered it to the heavens and conjured up small zephyrs to cool the air. Night sounds began – crickets and squatting toads chirruped and croaked.

The house was empty; David knew that Mr. Dhanraj was delaying the time when he would have to step inside.

"No, there was a misunderstanding some time ago. All forgotten now," he replied, avoiding the truth.

As they reverted to silence, David forced himself to think of Sumatee Dhanraj, as if it were the last thing he could do for her. He looked at the chennet tree close to the side of the house, quite twenty metres high, with bunches of ovoid green fruit just visible in the fading light. Sumatee was known locally as the 'Chennet Tree Mother'; although she had no children of her own, she was famed locally for her wisdom and knowledge pertaining to child ailments and matrimonial disharmony. When consulted, she would stand in the shade of the great tree on hot afternoons and dispense opinions like a doctor pronouncing diagnoses and issuing prescriptions at a surgery. On occasion, a small queue of anxious mothers, rejected wives or lovers would form out on the road waiting for consultation time.

David saw such a queue on one of his earliest visits to Ramdass Trace. He had no idea what was being discussed or why women consulted Mrs. Dhanraj but he assumed she attracted attention and received reverence for a good reason. He fell into a habit of collecting home baked cakes from his mother's kitchen table as a contribution to the afternoon tea that was always presented. David was not well acquainted with Mrs. Dhanraj in the early days as she would leave him and her husband alone. But then they were drawn together by David's own mother: she had followed him one day from the company estate to Ramdass Trace, her interest piqued by his propensity for taking cakes and pastries with him on long afternoon absences. She almost gave up on the pursuit due to the distance she had walked in the stifling heat and humidity when she saw her son turn off the Company Road past the pumpjack into the trace and march straight to number six, waving at a slender woman standing under a tree at the front of a neat timber house. It was too late to turn back; David's mother approached the woman only after she watched David climb the front steps to enter the house. In the space of fifteen minutes, the two women had spoken openly, exchanged minor confidences and confirmed that David was there as a guest on a regular basis, mainly as company for Mr. Dhanraj who was retired from Trinex and had a wealth of stories to impart to his willing listener. David's mother never returned to the trace after that day but she provided a constant supply of groceries from the company's estate shop, conveyed by David to number six Ramdass Trace whenever he visited. An informal, reciprocal arrangement ensued; Mrs. Dhanraj would send David home with local dishes, specially prepared, such as callaloo, dhal or fried aubergine.

David had not spoken to his mother about her conversation with Mrs. Dhanraj; there was a tacit understanding that they both knew she had followed him that day. He became aware almost immediately that Mrs. Dhanraj's attitude towards him changed as if she had learned something about him requiring empathy; he suspected she had been told of his sheltered, restricted life on the compound and had therefore realised his need to escape periodically to a different world. She initially showed some curiosity towards his daily life to confirm her view but then never again asked him anything about the estate or the people within.

Mrs. Dhanraj regarded David as a young companion for her husband; she knew older men liked to reflect on times and events that might amuse or bore a younger audience. She liked the calm, polite confidence of this boy; her acceptance of him as a surrogate son came later and gradually.

David had been informed of Mrs. Dhanraj's demise via a telephone call from the Trinex office in Santa Flora while he was in London; he travelled immediately in the knowledge that the funeral would follow quickly. During the long journey, as now, he pictured her as she was at her very best: wise from a lifetime of observing the faults and attributes in others, receptive without being intrusive, a close friend to all in the trace. From the early days he knew that he did not need a surrogate mother, his own mother doted on her only child without smothering his development, but Sumatee provided a willing ear to the frustrations of adolescence without ever prying into his home life.

David looked at his elderly friend in the faint yellow light cast from the single bulb inside the house. He decided to stay with him for the next few days, the worst period of bereavement, even worse than the time leading up to the funeral.

In the contained warmth of the front yard, the two men reminisced awkwardly, afraid that an old, personal view of Sumatee would offend or be misinterpreted. Mr. Dhanraj had brightened visibly when David offered to stay for longer than one night; David knew that no one else from the immediate family or circle of friends would enter the defiled house for some time.

When Mr. Dhanraj got up to walk over to the chennet tree and touch its rough bark, he carried away with him the suffocating miasma of loss, allowing David to channel his thoughts towards Girly. He did not want to dwell on the earlier confrontation; there had surely been a misunderstanding three months ago –had Jigs forgotten to hand the message to Girly, or had he deliberately failed to inform her of his hurried departure? There had never been any relationship between David and Jigs, cordial or otherwise. The briefest of greetings or polite nods had satisfied both of them.

Jigs had never been a factor in David and Girly's relationship either. Until now. During the three years David had been at university in London, he returned to his parents' bungalow once a year and spent as much time as possible with Girly. She never went to the Trinex estate.

David considered the time leading up to his first departure, the short period spent travelling around the island with Girly. She had an unsettling effect on him that he could never pinpoint or capture, a feeling of being constantly unsure whether she approved of him or was merely curious. She held a strange allure which became a fascination, even when she was dismissive, almost insulting towards his background.

He was sustained in his fascination during their travels by her occasional reference to the differences between them; he assumed she alluded to race and upbringing but he also knew from the first day that she cared nothing for these things in reality. She had tested him almost beyond temper and endurance in an obvious effort to find a reason to cast him away.

In the years that followed, he found it easy to combat her sometimes transparent baiting by the simple method of being the person he truly was and giving her no reason to suspect a hidden character or to search for a damning trait. As time passed, Girly had abandoned her attempts to excavate a facet of his character which would condemn him. His fascination grew as he was encouraged by her diminishing reserve until the point was reached when, as he returned from London after three years, an easy, close relationship developed which excluded any outside influences.

In due course, he was aware that his vision of her was selective – only the good characteristics remained in the forefront of his mental picture in which he chose to believe that they had grown and matured together. But in some deep, securely locked place within him, his admiration for her was tinged with an inexplicable melancholy which he found depressing, a feeling that it would end badly through no fault of his own. This may have influenced his inability to contact her when he was in London; he just could not find it within himself to ask directly why she had not responded to his note.

David looked as Mr. Dhanraj climbed the front steps of the yard up to the road surface. Evening relaxed, crossed its legs and watched them both from above through starry eyes. As a translucent cobweb of cloud crossed the half-moon, darkness consumed Mr. Dhanraj; his footsteps, at first tentative, became purposeful as his eyes adjusted to the lack of light and he walked to the Pump Man's house, standing outside, just as Ravi Bishoo had stood earlier. But there would be no welcome anywhere in the trace for Mr. Dhanraj on this evening or in the near future. Small lights flickered in bare windows on both sides of the road; insects buzzed around his head. He accepted that he was not acceptable because of the loss of his wife. Only David could provide a hole in the screen of isolation.

David listened to the footsteps receding along the trace with the occasional scuff of loose tarmac. He tried to look ahead but was inexorably dragged back to the past. Was he here to recapture something that was lost, already burned away on a pyre of misunderstandings or deceit? Strangely, Girly had only disappointed him once, on that occasion long ago outside the breakfast shed at Oropouche. It was the only time he had seen a vulnerability in her; he was disappointed by the nature of it, but more than that, surprised at how easily a comment from a stranger that should have had no significance quickly became a jolt in her mind, as if she should suddenly question their friendship and her own motives. David's gentle criticism of her that day briefly pushed him further away from her until she had time to recognize his innocence.

Now, his belief in a future here remained intact but it was tenuous. He revisited the day he left for London three months ago. Leaving a letter for her in which he asked her to walk away from her current life, even temporarily, had been ill-conceived, overly dramatic and unreasonable. Although this was clear to him now, at the time he had been hurt by her lack of response because their relationship leading up to that point had deepened from pale shades of hope to a richly coloured commitment. He had convinced her about the certainty of his ambition; already, the promise to hasten back to south Trinidad after university, despite her earlier cynicism, and fall straight into the arms of Trinex and Girly had been fulfilled. He repeated it whenever she asked, a reassurance she held, not as a comforter, but as a key to open up the years ahead. And it fell into place easily so that the reassurance became a guarantee during the time between his return from university and the sudden rush back to London. If she had been able to tell him that travelling to London was not inconceivable but at that time, impossible, he would have understood.

The brief, strained conversation earlier that day at the funeral told him little except that Jigs might have had a hand in her apparent confusion. She said nothing to explain. Looking back, did he expect too much? Despite her initial indifference, then explosion of anger, he dared to believe that all would be well.

David reflected on his attraction to Girly. In order to disentangle all the sentiments that did not really matter, the rebuffs and reconciliations now counting for nothing, he would have to consider the exact moment they first met on Ramdass Trace and relive an impression from long ago, misted and suppressed by familiarity. It would not come.

In the school at the Trinex compound, friends and acquaintances came and went. It had always been that way, part of a life he had regarded as natural in a community separated from the host population and based on a parent's employment. He had never found it an impediment to his aspirations; he had no time for issues beyond his control but stoically endured Girly's early disdain for his cloistered existence on the basis that she would eventually recognise the futility and welcome his independence and spirit. All he had was a depth of feeling, a positive belief in one corner of his mind, constantly visited, connected to a dwindling store of hope. He would stay here and devote himself to the task, for it would not be easy, aware that Girly would have withdrawn into her own familiar world and would only re-emerge on her own terms.

2 DARK OPIATES

Jigs Boodoosingh sat on the pale brown sands of Quinam Beach and looked out across the Columbus Channel. The sea here was blue, similar to the Caribbean along the north of the island and distinct from the brown waters of the Gulf of Paria to the west. He was alone, although much further along the beach two fishermen were pulling nets from a small white boat that was half in, half out of the sea. There were no religious ceremonies on the beach today; Jigs saw the water's edge smoothing the sand, pressing it flat and leaving it to sparkle in the sunlight. As the surf withdrew it bubbled over the surface then faded away.

Jigs knew of another Caribbean island where the lapping of the sea turned the sand a definite shade of pink. Was it Antigua or Barbuda? He could not remember. He told himself he would like to see that pink sand but it would mean a journey on one of those island hopper aeroplanes he had seen at Piarco. He would not travel. The thought of leaving home and spending a day or more away could make him drum his fingers on a nearby surface and induce rivulets of sweat on his back. He knew it was irrational, but any form of transport other than his beloved Ford car was anathema to him. He never understood whether it was just the mode of transport that concerned him or also the actual movement towards any destination beyond Port of Spain, which represented his maximum distance from Penal. A few minutes research once indicated he might be hodophobic; he did not bother to analyse the possible cause, he had never travelled far and did not intend to do so, despite the lure of things that appealed to him. Instead, he would picture the pink sand, smooth and soft beneath the gentle waves of the Caribbean Sea.

The previous afternoon, immediately following Sumatee Dhanraj's funeral, Jigs had hurriedly returned to the funeral parlour, packed an overnight bag, informed Mauva Tocks, the parlour's secretary, that he would not return that day, then set off for Angie's on Quinam Road. He did not want to see Girly again until he had time to assess the impact of David's sudden return. Now it was early morning on the beach that never closed, never let him down, and offered him time to think.

He walked to the water's edge in his bright green shorts, feeling the already warm sand on his toes. The constant, hypnotic sound of the waves a few metres away was punctuated by the occasional call of a mockingbird in the trees at the back of the beach. Jigs had made a mistake, he knew. He cared deeply for his sister, considering himself in *loco parentis* despite the fact that there were less than ten years between them. She was part of the 'Naparima Crowd' as he called them: former schoolgirls who remained friends and met frequently at the bars and coffee shops of the south; he also knew that most of the girls were insincere friends who travelled to San Fernando or Port of Spain daily to work in banks and insurance companies whilst laughing behind their hands at Girly's occupation.

Since their parents had moved to Arima and left the business in his hands, he found the role of older brother and senior partner sometimes stressful; Girly was not an employee or colleague in that sense – she was a family equal who now knew almost as much about the funeral parlour and its routine as he did but was nevertheless his junior in other respects. He had never experienced any problems in his relationship with Girly until David arrived. The first time he saw them together he knew she would change; he had an uncomfortable feeling that David would take her away and a fear that she would not come back.

During the times that David made his occasional returns from London, Jigs saw Girly grow less interested in her work, her close friends and Jigs himself. It was as though she stepped into a different world whenever he appeared, then stepped back when he was gone. But each time, he thought she became more confident, better informed, a young woman who expected more than Penal could offer. She appeared to be waiting for something to happen in her life, maybe something that had been promised, not a future that was nebulous but one bound to be different and encompassing a wider world than she was used to occupying. Jigs believed David would let her down but his sense of decency would not allow him to interfere, to tackle David and demand an explanation of his intention. As a result he did nothing until David entered the funeral parlour three months ago asking to see him. Up until this point, they had hardly ever spoken; a nod of recognition on the street, a polite 'good afternoon' when David came to the parlour to see Girly. But on that afternoon, David had been in a rush on his way to the airport. He left a sealed envelope with Jigs, respectfully asking that it be passed on to Girly as soon as she returned from a trip to Port of Spain. He would spend the night at an airport hotel before departing the following day. The note inside the envelope asked Girly to join him before he was obliged to leave the island. There was no explanation as to why he had to go so suddenly.

As soon as David left the parlour, Jigs had opened the envelope against his better nature but, he told himself, because he believed it to be a duty to look after Girly's best interests. He decided there and then not to mention David's departure to her; the very thing he feared for so long would happen if she went to Piarco – she would leave him, Penal and fly off to an uncertain future. Jigs had no idea what a sudden change of life abroad might offer because he had no inclination himself to pursue anything in which there was a degree of uncertainty, a chance on fortune, and he therefore found it natural and responsible to impose appropriate caution on his sister. He had replaced the note inside the envelope and dropped it into a desk drawer. He had also intercepted a call from London some time later, promising to pass on a message to Girly but found his throat constricted when Girly next appeared. He could not utter the words.

A warm sea breeze licked his legs, attaching spray and sand in an uncomfortable crust. He turned and kicked a small pile of loose sand in annoyance at his own inability to solve the new problem of David's return. He would have to face his sister very soon and provide a suitable explanation.

***

Later that morning when Jigs had returned to business, Ravi Bishoo stood on the damaged rough pavement at Penal Junction opposite the funeral parlour; the building wore a rainbow hat following a brief rain shower blown in from the east. He hesitated. Should he call in at Donna's bar for refreshment before his appointment with Jigs Boodoosingh? He remembered his last visit to Donna's and decided against it. He had simply forgotten to pay Donna for a small aperitif because his mind was occupied by an advertisement he had seen at Fong's Hardware Store, standing next to the funeral parlour on the corner of Clarke Road. The poster in the front window promised an impossibly green garden lawn if one purchased a new automatic watering system. Results were guaranteed. Ravi could never understand why, when his house was surrounded by so much green bush, his lawn was always brown. This was surely the answer. As he walked out of the bar and proceeded towards Fong's, Donna had hurried after Ravi on flat soles and with a breeze in her dress shouting: "Rum thief! Rum thief!" which to this day rankled with him.

Donna had caught up with Ravi at the *doubles* stall outside Fong's. A tethered goat bleated loudly as Donna harangued Ravi publicly; the *doubles* man enjoyed his discomfort. Ravi had paid Donna, insulted the *doubles* man and the goat then stormed into Fong's to discuss lawn irrigation.

Ravi now looked across the road towards Fong's store. The *doubles* stall and the goat were still there. He was surprised that the goat had not been slaughtered and curried but no doubt its time would come. The building which housed Fong's goods was unprepossessing and gave no clue as to the variety and volume of its contents. A red tiled roof covered walls which were partly constructed in red clay bricks and partly in unattractive grey blocks. Here and there, the façade was adorned with permanent pictures of religious symbols picked out in coloured tiles. Hanuman the monkey god was prominent, as was a depiction of Jesus Christ performing a miracle. Fong's message was that the store welcomed all denominations of paying customer irrespective of religion.

Behind the façade, the store was a mixture of chaos, untidiness and profitable retailing. A constant stream of buyers kept the cash registers ringing in all departments so that goods were never left on display for long. At ground floor level, the central foyer gave access to food, alcohol and snack counters on the right-hand side; to the left, Mr. Fong himself, a Trinidadian of Chinese descent, fussed over bolts of cloth and festoons of curtains from behind an imported oak counter which contained an embedded brass metric measure. Between these departments, one could walk through to the yard at the rear where Fong's became a builder's merchant. Stacks of bricks sat beside piled bags of cement and sand along with the ubiquitous galvanised roof sheets. As a result of the store's location on a corner site, builders simply backed their vans into the yard from Clarke Road and were served from a wooden shed without having to enter the main building to make their purchases.

At first floor level, there were further departments selling goods ranging from party hats to electric irons, garden tools to water pumps. And there was the doughnut bar, created and administered by Madam Fong. Ravi thought about her cinnamon doughnuts and strong Venezuelan coffee which he could almost taste from his side of the street. But no. He resisted. To the vocal annoyance of a pedal cyclist, a motor cyclist and a saloon car driver, Ravi jay- walked across the junction and stepped through the funeral parlour's entrance into the cool reception area where Mauva Tocks looked up from her desk and regarded him with a jaundiced eye. Mauva had been the parlour's secretary for over twenty years and her admiration for Mr. Boodoosingh senior had known no bounds. She had heard of Ravi's treatment of the funeral jacket and was personally affronted.

"I have an appointment with Jigs," Ravi stated, although this was untrue. Leaving Mauva open mouthed he walked three paces to open a polished, teak- veneered door into an office to find Jigs returning the telephone receiver onto its base. The room contained one large teak desk, scratched and worn with age, a desk chair which had punctured upholstery allowing stuffing to appear on each wing like bruised ears, and a sideboard upon which rested several framed photographs of burial caskets, each one an advertisement for the parlour's available stock. The walls were covered with red wallpaper; further framed pictures and photographs, dusted and polished, hung squarely on the wall behind the desk. There was no chair for a guest; there was one window through which strong sunlight illuminated the desk and Jigs' worried features.

Jigs held up a hand. "I have no time to discuss grass today, Ravi. There's a body to collect at Siparia and the police in San Fernando are releasing a suspected murder victim following post mortem examination. I must..."

"Not grass today," Ravi interrupted. "Important business." He held his letter from Trinex in front of Jigs' eyes. At the sight of the Trinex logo, Jigs twitched slightly in his chair. He looked at Ravi. Although they were not related, their families had been close friends for many years and saw each other often, mainly due to the fact that Ravi and Safina lived opposite Jigs' uncle in Ramdass Trace. Jigs had often wondered about Ravi – he had never seen anyone who looked so well and fit but was so short of energy. Ravi was athletic looking, not tall and he had no sense of sartorial pride. The slightly stained white shirt and creased flannels he now wore were typical. Jigs occasionally thought of taking Ravi onto the staff at the parlour just to allow Safina to take a break, but he decided against it. Ravi would be unreliable and no doubt appalled by the suggestion.

Jigs got up and walked towards the window. "What's the letter about?" he asked, making no attempt to take it from its envelope. He needed a few seconds to think. Outside, his pallbearers, Rishi and Raj, were throwing wet sponges at each other instead of washing the hearse. Jigs rapped on the glass to end the horseplay.

"Trinex playing the arse," said Ravi, throwing both hands forward through the air in a dismissive gesture. "Hell of a t'ing. They too conceited, you know. They asking to drill on our land for small rent."

Ravi's normally calm exterior was ruffled. He was not looking at Jigs as he spoke; he racked his brains to remember what Sagar Narsingh had primed him to say. It came to him. "Pump Man decide he can't take it on as a employee. It need you to go to Santa Flora, persuade Trinex to stop whole blasted t'ing."

Jigs sat down again at the desk; he pushed the envelope back across the surface. "Yes, I'll talk to them," he said quietly. Ravi blinked, unable to believe it was that simple. He rose quickly. "I gone," he said as he passed through the door, threw a broad smile at Mauva Tocks and scurried round to Fong's where he intended to reward himself with strong coffee.

Jigs had not expected Ravi to be sent as a Ramdass Trace emissary, but now that it had happened he was compelled to act.

He could no longer delay. He picked up the telephone receiver and asked to be connected to the Trinex area director at Santa Flora.

"Mr. Soames? Boodoosingh here from the Penal Funeral Parlour."

"Ah, have I just died?" Laughter bellowed down the line like thunder over the Central Range. The fact that Jigs had heard this type of comment a hundred times before prevented him from participating in the full merriment.

"Or are you asking for my measurements so you can plan ahead?" Further bellowing. Jigs would have happily thrown the telephone at a wall but he persisted. This was too important.

"No, I'm sure you are perfectly healthy. It's about Ramdass Trace." Jigs could almost feel Wendell Soames stiffen in every sinew.

"What about it?" The tone was now icy.

"The residents have asked me to represent them. I have to see you."

There was a pause. "Can you be here at three o'clock today?"

"I'll be there." The line died. Jigs considered for a moment then called Rishi and Raj in to instruct them to collect cadavers from Siparia and San Fernando that afternoon during his absence.

***

At three o'clock, Jigs parked the polished Ford in an appropriate bay outside an administration block that housed the Trinex Oil & Gas operation in Santa Flora. The site extended to approximately two hectares from Erin Road; to the left of the main entrance was a series of low, grey concrete buildings with flat roofs containing the doctor's surgery where Sumatee Dhanraj had met an untimely end, and staff quarters combined with the administration offices. To the right, separated by an open area with concrete road surface, were store rooms and piles of equipment including parts of oil drilling derricks, pipe casings, pipes and generators. There were also semi-complete oil pumps in condition ranging from seriously rusted to gleaming metal. On the far side of the stores a chain link fence separated two huge metal containers, black but dappled with corrosion patches; these received oil pumped locally from individual pumpjacks and stored it until transportation by road for refining at Point Lisas on the west coast.

Jigs stepped out of the car under a brilliant blue sky. The humidity pasted suspended grey dust onto his exposed skin, and held the scent of curried meat before him as he walked past the staff kitchens towards the plain brown door of the main entrance. A metal sign indicating that this was the district home of Trinex Oil & Gas hung slightly askew above the door due to a missing screw.

Five minutes later, Jigs occupied a seat in front of the desk assigned to Wendell Soames, local director of operations for Trinex. There was none of the earlier levity – Wendell Soames was businesslike from the outset.

"When we last met, you agreed to help me, to ease the way forward for Trinex in our efforts to place an oil pump in Ramdass Trace. I assume you have good news for me."

Jigs looked around the room; nothing had changed since his previous visit one month ago. It was a room of contradictions: the fan on the ceiling, totally inadequate, rotated lazily and creaked with insufficient power to disturb the heavy air; there was a pervading aroma of damp carpets but the floor was covered with broken edge tiles; wilting fresh flowers stood in a glass vase that contained no water. The room was functional and plain. Smooth plastered walls were finished with off-white emulsion, flaking here and there, marked and stained in several areas by human contact. Three metal framed windows in the only external wall offered a view from first floor level across the site road to the oil containers opposite. The chair Jigs occupied was narrow, uncomfortable and noisy. He wondered whether Wendell Soames deliberately failed to replace the chair; its dry note of complaint under the slightest movement could convey discomfort under Soames' penetrating gaze.

Wendell Soames was forty years old, a Trinex man since late teens, and fiercely determined to carry out the directions of his employers in Port of Spain. Within his dark features he used slightly bulging eyes to good effect, a double skewer on which to impale others and impose his will. He had emerged from humble beginnings, a shack on a dirt track next to a sugar cane field near Princes Town, to claim his current position at Trinex. His rise through the Trinex ranks had been steady but not spectacular. An early apprenticeship in metal working was followed by successful studies of the oil business in Trinidad and the wider world. He was sponsored for further development by Trinex and sent to university for a year in Canada. On his return he was seconded to the exploration section of Trinex in south Trinidad where he formed part of a team that made successful discoveries of oil and gas off-shore over many years. He was elevated to local director of on-shore development just in time to receive orders from head office to restart on-shore drilling in remote parts of the island. He was bent on implementing this latest directive from Port of Spain.

Jigs was drawn back to the previous meeting; he had been invited to Santa Flora on the pretext of being offered the oil company's funeral business now that Sadusingh's local undertaking had closed. Jigs had wondered how the level of business could be predicted but assumed that Trinex would recommend or persuade bereaved employees to its preferred parlour. Wendell Soames was a wily operator - he made it his business to locate articulate, suitable representatives of all villages and traces where he intended to implement his programme of well drilling and bend them to his will. Local enquiries had raised Jigs' name as a suitable contact for Ramdass Trace.

"Mr. Soames," Jigs began with a friendly smile. "You know perfectly well there was no agreement concerning Ramdass Trace. When we last spoke, you offered me an inducement; I did not accept any future funeral business if it was conditional upon any intentions on your part regarding Ramdass Trace. In fact, I believe that a new well in that area is a bad idea. The residents won't accept it."

Wendell Soames leaned back in his chair, eyeing Jigs like an indulgent father. "Let me explain something about my position," he intoned, now gazing at the dust covered glass of the windows. "The government needs revenue, Trinex has to provide. Drilling licences are issued on proof of oil reserves and a fair rent of land offered."

He was about to continue when Jigs asked: "Who decides fair rent?"

"Trinex."

"And if the land is owned and the owner does not want to rent?"

Wendell Soames smiled as if Jigs had failed to understand the whole principle. "Many years ago, the government gave oil companies the right of acquisition of land and water. You should look at the Petrochemical Industry Act 1962." He waved a hand in the air as if the legal details were suspended there for anyone to inspect. "However, compulsory purchase is not considered necessary and leads to delays. The government therefore supports temporary occupation of suitable land with proven resources to be exploited."

Jigs eased his position on the chair which responded with a loud crack. "Are you suggesting that if the landowners refuse, the government, through Trinex, will force them to lease their land?"

"Watch me. The land in question at Ramdass Trace is used for nothing. It's just bush covering several hectares. The owners never even look at it. We could drill a well there, two wells, quick sharp and locate pumps without anyone seeing them. We take great care in these matters."

For the first time, Jigs felt an anger rising within him at the blatant misrepresentation he had just heard. The words hung over the desk like noxious vapours.

"You are well aware that there are hundreds of abandoned oil pumps in south Trinidad dating back to the 1970's. The wells run dry in no time or are no longer producing enough oil so you leave the pumps to rust away. Trinex delays capping of the wells which contaminates land because they leak. Why does Trinex think it will be different this time? I suspect the cost of actually sucking the oil out of the ground is high, so why do you think that even more isolated wells are viable?"

Wendell Soames looked at Jigs thoughtfully. He had underestimated this simple undertaker, this dealer in death; it appeared that he was well informed. But there could be no retraction, no going back. "There is a new need for production areas to support our growing population. The island needs housing, roads, harbours, public works, not to mention employment. This is all done through taxation, especially of oil companies." Soames allowed his eye lids to half cover his penetrating stare so that he would appear more reasonable. "The government takes about half of oil companies' earnings. It's a major partner in all aspects of oil and gas. You see, it's our duty to smooth the path to the treasury. Besides, neither you nor I can stop this. It's inevitable."

Jigs thought he detected a sign of the burden placed on Wendell Soames' shoulders. His tone was not triumphant, he was not imparting news that delighted him, it was a statement of fact leaving Jigs in no doubt that the policy would be enforced.

Wendell Soames rose and walked to the window, glancing at the ceiling fan that was rotating uselessly. He was sweating profusely. The hollow, grating sound of metal pipes being moved out in the yard added to the increasing irritation that Soames and Jigs both felt.

He continued briskly, as if the growing weariness he felt should not be projected to his visitor: "It's true that some wells produce good returns at first, then cease in a few days or even hours. This is the risk that Trinex takes. The rents to the landowners are guaranteed. Also, we need Ramdass Trace because oil in that area is top quality. It always has been in the Fyzabad region."

Jigs thought the statement of facts had not addressed the issue of abandoned oil wells from a previous era across the island, and the associated land contamination. He was aware that much expenditure on land exploration was speculative despite the use of seismology; but although his knowledge of oil production was limited, he had the evidence of his eyes on his travels around the south to make his argument rational rather than an emotional reflex. There was, however, one example not far from where they now stood that could always influence his attitude. He saw the need for oil and its importance to the country but there was an image in his mind he could never expel when he thought about Trinex.

"You haven't answered my point about damage caused by abandoned wells," Jigs retorted. "Look at Ranji Village."

Wendell Soames turned from the window as if slapped on the head. "What do you know of Ranji Village?" he asked sharply.

"I've seen it and it's a disgrace." Jigs rose to indicate the interview was about to end. Wendell Soames composed himself, walked to the desk and produced a white business card from a drawer. He handed it to Jigs.

"Whatever our opinions, this drilling must proceed. I can get a government order. However, it would be easier if you would persuade the residents it would be in their interests to allow a smooth operation. As I can't supervise the projects in every trace and village myself, I have a local man to....implement the company's requirements."

Jigs looked at the card. He saw David's name in bright red letters.

Jigs was in thoughtful, depressed mood as he drove along Erin Road back towards Penal; dust from dirt tracks at the sides of the road found its way onto the gleaming surfaces of the Ford, irritating him further.

The discussion with Wendell Soames weighed heavily upon him. He should not have been surprised to find David's name on the business card; he was a Trinex employee in south Trinidad and to Jigs' sceptical eye David would not have returned solely for the funeral or to see Girly. The problem Jigs now faced was either to persuade the residents of Ramdass Trace that Trinex could not be stopped, would not be deflected, and to accept the well drilling and rent offers, which would not be increased, or to organize a campaign of resistance to force Trinex to take their business elsewhere. He could not be a champion for every trace on the island, but he could not close his eyes and do nothing for Ramdass Trace. He remembered as a small boy how he liked to wander alone into the bush at the back of his uncle's house, on and on through pockets of damp shrubbery, naturally formed, past shadowy dells into tiny, sun dried savannah, everywhere the soft sounds of small life, far away from oil wells. A thought came to him about David's role in Wendell Soames' intentions: Soames needed tools that would not turn in his hands, loyal enforcers. Jigs had to find a way of turning David and the solution might be found in Ranji Village. He was sure David would know nothing of Ranji as Trinex would not want employees or the public to be aware of what had taken place several years before. He turned the car onto the beaten earth front car park of a rum shop outside Quarry Village. As he stepped out of the car and into the semi-darkness of the hostelry, the burden of responsibility bore down on him. He ordered *dhal;* he also needed the dark opiate of a small rum.

***

The following morning, although the district of Santa Flora sweltered under burnished skies, a cloud of sadness had settled over Ramdass Trace that refused to be evaporated by the hot sun. A nightjar settled onto the bough of a tamarind tree next to Ravi Bishoo's house; it yawned and stretched a wing, preparing for sleep after hours of nocturnal foraging. The trace was out of sorts, at odds with itself, unable to shake off the gloom imposed by the recent funeral of Sumatee Dhanraj and the letters from Trinex.

The widow Dookie tried to lift her depression by baking. As she hobbled painfully on arthritic knees across to Sunil Jaggernauth's house at number nineteen, she carried a small bag containing coconut cake and sponge cake. Sunil Jaggernauth opened the door half way, accepted the coconut cake with a nod and a strangled smile, and then closed the door firmly without comment. Indira made her way to the Roopnarine house at number three where she found old Mr. Roopnarine in the side yard, almost naked, talking to a tree. She looked for Devendra without success. He sat in the living room with windows shuttered, brooding on what had happened at Mosquito Creek two days earlier. He considered David to be beyond the pale. The more he thought about it, he believed David could not treat Girly this way, reappearing and no doubt confusing her after such a long absence, not to mention that his own intentions had been firmly set aside, reduced to the status of 'runner up' in the competition for Girly's favour. He considered physical retribution, but he was no street fighter. Perhaps he would seek David out to initiate a verbal battle in which his dilemma would be explained, his honourable intentions would be evident and his greater claim for her hand beyond question. Besides, the house with gates at Penal Rock Road was still vacant and set aside for her when the time was right. Devendra was deliberating as to the best place to find David when he turned to see Indira Dookie leading his father into the room. He looked at the old man's vacant-eyed nakedness and sighed.

At Mr. Sagar Narsingh's house, the Pump Man was inspecting a further development in the gradual demise of the structure. He was due to call on Ravi Bishoo before proceeding with his Trinex pump inspections but something had caught his eye as he tried to make his way out of the front door. The wall above the door had sagged, making it impossible to open. His failure to deal with the bats in the roof had allowed them to urinate over the metal lintel above the door, causing it to corrode. The Pump Man had no idea that this was the reason for his inability to leave the house by the front door; he only saw one further defect for him to deal with when he had the time. But as with the discovery of all new failures in the property, it set off an alarm that transmitted as the voice of the house, mocking him, now assuming a face suspended in grey smoke. It berated him, demanded to know what he was going to do about the impending disaster of a collapse.

The Pump Man gathered his courage, defied the evidence of his eyes: he tried to open the door. Which was stuck fast. The grey smoke cackled and drifted across his eyes, forcing him to turn away. He hurried to the side door, stepped onto the external staircase without a thought for safety and barrelled his way, wide legged, down to ground level. The staircase objected loudly but held.

Ravi Bishoo saw the Pump Man hurrying along the road towards him; he lifted himself reluctantly from his veranda chair to make his report to a breathless Sagar Narsingh.

As they conferred by the roadside, Mr. Dhanraj was sitting alone inside number twelve. "Time to go out," he said to no-one but himself. "Yes, puttin' on shoe."

He went out. "See if anyone on road." He stopped – he realised he was loudly describing his actions to himself and he wondered why. When he reached the road, he trembled with the knowledge that he couldn't stand the silence that surrounded him. He was alone. Ravi Bishoo and the Pump Man continued their conversation without acknowledging Mr. Dhanraj. The taint of death still clung to him and would not be dispersed for some time.

*****

Girly Boodoosingh walked out of the Penal Funeral Parlour into a Penal Junction which, had she emerged an hour or so earlier, would have glowered at her beneath charcoal skies, but now the air was as serene and warm as in Santa Flora, a few miles away. She was oblivious to the bustle of street commerce whilst slaloming along to Fong's store on high heels, avoiding pools of muddy water from early morning rain settled into pavement depressions.

Within five minutes she was sitting alone at a first floor table next to the doughnut bar. She looked distractedly at Madam Fong who, with economic, graceful movements, operated the massive chrome coffee machine. Madam Fong always wore a Chinese robe, sometimes red, sometimes blue, with mandarin collar and short sleeves; her jet black hair was piled aloft in the shape of a doughnut, similar in size to those plated and perspex-covered on her counter. She glanced at Girly and not for the first time admired the young woman's bearing, style, composed demeanour, all of which were enhanced today by a jade coloured business suit. They rarely spoke despite being commercial neighbours; Madam Fong placed a glass of mineral water on Girly's table with a nod and a smile then slipped away.

Girly waited. After her aunt's funeral, she had left David at Mosquito Creek, somewhat alarmed that he might have been speaking the truth about informing Jigs of his departure, but none the wiser as to his reason for leaving suddenly. She had made good time in returning to the funeral parlour but Jigs had already gone and did not return that day. She knew he was in his office late the following morning but she decided not to confront him where he might escape by taking a telephone call or be distracted by business commitments. She therefore left a message for him to meet her at Fong's on this morning. She saw him climb the staircase and settle into a seat opposite her just as she was ordering her thoughts. Girly knew she had given him more than enough time to compose a story, an excuse, but he was an honest brother. She trusted him to be truthful.

Jigs spread his hands flat on the table. He looked as if something sour had touched his palate. "This is what happened. A letter for you was...delivered while you were out. I..."

"Where you put it?"

Jigs looked even more sour as Girly slipped into dialect, something she did when she wanted to irritate him.

"In my desk drawer." He looked away. "It's still there."

Girly waited. "The fact is I thought David would take you away. For a long time. Which is what would have happened." Jigs appeared as uncomfortable as he felt; his hands dropped to his sides, he slumped in his chair. Perspiration raised a glow on his forehead although the doughnut bar was cool.

"You thinking for me now?" Girly pointed to herself. She was pleased with her ability to remain cool in the face of what she saw as a blatant breach of trust and honour between family members. If this conversation had taken place three months ago, when the deceit was fresh, she might have grabbed him across the table and bawled into his face from a distance of five millimetres. But much had happened in the intervening period; she was no longer sure it mattered. The dull ache of abandonment she felt when David left had dissipated, any ghost of the unborn had retreated deep into a place from where she hoped it would never be released.

Girly saw Jigs glance at his watch every few seconds. Madam Fong placed a full white coffee cup in front of him, the top zigzag patterned with chocolate powder. In his wretchedness he left it alone. To make matters worse, before leaving the funeral parlour to meet with Girly he had absent-mindedly wandered into the embalming room, something he would never do when occupied by the embalmer from San Fernando whilst going about his business. Jigs entered just as a cadaver's blood and fluids were being drained by injection and vein opening; a tray of cosmetics was placed at the side of the slab. Jigs felt a tightening in his stomach, a crashing in his ears. In addition to all the other troubles he had to endure, this set his nerves on a precipice that could only result in a scream if he did not flee the parlour at once.

Jigs checked his watch once more. In his habitual manner of displaying frankness and openness he replaced his hands flat on the table.

"There will soon be a problem at Ramdass Trace. It will have long term effects if I can't help the residents. Trinex are determined to prospect for oil and David is their employee who will...co-ordinate the 'invasion'. I won't go into details." Girly felt the colour rising to her cheeks; Jigs sometimes dismissed her ability to grasp important facts.

"The point is, I don't believe he returned just for the funeral or for you." Jigs adjusted his gaze away from the coffee cup for a second to Girly's eyes, searching for a reaction. He saw none. "However, David did not have a chance to explain...anything to you. As I also have no idea why he left, I've asked him to come here now to discuss it once and for all. With you. I don't want this hanging over me any longer and I don't want to speak to him yet about Ramdass Trace." Another look at his watch.

Girly's eyes widened in amazement that her brother should take this upon himself without consulting her. She realized however, almost through sibling telepathy, that Jigs had other, unrelated concerns that were taxing him; he wanted to be rid of this problem of his own making. Now .

As she was about to protest, David arrived at the top of the staircase and walked towards them without hesitation. Jigs nodded as he left in a hurry with a speed to match that of Ravi Bishoo leaving his office the previous day.

Girly saw David avoid her eyes as he sat opposite. "So tell me what happened," she said.

3 THE OVEN HOUSE

When springtime arrives in London, winter is often tugging at its sleeve, holding it back, loath to let it go. But spring prevails eventually, even if it is early May before it finally shrugs off winter's unwelcome hand. Cold, biting winds become softer by degrees, dampness dries slowly as the air accepts a warmer sun. The transformation conveys something of an illusion: colours appear brighter as grey skies lift; lugubrious faces may assume an occasional smile. Yet nothing really changes. If nature awakes to lift the spirits of a busy population, then it is a passing phase. London's landscape and moods are changed by circumstances, not by seasons; this is not to say that society is completely unaffected by spring in particular: daily life appears temporarily less chaotic, commerce and gainful employment less of a grinding machine to be endured. After all, summer walks hand in hand with the progression of spring, and that is when London wears a handsome face, extends a friendly hand that guides its visitors through streets and squares, parks and avenues.

It was during such a period of temporary optimism that David turned into Gallery Street in central London on the day after his hurried journey from Trinidad. He paced slowly along a brick paved pedestrian route, a safe haven from the threat of vehicular traffic, passing an eclectic mix of retail outlets ranging from a café which also sold cameras, to a bookshop specialising in the occult. The buildings of Gallery Street formed terraces either side of the pedestrian way, mostly comprising mid to late Victorian, four storey residential properties but all with shops at ground level. Front elevations were finished in brightly painted stucco incorporating decorative stonework window surrounds and ornate stone balustrades at roof level.

An old man sat morosely outside a café in the spring sunshine; his best years had walked past his eyes leaving him alone with nothing but caffeine and fading memories. David nodded to the blank face. Received no response. As he passed along the sunlit terraces, the International Gallery came into view at the end of the road standing opposite the junction with Gallery Street: Victorian Gothic appearance surrounded by low, grey brick walls carrying black metal railings between piers. David was not looking at the gallery. He was focused on the penultimate building in the terrace to his right: cream painted stucco and white stonework with the Oven House restaurant occupying the ground floor. Gold letters on a red background fascia confirmed the identity of the business.

David reached the building, pushed open the front door. It shivered on its worn hinges. He walked in, the door relaxed and settled quietly into its frame.

The Oven House was not just a restaurant. It provided a diversion for London's busy workers, visitors from out of town, and local residents. Clients ranged from bank managers to back street dealers, insurance clerks to street corner hustlers. The only criterion laid down was that the customer had to pay the rate for the time of day, and therein was the essence of the Oven House. You turned up, paid for lunch or dinner; the difference between the two was a pecuniary chasm one would not have believed unless one had visited before four o'clock and after six o'clock.

Quite simply, the Oven House was a diner and patisserie at one end of the scale, and a restaurant with a first rate chef at the other. It was open every day except Sundays, when the tired emporium rested its hotplates, cooled its grills and microwaves, turned its back on a hungry clientele. The common element was the premises but that was all. Even amongst London's many restaurants, it was unusual. The name did not change from lunch to dinner but during the 'closed' period between four and six p.m., there was a metamorphosis.

It was just after midday when David surveyed the empty room from a corner table. It was arranged for lunch with twenty tables of polished wood placed erratically in the available space. There would be no table cloths until evening when five tables would be removed. Wall and ceiling finishes could not change or be upgraded when the Oven house was shut; they were therefore unremarkable in content and design: colour washed plaster in pastel shades with stained wood dado panels that darkened the room somewhat but did not detract from the feeling that this was an unusual venue in keeping with the other businesses David had passed along the street. The ceilings were high, decorated in early twentieth century style with fibrous plaster mouldings depicting fruits and the occasional cherubic face along the perimeters. The ground floor element of the façade contained a large glazed panel, misted in manufacture to shield the diners sitting next to the window from passing, prying eyes.

David should have been alert and attentive to his surroundings and the microcosm of life around him, a young man like any other who gained experience by observing, questioning, taking part. Today, as customers began to arrive, he felt the bustle of the place begin; it was like a well rehearsed play with participants all knowing their roles thoroughly due to daily repetition. Some walked directly to what were clearly familiar tables, favourite locations in the room where the view or the relative privacy were important to them. But David was unable to fully absorb the growing atmosphere, take in the small changes as the minutes passed: he was feeling very ill and he was unsure whether he could make it out of the restaurant. He saw a man enter the room, scruffy and unkempt, making a beeline for a table in the opposite corner. It was a beeline making no concession to objects that might impede his progress – chairs were nudged, tables pushed, cutlery jostled. A neat orderly room was suddenly ruffled before a customer had been served.

David would normally have looked upon this minor invasion with some amusement. But now he could not concentrate on anything for more than a few seconds due to the debilitating illness he had carried for three days. He looked down at the written review he had found in a London guide:

'*By day, the Oven House offers basic fare comprising mainly hot-plate selections designed to satisfy the appetites of London's artisans, professionals and tourists who gather to feed rather than educate their palates. By night, the transformation is truly amazing: an atmosphere is created by means of low-level, recorded crowd chatter on a discreet public address system and the constant faint aroma of summer flowers. Dishes ranging from saffron risotto to red mullet or chateaubriand may be ordered from a seasonal, à la carte menu and an ever changing specials' list compiled by the remarkable Armand Fournier. There is also a reserve menu containing rarities such as zebra and kangaroo.*'

As he read further, the words blurred until the sense became apparent nonsense. Did the review really confirm that conjurers drifted between tables during the evening? Card tricks and magic wands? The article continued to expound the novelty value of the Oven House in a city where restaurants battled each other to find the quirk, the edge that might just be the difference between failure and keeping the doors open.

By now, David knew he had to leave. As he rose, he saw a waitress approach the scruffy man in a far corner. She had stepped out of a lobby next to the kitchen where racks of cutlery stood side by side with piles of snow white serviettes (paper for lunch time, damask for the evenings), rows of condiments on beechwood trays, short towers of crockery in three shades of blue. The man sniffed which produced a sneeze and a projectile of extraneous matter settled on the waitress's shoe as she arrived at the table. David did not wait for the next scene; he walked slowly from the room without having placed an order. As the new owner of the Oven House restaurant and a long lease on the small apartment above, he should have been assessing the future, deciding how to apply his new found wealth. Instead, the sickness inside him sapped his spirit and his ability to think clearly; for the first time, he was alone and unable to look after himself. The thought that he might be seriously ill carried him to a point of near panic as he left the restaurant on Gallery Street.

A distinctly cool gust of wind hurried along Gallery Street towards the International Gallery. David closed his short coat around him and viewed the pavement through rheumy eyes, trying to recall the pedestrian route he had worked out in the restaurant. He set off on aching legs endeavouring to ignore the fever which gripped his vitality and squeezed it almost to the point of submission. This was not influenza – something more serious had taken hold although some symptoms were similar.

He turned into Great Russell Street, then right into Bloomsbury Street leading to Gower Street, past busy pavements, shops and commercial enterprises, none of which attracted his attention. He concentrated as best he could on his destination but his thoughts were wandering, indistinct, focusing intermittently on the pain in his back and the pounding in his head. By the time he reached the plain, brick and tile panelled building off Capper Street, David was near the end of his endurance; it had been a long walk for a sick person, even a fit young man. He pushed open the entrance door of the Hospital for Tropical Diseases and promptly collapsed onto the floor.

***

David resurfaced from a dreamless sleep the following day still feeling very ill but in the relative comfort of a hospital bed. His first thoughts were mixed between a fear of having to return to the streets and the empty apartment above the Oven House in his present condition, and the lack of meaning to the two words which continually repeated themselves in his head before his collapse. At first, 'brown water' held no sense in his consciousness but would not leave him, as if they were a puzzle to be solved before he could understand his predicament.

A doctor approached his bed-white coated, bouffant hair-style and a smile to either project a confidence in his own ability or make him the possessor of an important piece of knowledge he was about to impart to his patient. David found his eyes directed to the doctor's hair which seemed to be living a separate life to its owner. His father had once told David that he could never take anyone who wore a toupee seriously. This was not a toupee but David thought the style detracted from the doctor's credibility. So when the doctor sat on the edge of the bed and said: "Sir, the diagnosis is clear. You have yellow fever," David felt he had resurfaced into a comedy sketch which would soon revert to an hallucination induced by his illness.

"Yellow fever? I thought it was the water. Poison." David tried to sit up but gave in to his aches.

"The water?" The doctor's smile was replaced by an amused frown.

"Yes, brown water from the tap. They said it was quite safe. Brown water, slightly ....fizzy."

The words had tumbled out unbidden to explain why 'brown water' occupied his recent hazy thoughts so much during his arduous walk to the hospital.

The doctor looked at David closely, searching for a yellow shade to his skin. He saw only a sun tan given an odd greyish mix by the virus. "You must have been abroad recently."

"Trinidad. I live there."

The doctor spread his hands as if all was now clear. "It's in the zone. Look, yellow fever is a virus spread by the bite of a certain mosquito. It's more common in Africa but also found in South America. Trinidad is just within the South American zone where it might be prevalent." The doctor assumed a severe expression. "If you've been living there, you should have had the vaccination. We took a sample of blood that confirmed you have the virus," he continued accusingly.

"I feel terrible. Headache, pains..."

"Yes, yes, all normal symptoms. You'll have to stay here for a while. There is no specific treatment and we have to ensure that when the fever breaks it doesn't return because then it could become really serious. Liver damage and other things you don't want to hear about. On the good side, if you survive there will be no lasting damage and you will have lifelong immunity. You'll be able to go home."

The penultimate sentence was delivered with a roguish smile as if to soften the blow of what the disease was capable of inflicting. The doctor left David alone in the small single ward; he looked at the two tone grey walls, clean and functional but drab in the weak spring sunshine filtering through the dust smeared window glass. He searched around the room for a glimmer of interest to lighten the depression rapidly overtaking his thoughts; the virus and drugs he had received overpowered him inducing a deep, long slumber.

Much later, David awoke to find the single, private room in semi-darkness. A small, pale lamp on the wall behind his bed provided only a shallow arc of light so that the far limit of the room could not be easily discerned. There was no internal noise; silent shadows closed in on his isolation. He assumed that this was an emergency single room from where he would be transferred into a large ward. He felt a slight improvement in his condition due to the easing of the fever. He needed to think; he was a young man normally able to calculate clearly and with a degree of perspicacity but so much had happened in the last few days, a confusion of illness and yearning to be elsewhere, the disappointment of leaving Girly and her failure to respond.

As he reached for the glass of water, crystal clear and pure, on the night stand next to the bed, he was reminded of how the recent sequence of events had begun. Several days before, he had arrived home from work with Trinex to his parents' bungalow on the oil company's compound to find his mother peering at a drinking glass half full with a pale brownish liquid she had just drawn from a tap. She explained that the whole estate was affected and residents were demanding answers from the Trinex property division responsible for maintaining the buildings and services. Trinex had investigated, assured everyone that the water quality was fine and the filtration system (a small enclosure at the back of the estate comprising a low, fenced-off building housing electronic filtering equipment for a large external storage tank) was operating effectively; the discolouration was a temporary, non-harmful event and not hazardous to health. David had drunk a small quantity of the water, reassured by the Trinex statement. He detected a slightly oily or gasoline-like aroma, the water also appeared carbonated, as if soda water had been supplemented by a very small addition of petrol and mud. It was only after he had opened other taps and the bathroom shower control that the extent of the pollution became clear. David's mother had walked across to the estate shop to demand vast, free quantities of sealed, bottled water but found supplies severely depleted since the onset of the pollution that morning.

David had thought about the likelihood of underground pollution of water from an undisturbed source, such as the local aquifer, and decided it was not possible. There had to be a reason for the sudden influence on the water supply. A short distance from the estate near Fyzabad, Trinex had recently erected a drilling rig close to the road and started to excavate, depositing extracted material into adjacent waste pits. David decided he would tackle Wendell Soames on the subject the following day. That night, David had experienced the first symptoms of his impending illness and attributed the cause to the water. The next morning, he intended to combine his visit to Wendell Soames with a consultation about his symptoms at the Santa Flora medical centre. But as he was about to leave the bungalow, he received a telephone call which would change his plans drastically and throw his immediate life into turmoil.

The glass by his hospital bedside was empty, the adjacent jug half full. Despite its clean taste, he detected harmless minerals in the water. He thought back to the news he had received on the morning after the first panic at the Trinex compound. Resident employees demanded action from Trinex –everyone seemed to attribute the cause of the pollution to local well drilling. After all, these were informed people who were not prepared to accept the company's word without full investigation. Meanwhile, David's parents were considering leaving the compound until the problem was resolved. David could not think about Trinex now; the telephone call from London informed him that he was about to benefit from the terms of a will made by a hitherto unknown aunt, his father's sister, who had not apparently bequeathed property or pecuniary advantage to her brother, and David should present himself at the offices of Anthony Stokes, solicitor, in London as soon as possible. David's father, completely unsurprised and unaffected by his disinheritance, had urged his son to leave immediately, ignore the possibility of infected water as a cause for his progressing illness, and seek advice in London. His father did not believe that the murky liquid passing through the water system at the compound could have had such an immediate effect on his son.

David had contacted Wendell Soames, explaining his intention to leave immediately and with the hope that his absence would be brief. He thought about Wendell Soames, the man who had taken him onto the Trinex staff in the local exploration department as soon as he returned to Trinidad from university. David was grateful for the job at the time but the sharpness of his gratitude had been dulled during the several months with Trinex as he became acutely aware that he did not agree with the destruction and potential local disasters caused by exploration on land. The company's attitude to temporary land acquisition made him realise he could not sustain the loyalty required by Trinex if it continued unchecked.

On more than one occasion David had heard Wendell Soames expound the theory "We can't afford the truth. Nothing would ever get done because truth gets in the way." David doubted this was original but it perfectly represented Trinex's current thinking.

The London traffic noise hummed outside the hospital window. Room shadows kept their distance around the bed. David suddenly felt an insecurity; this was not homesickness because he felt quite at home in this city. But it was a yearning for his first home: he missed the night noises from the bush near his parents' bungalow, the spasms of scent from bougainvillea outside his bedroom window, the breaking of a hot dawn with steam rising from rough grass pastures where treasured cattle grazed next to silent waterways. The heat of the room and raised body temperature rendered him unsure of his clarity of thought. His head maintained a crushing ache; he cursed the lack of a simple vaccination which would have prevented the debilitating ague that now afflicted him. How had his parents omitted to arrange for this basic requirement of life in the tropics? As the illness had taken a firm hold on him, his eyes were full of sickness and fear but now sorrow bit the edges of his anxiety; *"treat the symptoms, that's all we can do. The recovery is up to you,"* the hospital doctor had advised that morning. Where was Girly now when he needed her? Far away across the roofs, the streets, thousands of miles....David relapsed into deep sleep once more as dawn spread its light over London.

***

Three days passed rapidly in fitful sleep, half-awake discomfort and pain, periods of lucid awareness and occasional nightmares in which he was alternately attacked by clouds of mosquitoes emerging from a bubbling brown-water swamp in Caroni, then sinking into an oil pit on the Fyzabad Road with an unexplained immobility of hands to lift himself out. Hospital nightwear was periodically soaked in perspiration. Nurses came to his side regularly – brisk, intense and capable but no specific treatment was administered; medication was given for the symptoms. His continuing isolation puzzled him because the fever was not contagious. It suited him to be alone.

On the fifth day, the same doctor who had informed David of the diagnosis visited his patient, pronounced himself satisfied with progress but warned that bed rest would be required for several days more. David noted the formerly extravagantly coiffed specialist now sported a flattened, swept hair-style; he assumed the doctor had been caught outside in a rain shower.

As it was difficult to maintain threads of thought and make decisions, David decided to write down his ideas and intentions so that nothing could be lost to the fever if it returned:

On leaving the hospital he would have to visit Anthony Stokes to receive details of his aunt's will and presumably keys to the apartment above the Oven House restaurant. He had no idea about her wishes for the business; perhaps this would be included in the terms of the will.

Before leaving his parents, David had attempted to find out why his father had been omitted from his sister's will and also how she came to be the owner of a central London business which she was prepared to leave to a young, inexperienced nephew she had never seen rather than her only brother. David's father had been reticent, expressing a vague opinion that as the siblings had not been close and not met for many years, there would be no reason to endow him with a business and property. Also, he had lived abroad for many years working in the petrochemical business – he saw no reason why his sister, with no other relatives, would not entrust a young nephew with the responsibility and at the same time bequeath a great advantage. David would have to ascertain for himself whether the apparent windfall was truly an unexpected boon in his life or a burden. He assumed there was more to the brother-sister relationship and its effect on the will but he decided to take it no further. His father declined to explain how the aunt had acquired the London property.

It was with a feeling of surprise and no little excitement that David had set off from Trinidad to London, the drama in his life offset by the creeping illness.

David wrote a short list of items to discuss with Anthony Stokes before moving on to consider his position with Trinex. One major factor he could not fathom was why he had not been informed of the will until after his aunt's funeral. Anthony Stokes had been quite clear during the telephone conversation that the funeral had already taken place. David's father had been vague as to why he, the deceased's brother, had not been informed either.

David would soon have to make a decision – at this point he could not contemplate staying in London indefinitely, but with the inheritance came a responsibility to restaurant staff and to the aunt he never knew. He dearly wanted to return to the Caribbean, Girly and the life he had established with Trinex over the last few months. The fact that he now had grave doubts about Trinex created a further dilemma.

During the long lonely hours in the hospital room, David rehearsed the conversation he would eventually have with Girly, adjusting his tone, manner and content to reflect her attitude. It wasn't satisfactory. He had telephoned his parents, assuring them his recovery was progressing; he was informed that Girly had contacted the bungalow once, was told that David was in London, and no further calls were received. Why had she telephoned the bungalow when she knew he had travelled several days ago?

He would have to make a call to Penal; he imagined Girly at a work desk in the dated funeral parlour, no doubt arranging for yet another body to be reduced to ashes. He realised he had never been concerned about anything in her life in a critical way. A small force pushed inside him, twisting a sympathetic urge which translated as a feeling of loss; he might be away for a long time and clearly she had no intention of joining him in London. He had been away from her for long periods before while at university so perhaps she had finally decided their lives were too dissimilar. His sudden disappearance, which he had tried to explain in the letter, may have proved to be a step too far.

On a warm spring morning with parallel lines of yellow sunlight illuminating his dull room, David was drawn into a reverie which was a recent personal history with no conclusion, aching precious hearts, liaisons full of whispers and soft touch, private as a lover's note. Whenever he was with Girly, right from the very first, he tried to project a confidence he did not always feel; he was in awe of her ability to engage casually, disconcerted for no apparent reason when she habitually alternated her gaze between his eyes and lips when he spoke. The attraction was there from the very first day in Ramdass Trace but he could not dispel the feeling that she was beyond reach. He had decided at an early stage not to project any trait or aspect of personality which was not true; she would immediately see through it and in any case he believed it was not within his character to mislead. She would have to accept or reject him as he was but he was determined to work at the relationship through good and difficult times; during long separations when she might have given up on him he wrote long letters regularly. During brief visits to Penal he feared she might send him away. But she never gave up on him, she offered a drip feed of friendship and affection which suddenly became a closer bond, as if his absences fed a growing regard, culminating in one defining evening together in Ramdass Trace, barely one month ago, when, in the warmth of the dry season and close to the rhythmic sounds of the oil pump on widow Dookie's land, the world appeared to pause and give its approval to a union which produced nothing but a fleeting glimmer of life, later lost in damp leaves and black soil, while the bush averted its eyes.

The sunbeams in his room lifted into the far corners and melted away the shadows. David looked at the constantly moving dust particles in the sharp light. He was restless, becoming depressed by inactivity and the loneliness of his thoughts. He had to accept the fact that his relationship with Girly could change irrevocably, each with hopes and expectations unshared by the other.

***

As there was no-one to advise him, David decided to follow his own judgement; he left the hospital one hour later against the advice and wishes of the now re-bouffanted doctor. He made his way to the office of Anthony Stokes who welcomed him effusively, wasting no time in producing the file containing the last will and testament of David's aunt.

David looked around the office; it was located on the first floor of a modern office building of three storeys wedged between two beautifully preserved and maintained Victorian villas within walking distance of the Oven House restaurant. Although it was a disaster of town planning, the building was also impressively maintained; sadly it could not hide its 1950's design. The room occupied by Anthony Stokes was square, decorated with red and silver flock wallpaper, adorned here and there with framed cartoon prints of wigged and gowned barristers from another era. The oak desk and chairs situated in the rear third of the room were scratched and marked on several surfaces and large enough to be distinctly out of proportion with the room size.

Anthony Stokes was a junior partner in the legal practice that occupied just one office in central London and normally dealt with family law matters. He was in his mid-thirties, a large, shambling figure in an ill-fitting suit; it appeared to have been made with too much material, as if allowing for shrinkage at some future date, or made originally for a different person. He was made aware of David's recent illness but refrained from commenting on the misfortune of it or David's current appearance; he considered that his new client should still be in hospital. He was not entirely mollified when David read his thoughts and informed him that there was no possibility of contagion.

The solicitor began speaking at a pace to suggest this was a straightforward matter to be concluded quickly so that the sick person in front of him would remove himself without delay.

"As I mentioned previously on the telephone, your aunt's will is perfectly clear: you are the sole beneficiary of a business and residential property." He looked at the papers in front of him. "There is no cash to speak of. Our fees have been settled. Over the next few days, I will send you forms to complete. You've provided proof of identity so I can give you keys to the apartment today. Have you seen the restaurant yet?"

"Yes, I went there before I became ill. Can you tell me anything about the business, how it's doing? I don't know anyone connected with the daytime or evening operations."

Anthony Stokes sat back in his chair. He pulled the lapels of his jacket downwards so that the excess material sat more comfortably around his neck. "You need to see Ronny...er, Veronica at the restaurant. She runs the whole thing: daytime, evening, everything. More than that

I can't say and you probably have to speak to the restaurant accountants to find out how things are with the business financially."

David received the keys to the apartment in Gallery Street and was about to say his farewells to the solicitor when he remembered the short list of items he had made in hospital. He was perspiring freely despite the even temperature in the room; the virus was loath to leave its host. In spite of the doctor's dire warnings about the serious consequences of a possible relapse, David could not think about returning to the hospital at this point. He felt compelled to make his way to the restaurant, where he now had a contact, and assume his responsibility for the business and its staff.

Anthony Stokes had covered most of the questions on David's list. There was one final enquiry. "When we last spoke, you said the funeral had taken place a week or so before. As you knew about the will a long time ago, why did you not contact my parents or me earlier so that we could have travelled in time?"

The solicitor looked puzzled, a three-line frown appearing on his forehead. "I telephoned your father two weeks before I spoke to you. I told him his sister had died in hospital and gave him the funeral arrangements – cremation in accordance with her funeral directions in the will and the date and location of the funeral. Your father told me the family could not attend and asked me to telephone you directly a week after the funeral concerning the will. I told him you were the sole beneficiary and he seemed unsurprised."

David wiped his brow with a handkerchief. The aches and pains in his body had relented but the basic medication he had been given on leaving the hospital was struggling to keep his temperature even.

"Did you meet my aunt? You see, I have no idea who she was as a person. We never met even when I was at university in London for three years. I didn't know she existed until recently. My parents seemed reluctant to talk about her before I left, as though she was a stranger who happened to be a relative."

Anthony Stokes appeared to consider his words carefully. "I met her once, when she came here to make the will. She was clear that you were to be the sole beneficiary even though you weren't in contact. I got the impression that she may have made certain private cash arrangements outside the will with another person or persons but she wouldn't talk about it. That could explain why there is very little cash left now."

"And the funeral? Do you know who was there?"

"No. I couldn't attend. You should speak to Ronny."

David left the solicitor's office and made his way by public transport to a residential building owned by a London university one mile west of the Oven House. There, he collected luggage left to an old friend's safe keeping since his arrival from Trinidad. He retraced his journey back across London to the restaurant but first entered the door at the side of the glass frontage with the keys given to him by Anthony Stokes. The street door led to a short passage and staircase to the first floor where there were two internal doors for the two apartments; the staircase continued up to the next floor and, David assumed, further accommodation. He let himself into the front apartment, setting his luggage down in the short corridor. He walked into the living room at the front of the building. The room was bright with expensive-looking but dated furnishings. Wall and ceiling finishes did not look recent. David checked each room, confirming that it was a one bedroom apartment in serviceable condition, not to his taste and style but liveable. He assumed his aunt had been the occupier until her recent death although there was no evidence to confirm this: there were no personal effects, clothes or clues to her existence; the rooms had been cleared except for furniture and carpets.

The bedroom was at the rear of the building with a window view over a rear yard where boxes and crates associated with the restaurant were stored. Further on past the yard, the backs of buildings in the adjoining road stood starkly black in shadow against the pale blue London sky. David made a mental note to buy essentials for the property: bed sheets, towels and sundry items for what might be a long stay.

***

By the time the last customer had left the Oven House's afternoon period, Ronny had already arranged and prepared several tables for the evening session with laundered table cloths, cutlery and napkins. She usually expected the waiting staff to carry out the transformation, but she was short staffed and it was almost four o'clock.

As she was about to walk across to the main entrance to lock up, a young man opened the door and stood in front of her. He was tall, wide-shouldered and unwell. She knew instinctively who he was.

"I'm David, I...."

"Yes," she said. "I know who you are."

"Veronica?"

"Ronny. You look ill."

David shrugged. He was getting used to the idea that his recent debilitation would be reflected in his features. "I'm recovering slowly. I should have been here days ago. I went to see Anthony Stokes this morning. He referred me to you." There was no way of knowing how he would be received at the Oven House so David decided to say as little as possible initially and let Ronny lead him in acquiring whatever knowledge he needed.

They sat at an unprepared table where the same waitress David had seen several days earlier set down two cups and a full tea pot before them. Ronny looked at him, deciding where to begin so that she would only reveal enough to gauge his intentions for the business. That was her prime consideration.

"I manage the restaurant in all its forms," she began, "but I can't be here all the time. It's too much for one person. Your aunt had no interest in the business, leaving it to me." She looked at him quickly wondering whether he was about to misinterpret the factual error. There was no evidence he had considered the mistake. "She left ownership to you, of course."

Ronny was in her late twenties with short fair hair cut close at the sides and back; her features were pale and even, showing no sign of premature ageing but she looked tired. There was no sparkle in her eyes. She sipped tea then removed the cup from her mouth, leaving a small crimson lipstick smudge on the rim. She looked at David and felt what she had expected to feel when she knew for the first time that a young, inexperienced heir would be arriving from abroad: he would be of no help to her with the restaurant and be even less interested. The important factor was to ascertain his long term intentions.

She studied the new proprietor surreptitiously while he glanced around the room; he was clearly still suffering from whatever had caused him to be several days late in arriving. Anthony Stokes had told her to expect David during the previous week. She sensed there was an inquisitiveness about him which might be the product of a lively mind that could be channelled to take an interest in the business. He also displayed, in the few minutes they had been acquainted, a slightly disarming confidence which was unexpected. She decided to take a direct approach.

"Have you seen the apartment upstairs?"

"Yes, and I've been in here before but I couldn't stay."

As he offered no further explanation, Ronny let it pass. She projected a soft voice with no discernible accent. "Let me tell you what happens here and what I know about you so that you can tell me what you propose to do." She waved her hand in the direction of the restaurant as a whole; she was determined not to sound proprietorial, assuming he would consider her an employee. "I've been here for two years, during which time nothing has really changed for lunch times but the evening menu and procedure are completely different. Your aunt gave me a free hand to alter that part of the business; I brought in Armand, the chef, and together we've made it quite successful."

She regarded him closely to see if he was following; his green eyes were locked onto her lips. A brief, self-conscious bite on the inside of her bottom lip annoyed her. She looked away. "However, the lunch period, although busy, makes very little. It's just always been a day-time diner and your aunt did not want to close that part. If we increase the menu prices, people go elsewhere because there is plenty of day time competition."

David nodded in agreement. Although he had no knowledge of the local dining facilities, it made sense that competition would be fierce in this part of London.

Ronny waited until David refocused on her eyes. "The fact is... it's hard work for me and I can't sustain it for much longer. I have to spend many hours here and I'm on call upstairs when I'm not actually in the restaurant."

"Upstairs?"

"I have the apartment next to yours. I rent it," Ronny added quickly.

The waitress cleared the crockery from the table; all tables except the one David and Ronny occupied were now perfectly set for the evening. The floor had been swabbed whilst tables were rearranged.

Ronny stared at David, holding his gaze, impatient to hear something positive. There was no placatory nodding, no patronising half-smiles. She thought he had made up his mind. Ronny buttoned up her jacket, leaned forward with one arm resting on the table. It was intended to be a business-like gesture to cut through the preliminaries. "Look. I know you live abroad. You've inherited the restaurant and apartment upstairs. What I need to know is, are you staying? Do you intend to participate, or can I hire some help?"

David also leaned forward. He placed a hand on the table with which he brushed away a lunchtime crumb from the surface. Outside, the late afternoon was darkening the buildings opposite; street lamps began to flicker in response to the fading light. The glow of the wall lights in the room became brighter as time passed. When they sat down, the restaurant had been quiet. Now, the kitchen activity was building towards the preparations for evening; sounds of metal objects touching and colliding were mixed with a hum of low conversation.

"I expect you know more about me than the fact that I live abroad. That doesn't matter." David thought for a moment. "Do you want to own the business?"

"I've invested two years in this. I can walk away today if necessary, but I need an objective, a reason to stay. Your aunt took no active interest recently but she alone knew the exact financial situation and kept it to herself. You have to find out how things stand." Ronny looked at him closely. "What did you mean, 'Do I want to own the business'?"

David ignored the question, as if regretting asking his own. "From tomorrow, I'll be here every day. Let me follow you afternoon and evening so I can learn what happens. In a week or so, I'll be of help so you can take more time away. After that, we'll decide which way to go."

"You're not leaving soon, then?"

"No, not soon." Ronny thought he looked sad at the prospect of staying in London; she watched as he levered himself out of the chair on aching joints and walked out of the restaurant.

***

Outside on Gallery Street, there was no retail outlet for the essentials David needed in his new residence. He decided to stay on foot, feeling better in the cool early evening air. Taking a similar route to that of his recent trek to hospital, he found everything he needed close to Gower Street then returned home, ignoring the restaurant. He spent two hours making the apartment habitable before sitting down on the luxurious but old fashioned sofa. His eyes searched the corners and surfaces of the room trying to gain a sense of the person his aunt was, but there was nothing; it was vacant, impersonal, sad. He had deliberately refrained from asking Ronny any questions about his aunt – that would come later when she was reassured about his intention to take an active interest in the restaurant. The problem was, he could only look at the short term; he was becoming more and more resolved to return to Trinidad. It was a question of when. Later, as the apartment chilled with the advent of night, he unpacked the contents of a small travel bag into a four-drawer oak unit in the bedroom. Inside the second drawer he found a black and white photograph which must have been missed when the apartment contents were cleared. David studied the photograph briefly then put it to one side.

The following morning, he stepped out of the apartment onto the communal landing, dark and windowless; illumination was only available if one remembered the push-button, timed lighting system. At the end of the landing, a muffled rattle of lock and chain was followed by Ronny opening the door to her apartment; they stopped, facing each in silence until David produced the photograph and handed it to her.

"Have you seen this before? " he asked evenly. "I found it in an empty drawer and wondered if you knew who the people are."

Ronny took the picture, barely glancing at it before placing it on a small telephone table just inside the apartment. "I'll look at it later," she said, locking the door before preceding David down the staircase.

***

They spent the morning together in the restaurant discussing the daily routine, introducing David to the staff, procedures and accounts. David absorbed as much as he could in four hours until his head buzzed and he sought the sanctuary of his apartment. There, he made two telephone calls to Trinidad where it was still early morning: firstly, he spoke to Wendell Soames at Trinex, apologising for his continued absence and assuring his employer that he intended to return as soon as possible to resume his agreed duties. Wendell Soames reluctantly acceded to his request for more unpaid time away with the caveat that the position would not be available indefinitely and he should 'find his backside home, quick sharp' which did not affect David unduly. Secondly, he called his parents, a call that turned out to have fortuitous timing as they were in the process of leaving the Trinex village, having rented a house at Galeota Point in the far south east, remote, sparsely populated but close to the Trinex outpost where helicopters transported staff to offshore platforms.

David's mother informed him that the Trinex residents had rebelled in the face of the company's assertion that local drinking water was safe. Preparations were in progress for a full evacuation, many employees having already transferred to temporary accommodation near San Fernando where ample rentals were available, costs to be charged to Trinex although the company was currently unaware of this intention.

Later in the day, when David awarded himself an hour away from the restaurant, he walked to the local library, obtained a limited-time pass to use a computer, and opened the attachment to an e-mail his father had sent regarding the chaos near Fyzabad. The story of recent events was set out clearly with a flavour of the absurd way the picture had unfolded since David left. It was clear to all concerned that the local oil drilling near the compound outside Fyzabad had a direct bearing on water contamination. A rushed, preliminary report had found its way to residents indicating that the only way a water source could be affected was by a leak to pipe casings at the well during drilling. The mild scent of gasoline in the water to the residents' taps had abated but it was still off-colour and clearly a level of pollution persisted. Whilst the water was not currently considered harmful, the long term effects could not be predicted. Also, the content of benzene and petroleum hydrocarbons in the water was marginally above health concern levels. David's father had been to the oil well nearby and the filtration plant inside the compound; he reported that the system was bearing up but would not remove contamination unless drilling was halted. It was clear to him that drilling with leaking pipe casings and dumping extracted matter into waste pits was responsible for the emergency. It was on this premise that residents had left, which in turn led directly to a bizarre turn of events.

Almost as soon as the first compound residents had left the site, a series of burglaries swept through the empty properties and, although still open to remaining customers, the general store was relieved of much of its surviving stock via the rear door usually reserved for deliveries. Speculation had it that the instigators of this brazen theft comprised a band of teak tree fellers. Emboldened by mind-bending strength rum, they had just enough cash to persuade the security guard at the site entrance and the shop staff to take longer breaks. This had provided ample time to fill their flat bed trucks with booty on several occasions. There had been a sudden rush of second hand furniture and goods available around Fyzabad which found their way into the homes of local villages and back traces. Violence had not accompanied the felonies but the Trinex property section had been placed in a quandary: residents would not return until the water supply was pure, thefts would no doubt continue despite additional security personnel being ferried on to the site, and the oil well drilling could not be stopped as it was firm company policy.

David's father concluded the missive with a promise to forward his new address in a later e-mail. In a postscript there was a note that Wendell Soames was beside himself with rage at the leaking of what should have been a confidential report on the compound's water supply; it was apparently common knowledge that he promised terrible retribution on the culprit, when found. David's father asked about his son's health. He did not mention the restaurant or inheritance in general.

David thought about Wendell Soames; he had seemed calm enough earlier in the day on the telephone but David knew he could be two characters, possibly with schizophrenic tendencies, at once calm and understanding but tyrannical if crossed. Even at this distance, David could imagine the Soames ire at the idea of betrayal by someone leaking the water quality report relating to the Trinex compound. David knew he was not indispensable but clearly Soames considered him to be of use. David's new found independence meant he could take his time over a decision as to when he should return. Wendell Soames was the very least of his current considerations.

He considered making a call to the Penal Funeral Parlour or, as his fingers hovered over the computer keyboard, sending an e-mail to Girly. It would surely remove the anxiety he felt, but he couldn't make himself do it, and it would become more difficult as time passed.

***

On returning to the restaurant, David met the staff for the evening session. In the kitchen at the rear of the building, walled with spotless, stainless steel panels, was a sterilized area without character, equipped with similar material sinks, counter tops and utensils; activity was suddenly heightened by the arrival of Armand, the chef, resplendent in kitchen whites offset by a yellow cravat apparently supporting a neat, pointed beard. Earlier, David had been introduced to Max, the short order lunch time cook and his latest assistant who was unlikely to be employed for long. Assistants never stayed; they could not support Max's whims, insults, irascible nature. They left, usually during a lunch time opening, with much rancour, hurt pride and throwing down of hygiene hats. It never occurred to any assistant to return Max's vitriol in equal measure. Not only would it have been tolerated, Max would have respected the resolve, seeing it as part of the kitchen verbal jousting he thought was vital to creating long-term harmony. But either they could not be bothered or they anticipated termination of employment should a cross word be spoken. As a result, the local catering agency supplied a regular line of cooks who became fodder for Max's truculence and spite. Max had been unimpressed by David's introduction, possibly assuming the new ownership of the business was a passing phase which would have no direct bearing on his own realm - the kitchen that he ruled from morning to afternoon with little interference from Ronny. There was virtually no connection, no interaction between Max and Armand, the former having no interest in the evening performance and Armand considering Max's culinary skills beneath contempt.

In a way, Armand had a point. He was dismissive of short order cooks generally, hating Max's use of the kitchen. The lunch time menu, guaranteed to give Armand dyspepsia if he ever examined it, included anything that could be hot-plate heated in short time, flipped with a spatula or lowered into a basket of boiling oil then raised before complete dissolution took place. There were daily specials, repeated week after week, which were usually delivered in the form of a short crust pie containing the butchered product of quadruped or fowl, microwaved until it was assumed that the refrigerator chill had been elevated to an acceptable temperature. Amongst favourites in the heavy winter category were a watery casserole and lamb stew, although 'favourite' would apply only to the frequency on menu rather than repeated requests from table occupants. Pancakes, as thin as possible, were offered with a tinned fruit supplement accompanied by aerosol cream or economy grade ice cream. All this was served at rock bottom prices to fill the tables and made little profit. The day-time Oven House also considered itself a patisserie: pastries were not made on the premises but bought fresh from a nearby family bakery or, when the baker was on holiday, ill or unable to raise himself from his bed in the early hours following an alcoholic lapse, cakes in cellophane wrappers were purchased from a supermarket, placed on beechwood platters and allowed to fester in a glass cabinet next to the cash register unless purchased by clients on their way out of the restaurant. It was at the direction of Ronny's former employer that Max reigned and nothing changed.

By contrast, Armand considered himself an artist; more importantly, this was also Ronny's opinion. She had tempted him away from the kitchen of a major London hotel where they both worked for a while, recognising his potential purely from the verbal complements of customers she heard in the course of her duties as restaurant under-manager. He was then sous chef to a renowned London food icon. She had promised him a free hand on the menu if he came to the Oven House to work evenings only. Armand had accepted because he liked the idea and he was platonically in love with Ronny; he never asked how she obtained the position of restaurant under-manager and she never discussed it with him.

From the outset, the Oven House thrived under Armand's imagination and Ronny's management, if one ignored the diner operation. Ronny broke into the central London market with targeted advertising, snappy promotion and most importantly, Armand's culinary vision. In his hands, a simple lemon sole became a piscine poem; lamb with apricots, possibly to some an unpalatable combination, fused like no other ingredients with almonds and mint into a superb *maroc tagine*. Armand was unstoppable in his self-belief, flair and success with customers, amongst most of whom he was revered, but hampered, frustrated and vexed by the abomination of the diner operation which, he informed Ronny at every opportunity, had to go. He received a sympathetic ear, qualified by the realisation that the previous restaurant owner would not allow it to happen. Now, on change of ownership, Armand intended to resume his assault on Max's domain.

David spent the next three days observing, questioning, shadowing Ronny until he had a reasonable grip on how the Oven House worked. His initial fascination was then blunted slightly by the realisation that, like all businesses, the Oven House existed by routine, essentially the same formula each day varied only by the time of day one was actually in the dining area or kitchen. Colour was added to the mono-chrome of regular procedure by the people who frequented the establishment: staff and customers.

At the end of the first week, David took Ronny aside and arranged to meet outside the restaurant on a Sunday morning. His main idea was to discuss his initial impressions of the Oven House, but he was also increasingly frustrated at her reluctance to answer directly any questions about his aunt. They ambled slowly and undisturbed in the perimeter grounds of the International Gallery which was closed to the public for the day.

"Two things are clear to me already, even after a few days," David began. "The afternoon diner can't continue in its present form. I would prefer Armand to take over the whole menu, afternoon and evening. Do you think he'll do it?"

Ronny stopped and sat on a bench opposite a side elevation of the gallery. The grey stone walls, recently cleaned and relieved of city grime, almost shone in the morning light. She did not hesitate.

"I was hoping you would reach that decision. I'm sure Armand will do it, he's been badgering me for months. It will take some time to make the change, and you can leave Max to me. I'll help find something for him elsewhere and we'll keep the day time staff."

She had clearly considered the possibility of David's decision and was prepared to make a pitch for the conclusion he had reached on his own. They looked at each other with half-smiles, knowing it would not be necessary. David noted the immediate change in Ronny's attitude: she became suddenly enthusiastic, whereas previously she had been careful, measured in his presence, only prepared to divulge essential information. She was animated in her vision of how the Oven House could evolve, take its place amongst the premier establishments. Either through lack of experience or enthusiasm for the restaurant business, David could not share her future aspirations, but he was gratified that he had found a way through her reserve.

He looked at her closely when she spoke. She appeared friendly, at ease. Familiar. He wondered about Armand, probably fifteen years older than Ronny, and noticeably receptive to her ideas and authority. He detected a bond between them but no intimacy; there was also no indication in the time David had been in London that she was close to anyone.

"The other thing I wanted to mention...you have to tell me about my aunt."

Ronny switched from open, free association of ideas to what might have been a rehearsed speech containing a rehearsed order of facts, as if anticipating his every question and attempting to cover the subject without getting involved in a drawn out conversation. But there was also a hint of frustration in her tone, as if she wanted to say more but imposed a restrictive ring around her words in case something unmanageable should result and give him cause to probe further.

"Your aunt contacted me when I was working at a hotel about two years ago. Told me about the Oven House, how she wanted to change it partly but not completely. I joined her and managed to get Armand a short time later. She owned the business solely but was losing interest. When I started, she shared the duties with me but became distracted, and later less able to help because she was ill. It was progressive to the point that eventually she was unable to come downstairs. I had no idea about the finances, as I mentioned to you before, because that was the only part she kept to herself. Near the end, she told me you would inherit and I should wait for you to arrive. You did, several weeks later."

If there was a slight note of bitterness, David thought she hid it well. He had noticed Ronny's habit of conversing in straight-faced facts; he assumed the mask hid true feelings or was a method to prevent probing of details. She told him his aunt's last days were spent in a hospice which Ronny visited until the end. Her business affairs were handled by accountants and Anthony Stokes. The funeral was poorly attended: restaurant staff and no relatives.

"You know I wasn't informed about the funeral date?"

Ronny shrugged, as if it were of no importance.

"Tell me what she was like...who was she?" David leaned forward with hands on his knees. Ronny hesitated only briefly, looking into the distance at the edifice of the gallery.

"Christine Morris was in her early fifties,well educated and informed, but introverted and rather distant. I don't know of any close friends. Her wealth....well, you know what property she owned. Everyone at the restaurant liked her – staff, customers..."

"And you?"

"We got on well enough." Ronny stood, looked left and right before moving off back towards Gallery Street. "I can't tell you much more. If you want to know why she left everything to you, I can't help. I didn't ask her and now it's too late."

"But did she ever discuss me, my parents? What happened to her personal effects? The flat is empty. Was there ever a husband, partner?"

"Anthony Stokes arranged all that," Ronny replied stiffly, referring only to part of the question.

David shrugged off his usual good manners, stopping her in the street with a hand placed lightly on her arm. "Is that it? All you can tell me when you knew her for two years?"

Ronny removed her hand. She looked squarely into his eyes; there was a slight tremor in her voice. "It's just too late." She repeated her previous assertion but this time David saw a small pain flicker behind moist eyes. He watched as she walked away, square shouldered, at a fast pace past Gallery Street and beyond until her emerald green coat was lost to sight amid the flocks of London tourists.

***

The familiar path from apartment down to restaurant became a routine six days each week for David, and on the seventh day he transported himself as far away from Gallery Street as he could, visiting old university friends, rediscovering pleasant haunts, intentionally keeping away from Ronny. They met occasionally on the staircase outside their apartments, hiding feelings behind business chat, never discussing what David wanted to know most. On passing the open door of her apartment one day he noticed that the photograph had been removed from the telephone table. When he raised the matter with Ronny, she was blunt: "I can't ask Christine now, can I?" she said dismissively.

Life followed a regular pattern as the days multiplied into weeks.

David decided he had to make every effort to assist Ronny in the restaurant changes, making himself available for staff, never flinching from awkward questions, ensuring he personally informed Max of his intention to close the diner element of the business despite Ronny's earlier offer to deal with Max herself. In the event, she soon found him a position elsewhere and the changeover happened earlier than expected.

During the second week of David's stay, he had visited the restaurant's accountants. There was nothing to dissuade him in relation to the business finances – his decision to follow his inexperienced instinct regarding Armand's potential was likely to be vindicated. Moreover, when the time came for him to leave, David would not have his conscience troubled by a debt-ridden operation.

However, there was one matter which was mentioned, causing him to swallow deeply before responding: "I don't have it." His accountant had raised the spectre of tax on his inheritance, a gain which could not be dismissed by claiming normal residence abroad.

"You will be a 'deemed domicile'. You were born here and lived here quite recently," he was informed. "You can't avoid it."

The conclusion was that David would have to sell the apartment to pay his tax liability. The location of the property would ensure that he would still be a wealthy man after a sale, but he would lose his newly found base in London. He left the accountant having also decided what to do with his remaining asset, the Oven House restaurant.

***

The permanent change to the Oven House's future coincided with early summer in London. Ronny decided to take a week away from the restaurant. She did not tell David where she was going and he did not ask. Late one night, the eve of her trip, they sat together in David's apartment discussing his routine for the week ahead. Ronny already seemed more relaxed than he had seen her since his arrival; he dared to believe that the help he provided and the Oven House's full emergence into a serious restaurant was at least part of the reason for her sunnier demeanour.

Ronny still exhibited a quiet reserve whenever their conversations veered away from business. She clearly had no intention of discussing whatever private life remained to her outside the long hours spent in the Oven House. The following morning she left without a word and contacted no-one for seven days. She returned to work with, in David's view, a subdued attitude which was not dispelled as the first day proceeded.

David spent some time that day relating details of what had happened during her absence:he had finally engaged her preferred candidate for the position of restaurant manager to spread the load; interviews had been carried out before her time away. In the quiet of late afternoon when the dining area was empty and they sat together at the same table they had occupied when they first met, he also told her he was selling the apartment, not by choice, but out of necessity. He would stay in London until this was concluded, which might take some time, then reconsider his options. The truth was he had decided to return to Trinidad as soon as possible but there was one further matter to complete.

"I think the restaurant will do very well if you and Armand continue in the way we've decided to proceed. But I think you also need an incentive. We should move towards you taking control of the business, maybe over a period of time, and I'll retain forty nine per cent. We can agree the details of how you can buy in, but I'll make sure it won't ruin you financially. You may even ask Armand to join you." David looked for a reaction, not initially to his offer, but to see if there was a glimmer of response to bringing Armand into the potential agreement. He saw none.

Ronny rose from her chair, called an instruction through to the kitchen and returned to face him across the table. "What is it that makes you want to return to Trinidad? You have everything here, given to you. All you have to do is stay and make it work." She looked down at the table, possibly regretting too much emphasis on his good fortune.

David decided to tell her, for the first time, about his life and potential career in the Caribbean, not omitting the uncertainty of it all. He told her of his fears for the role that Trinex might impose on him; he related most of the details concerning his relationship with Girly. If he looked for advice, none was forthcoming. Ronny maintained that indefinable reserve David had noticed since the first day.

"I'm very happy to continue here, and thank you for the offer. You're retaining an interest in case you come back – I can see why." Ronny then hesitated, glancing right and left as if in a moment of indecision, as if she wanted to tell him something new, something that had been on her mind and would change everything. But it would not come. The thing that he believed was troubling her obstinately stayed where it camped in her reserve, unwilling to vacate its entrenched position. He wondered if it were a question of trust that held her back, an inability to confide in a still recent acquaintance. He hoped that if he stayed long enough, the barrier would fall; she did not seem unhappy, just preoccupied by something she could not share.

And then, everything did change. After three months in London, during which time David reported regularly to Wendell Soames at Trinex but did not contact Girly, he received a telephone call one morning from Trinex in Santa Flora. He expected to be berated unmercifully by Wendell Soames and told that he was no longer required. Instead, he was informed that Sumatee Dhanraj had died and the funeral would be soon.

David did not consider why the Trinex staff were passing on the message; he could not know that Wendell Soames, having heard of the sad event at the Trinex medical centre that day, had specifically asked for a call to be made to David in London, expecting that the news would hasten his return. He was keenly aware of David's connection with Ramdass Trace; it suited him perfectly.

On a bright summer's day, David lifted a suitcase downstairs to the pavement outside the Oven House and waited for a taxi. At the close of business the previous evening, he told Ronny he had arranged a flight ticket for the following day; he told her the reason for leaving, giving no indication of when he might be back. They parted with a promise to meet out on the street before he left.

As a black taxi arrived at the restaurant, Ronny appeared next to David. She was strained, almost in a panic. There was a tiredness in her eyes as if she had not slept since they parted late the previous night. As David climbed into the taxi, she clasped his hand and forced a white envelope between his fingers. "Try to come back," was all she managed to say before hurrying into the restaurant without looking back.

The taxi left Gallery Street taking a familiar route west towards the airport; David opened the envelope. It contained a folded letter of several pages and the photograph he had given Ronny all those weeks ago. They had never mentioned it since. The picture showed a woman in her twenties holding a baby. A girl of about six years stood by her side. David reversed the photograph where, on the plain white backing, he recognised Ronny's neat handwriting:

Your aunt was not your aunt. She was your mother.
And your mother was my mother.

4 DHARMA ILLUSION

On the long flight away from London, David read Ronny's letter several times; the sense of shock, disbelief and even anger was not assuaged by each reading. He found it impossible that his beloved parents, now not his parents, could have deceived him for so long. He wanted to disregard Ronny's claim but something told him it must be true. Her attitude towards him since they first met, a reluctance to engage, was no indicator of what her letter revealed. The words, however, just had the ring of truth, and there was the photograph. The small girl in the picture just looked so...familiar.

He began to read the letter again as if something might appear between the lines to cast doubt on its veracity, to reinstate the position he held in life several hours ago and in all his previous years.

David,

There is no easy way to write the words that will have such a profound effect on your life so I'll just give you the facts, the answers to your questions, and with an apology for not being able to tell you face to face when all along I knew you were unable to understand the situation you found yourself in when you came to London. As you have probably guessed by now, the photograph was left in the apartment for you to find; I probably hoped that if you enquired about it, there would be an easier way for me to tell the story, but I couldn't do it.

I have no doubt your parents will be aware that, by now, you have discovered the truth. When you have read this account, I sincerely hope you will still regard them as parents because, although you will no doubt feel they have misled you for so long, you have to consider why they found themselves in a dilemma when you were so young.

Christine Morris married our father thirty years ago. I know little about him except that he had been very wealthy, then less so, but owned the whole building in Gallery Street when he left our mother as you see her in the photograph. I think your 'father', Christine's brother, may have taken that picture. Anyway, our father went away permanently, Christine either did not know where or would never say but he never came back. She obtained sole ownership of the building by transfer – apparently he communicated for a while through a solicitor then disappeared. I have kept his name whereas you have Christine's and your 'father's' name.

Christine told me that initially she coped but as time passed the responsibility of the business and two children overwhelmed her. She sold the properties at the top of the building to keep the diner in funds for many years. Although she never fully explained the reason for giving you up, I have concluded that her brother offered to take you with him when he travelled abroad to work because the depression she was suffering proved too much. Why she kept me with her in London, I couldn't say.

David broke off from the letter to reflect on his early life; he had no memory of London as a child – he must have been taken as a baby. And Trinidad was the only country he knew from the past. He continued to read with a sense of awe that the family arrangement and its continued deception had endured.

I believe there was a family agreement that you would be returned one day, but it never happened. You will have to ask your parents why, although Christine told me, with some bitterness, that they refused to bring you to London, and swore to tell you that you were given up to them if she tried to contact you. This, of course, would have been true but no less devastating for Christine as a mother. She did receive occasional reports from your 'father' about your life, your progress, but she never tried to contact you. He will have his own reasons for maintaining this situation after you became an adult.

For my part, I left Christine several years ago – we had occupied the first floor of the building above the Oven house – to pursue a career abroad but I couldn't leave permanently. On my return, we converted the first floor into separate apartments and yes, she gave me my apartment in case you were wondering. It's not rented as I told you.

When she became ill two years ago, I returned to the Oven House – I was working in London at a hotel as I mentioned a while ago – on condition that I would change it as I saw fit. She half agreed and that is the position in which you found me three months ago.

Christine deteriorated in health gradually. She employed a nurse until the end; the nurse kept in contact with your 'father'. It's odd to think that when you were at university here, you were probably within walking distance of us at Gallery Street, but neither of us knew. No doubt your parents were careful not to reveal this to Christine.

I was surprised your parents did not accompany you to London for the funeral. Towards the end, Christine only communicated with them via Anthony Stokes. It was a terrible shame they could not be reconciled; I might even have discovered an uncle and aunt. Isn't this just silly and complicated?

Christine told me the details of her will a long time ago. She was adamant you would have the restaurant and the remaining property. I'm sure you will guess that she entrusted me with her remaining money to invest in the business. Although you might expect siblings to be treated equally by a parent, your absence and the fact that I left her for several years probably affected the will. There is no bitterness on my side – we have an apartment each and will share the business in due course.

On several occasions, Christine suggested I might try to contact you; she believed you would have travelled to London straight away if you knew about her, especially when she became very ill. Somehow, I always dissuaded her and now that it's too late, I can't decide why. Everything just seemed too difficult to explain – maybe I should have left it to her but I didn't want to have to pick up the pieces if you rejected her. Not so close to the end.

Now that we've known each other for three months, I suspect you will come back, despite the fact I know very little about your other life. There's no need to explain, call or write – just turn up one day, exactly as you did in the springtime.

The letter ended abruptly without signature or words of sorrow, consolation or regret. David looked out of the small window on his right; the aeroplane was descending into St. Lucia, the only stop on its way to Trinidad. There would be a one hour halt, then a further hour's flight into Piarco where he would hire a car and head south.

Although the depth of his anger towards his parents was lifted somewhat by Ronny's explanations, there were still too many unanswered questions. He reflected on the position his parents encountered when they carried him away; with Christine unable to cope, they possibly felt there was no alternative but to sustain the lie when he entered his teenage years then adulthood, but it wasn't logical. Now, they sat in Galeota Point and were no doubt wondering when he would return to the island and whether he would see them again. They must have prepared themselves for his discovery, yet there had been no reticence, no change in attitude whenever he telephoned from London.

An hour passed in deep thought; the aeroplane thundered down the runway on its final leg of a long journey. David decided to concentrate on the immediate reason for his return, putting aside personal anguish until after the funeral of Sumatee Dhanraj.

5 THE SOUND OF TEARS

When Jigs Boodoosingh left Fong's doughnut bar in great haste, a wave of relief washed over him until its cool, refreshing influence dissipated in the midmorning heat. He could leave Girly and David to sort out their own differences, almost irreconcilable though he considered they were. There were weightier matters on his mind now that he had almost squared things with Girly. There would certainly be some fall out later and she would confront him, but the hard work had been done.

Jigs collected his car from the funeral parlour yard; he was gratified to see that Rishi or Raj had wiped over its perfectly preserved surfaces that morning. He left the yard in a hurry, turning onto Clarke Road then Erin Road, pointing the car in the direction of Santa Flora. He had arranged to meet the Pump Man at his house in Ramdass Trace; he found him, ample and exhausted, on his veranda with a glass of his favourite grapefruit juice at his elbow. He drank greedily until a bubble of gas rose within him, escaping through full lips with a sigh. The Pump Man had just returned from his early morning labours reading dials and gauges on oil pumps in the Cedros area close to the Southern Main Road. His doleful mood had not been lifted by the coastal scenery which might have soothed his troubled mind: unspoilt empty coves fringed by coconut groves in a landscape unchanged for centuries by humans or unnatural interference. This remained unnoticed while his thoughts were concentrated on the impending occupation of part of his land. Each oil pump, carefully or by chance tucked away from the highway, coast and casual visitors' eyes, reminded him of home. These were working, producing pumps, but Sagar Narsingh was acutely aware that there were hundreds of idle, rusting piles of scrap iron which scarred the island. More to the point, the immediate surrounds of each pump were tainted or poisoned by the inevitable small oil spill from live or redundant pumps alike. He might not have been able to articulate the irony of damage caused by that which gave the republic its wealth but he was nevertheless sensitive to the issue and of being employed by the force that was inflicting on him so much mental turmoil.

Jigs mounted the steps to the veranda; Ramdass Trace was quiet except for sundry birds calling their partners and the ticking of his cooling car engine. Jigs explained the finer details of his meeting with Wendell Soames so that Sagar Narsingh could be in no doubt: although Jigs would do his very best to thwart the Trinex invasion, it was unlikely to be rewarded.

"I feel I blight," responded the Pump Man, sagging deeper into his chair. "They take away my land, and the house take itself away." A *jackspaniard* buzzed angrily around his head before disappearing through the open door into the house.

"That is said to be a lucky sign," Jigs prompted, following the flight of the wasp with his eyes.

"I don' feel lucky," was the reply. "I expec' Soames on his high horse now, ready to move in wit' drills."

Clearly, the Pump Man was inconsolable. "We'll arrange a protest," Jigs offered, "and when we find the actual locations of the drilling, we'll do what we can to stop it. I'll obtain legal advice before they start." He sounded more enthusiastic than he felt but the sight of the Pump Man's suffering made him overstretch his own expectations. Sagar Narsingh looked reduced, stricken, swamped in a sea of misfortune. He explained to Jigs his love for his home and the land that surrounded it, the responsibility he felt to his family who had entrusted it to him; he also bemoaned the fact that he was powerless to engage with Trinex or meet the need for repairs to his house.

Jigs tried to ponder the problem from a neutral perspective. On one side, it was a high-handed approach by Trinex – he didn't bother to mentally revisit the details of his interview with Wendell Soames. He had made his views clear about invoking government backing for the occupation and development on and under private land. But on the other hand, Soames' exhortation to Jigs for help in achieving a higher objective than the preservation of unused bush could be compelling if it were not for Jigs' certain knowledge that the way Trinex implemented their aims was, at the very least, cavalier and without a sensitive approach. He decided that there would be no common ground with Soames, no alternative way that would appease Ramdass Trace residents. He could only try to minimise the effects of what was about to happen. To that end, he decided to call a meeting in the trace of all those affected as soon as Trinex detailed the actual proposed drilling sites. Meanwhile, he would leave Wendell Soames alone but concentrate his efforts on persuading David that his employer could not be trusted to treat the land in a responsible way.

The Pump Man shifted in his seat, leaning forward as if to include Jigs in a private thought. "What I can do wit' this place?" he asked. "Family pass it on but I stuck wit' responsibility. I can't sell now – who would take it? I have Trinex on my tail. If I make trouble for them here," the Pump Man threw an arm towards the rear of the house where oil extraction would take place, "they sack me."

Jigs considered for a brief moment. "Leave it with me. I can help you with the house." He looked away, slightly embarrassed by his own show of altruism. He saw the leaking tank next to the house, heard the drips of water as they hit the earth below. A grateful Pump Man brushed away a tear from each eye.

***

Fong's Hardware Store was busy. A din from the ground floor emporium joined raucous shouts from the yard at the rear to rise like an ocean wave in a storm to first floor level where a more refined chatter hovered over coffee cups and cakes.

Girly Boodoosingh was stunned. For more than an hour, between interruptions from the funeral parlour via her cell phone, she had listened to David's story with a growing sense of awe. He told her everything that had happened to him in London with a casual detachment as though it had happened to someone else. Girly sat back in her chair, glanced around the room then leaned forward slowly to impress upon David that she had absorbed everything, understood his position but what it all came down to, as far as she was concerned was this: "Not one call to me. In three months. You left a message which I did not receive, but not one call. You said you only came back for the funeral, so why are we here now?"

Girly was aware of his discomfort; she was not going to make this easy for him after so long.

"I stepped suddenly into a different world as soon as I arrived in London. There was so much to do, to learn, and I was very ill. I just couldn't do it," he said hopelessly, as if the act of dialling a telephone number was beyond him amongst all the other things he had to do.

"You called your parents, though." It was a guess.

"Yes," he conceded, "but that was because they knew I was sick. I had to tell them I had recovered."

Girly pondered his response and smiled at how inadequate it sounded. She repeated her earlier question. "So why are we here now?"

David appeared to be nonplussed for a moment, searching his mind for confirmation that he had already answered her. "It's difficult. I came to tell you everything, explain....I'm still contracted to Trinex so I had to come back." He stood up suddenly in what was almost an aggressive manner; his calm confidence evaporated in a loss of expression, an inability to convey an answer to her about that which bothered her most, a similar mental block to that which overcame him in London and prevented him from making contact.

He made an excuse, looking at her directly: "My life has changed completely. I still don't know what to make of it."

Girly watched him retake his seat. He pushed a hand distractedly through his fair hair. She suddenly understood that the last three months had left him in a fragile, confused place, but she was not prepared to consider the lack of communication as a mere aberration on his part. By contrast, Girly felt no confusion about her life now, no sense of needing David to help her make desperate changes. She was not a victim in a Caribbean dystopia; she did not see him as a passport out of Penal. Also, she was not prepared to recall past events with him. He must never know about her loss.

"You know, you have one foot here and one in London. You have to make up your mind what you want. But don't look at me."

Girly gathered her purse and cell phone, nodded to Madam Fong who looked on benevolently, and prepared to leave. David withdrew several dollar notes from his pocket; they were screwed into an untidy ball. Girly watched him unravel the creased, tattered paper into a presentable condition to hand to Madam Fong. It was typical of him to unconsciously exhibit a casual disregard for money, a trait which she had long ago found both irritating but strangely attractive.

"If you had received my letter, what would you have done about it?" he called after her as she descended the staircase. She left through the main entrance without an answer or a goodbye but despite all she had heard and the disappointment that he had not returned with a satisfactory explanation to force her into regarding the previous three months in a different light, she was unable to completely fight down a small sense of joy to accompany her at her desk in the Penal Funeral Parlour. She would mull over the details of David's story later; she was amazed in particular at the revelation his parents were, in fact, his uncle and aunt but she had been careful not to show any great interest. Her long standing anger did not afford him the solace of a sympathetic ear.

David remained at Fong's for long minutes after Girly had departed. He passed the crumpled dollars to Madam Fong whilst taking some notice of the increased activity around him at the doughnut bar. The conversation had become more animated when a group of evangelists from the Penal Presbyterian Church occupied two tables adjacent to the counter; they were discussing the means by which they could persuade the Penal unfaithful to attend church the following Sunday. In reaction to a damning verdict on their recent efforts by the pastor, Reverend Sproule, they sat with doughnuts and sugared smiles in a state of chastened excitement. From the pulpit of the church just outside Penal, the Reverend Sproule had called into doubt their commitment, questioned their moral compass, failed to discern a backbone between them and considered them unworthy of God's love unless they followed his way out of their complacency. But even as they cringed beneath his lacerating barbs, they were filled with a determination to go out into the Presbyterian heartland of south Trinidad, find and persuade faint hearts to fill the church. The pews should be crammed, the collection box should overflow.

David heard the excited, dough-filled mouths, gleaned enough from the conversation to wish that his own mission was as straightforward. As a result of his own ineptitude, he was no further forward in expressing his innermost thoughts to Girly; he was shaken by her lack of empathy but could not decide if it was deliberate or the result of genuine disinterest. At least he had managed to convey every detail of his recent life so she could be in no doubt as to what had happened to him. He looked at the wall clock on the far side of the room; it was time to report to Wendell Soames at Santa Flora. He left Fong's feeling more dispirited than when he arrived an hour or so earlier.

***

By the time Jigs Boodoosingh left the Pump Man at Ramdass Trace, he judged that he had allowed adequate time for Girly and David to conclude their meeting in Penal. The outcome was of little interest to him at this time as his assumption was that Girly had moved away from any previous commitment to David with the passage of time. Besides, he had noticed in recent times the interest of Devendra Roopnarine in his sister, an interest he intended to encourage.

He drove the short distance to the Trinex centre at Santa Flora, parked his car away from the administration building and settled in his seat to wait. David had mentioned earlier that he had to report to Wendell Soames after the meeting at Fong's. Jigs used the waiting time to consider the way forward with his plans for Ramdass Trace; he assumed there would be no imminent move by Trinex to press ahead with their site preparations, in which case he had time to organise his thoughts and plan a way out of the problem. Unfortunately, beyond an idea to convert David to his side, he really had no clue how to take on Trinex effectively. Also, David would have a minor role in the overall process. Jigs needed a lever to force Wendell Soames away from Ramdass Trace onto another track. The legal arguments would be lost and Trinex would not be delayed or deflected, not with government backing for their policy. Until he could think of the perfect argument or action, he would have to revert to his current idea – take David to Ranji Village.

Jigs also had a vague notion that there must be a meeting, a rally in Ramdass Trace to stir the hearts of residents into believing there could be a way out of this potential disaster. On the sixteenth day after the death of his aunt, Sumatee Dhanraj, there would be an 'open house' at number twelve Ramdass Trace, a celebration of her passing and a welcoming back into the fold of his uncle. Jigs was just congratulating himself on finding a perfect opportunity for gathering residents together when he saw David's hire car turn into the car park in front of him.

David got out of his car and turned towards the administration building; he stopped in response to a shout from Jigs: "David, come. I have something to show you."

David walked quickly to the polished Ford. He put a hand on the roof paintwork and leaned down to the side window. "I'm late for an appointment. What is it?"

Jigs looked pained as he eyed David's hand on the roof. He opened the passenger door. "It's urgent. Wendell Soames can wait."

David hesitated, looked down at his feet as he scuffed the worn car park surface with the sole of a shoe. "It's important," Jigs urged, "and nothing to do with Girly." With a sigh David climbed reluctantly into the passenger seat. Jigs started the engine and manoeuvred carefully out onto the main road.

"I won't talk about Girly. I don't want to interfere." Jigs ignored the involuntary snort of disbelief from his passenger. "This won't take long, maybe an hour." The car motored onto the Siparia Road.

David looked at Jigs, noticing how carefully he handled the car. "Tell me why you didn't pass on my letter to Girly. You can be honest as it probably doesn't matter now."

The car veered smoothly to the left to avoid a deep depression in the tarmac. Jigs corrected his steering before replying. "It was a very bad error of judgement but you have to understand...I really thought she would go with you and not come back. You and I have never spoken seriously before and now is not a good time. I withheld the letter for the best of reasons because I'm her brother but more like a parent."

Jigs was presented with a burden when his parents retired to Arima. There was little notice, as though duty and obligation were packed away in a frequently used cupboard for Jigs to find as soon as the parents were out of sight. They decided one day that Penal and the funeral parlour were no longer to be the centre of their world. The house in Arima had been bequeathed several years earlier to Jigs' mother and was found to be a perfect antidote to the claustrophobic apartment above the business premises. They left in the carefree knowledge that Jigs knew his role, he would assume responsibility for Girly and the parlour; a safe and profitable future stretched out before their offspring. They could do no more.

Jigs never openly revealed his dislike for his father's profession, merely hinted at it from time to time, noticed by Girly, and his lack of participation in some aspects of the work illustrated his reluctance. But he continued, aware that the business prospered and it was expected of him. He never saw Girly as a burden, however; he assumed his parental mantle with an initial light touch, only becoming a heavier hand employing deceit when David became a regular feature in Girly's life. Jigs convinced himself his sister would not cope with a life abroad, unaware that he was transferring his own phobia to Girly.

"She's my age, not a child. She can make her own decisions." Some of David's frustration created earlier in the day by his inability to connect with Girly now surfaced in this unexpected opportunity to corner Jigs and elicit a satisfactory excuse for his interference. "Why didn't you just ask me what was in the letter?"

Jigs turned onto the Fyzabad Road soon after the centre of Siparia. The engine throbbed pleasantly, the wheels proceeded slowly towards the village of Thick. Jigs drove as if he were in one of the parlour's hearses en route for Mosquito Creek. "Yes, I see that now," he replied disingenuously. "Leave it to me. I've already admitted my error to Girly. I'll talk to her again."

David wondered whether Jigs might be the sort of person who often said "Leave it to me" but failed to deliver on his promises. He studied Jigs whilst appearing to survey the road ahead and at the side. Jigs was the sort of person one found difficult to dislike on first acquaintance; he had a friendly charm, appeared to take you into his confidence when speaking. There was no obvious guile even if David was not impressed with his blatant positioning in his relationship with Girly. David also saw a fussiness in Jigs' general demeanour which he felt might be related to his profession, but Girly had once told him that Jigs found the business of undertaking distasteful and almost unbearable. He compensated by delegating as much of the parlour's routine as possible. David smiled to himself at the thought of a reluctant undertaker.

Just before Thick, Jigs turned left away from the road onto an unmarked single track; there were no road signs of any type, the road surface was substantially covered in foliage and green matter which encroached from the margins. The car wheels left dark lines in the previously undisturbed layer.

"This is as far as we go," Jigs said, pulling the car over to one side and opening the door. He walked to the rear of the car, opened the trunk and lifted two pairs of boots, placing them on the ground. As David joined him, he looked at his casual brown shoes. "You'll need these," he said, handing over a pair of boots.

David looked around. There was a continuation of the track heading west, covered more densely by the overspill from the bush on either side. There was no indication of where they were.

"What is this place?" David asked, glancing at his watch, thinking about Wendell Soames waiting at Santa Flora.

"Just a short walk then I'll explain everything."

They walked quickly along the track, narrow and dark with overhanging vegetation, until it began to widen. David was suddenly assaulted by the change in the air, heavy with rank decay and crude oil, sickening and cloying, like a foul lacquer on the tongue. The track finished at an opening in the bush, leading to a large clearing; it was once a small village, now ruined, abandoned, a desolate place not fit for habitation by human or animal. There was complete silence.

David stopped in shock at the scene before him. Several timber houses and shacks remained around the central clearing, all dilapidated, looted, empty. A small lake of black, glutinous oil had spread out from a still, silent pump fifty metres from the dwellings on a steep rise; the oil found natural boundaries as it slipped down the hill in the form of perimeter earth mounds and obstructions until it settled and congealed in a shiny mass on what was previously a village square.

"What happened here?" David asked, looking at Jigs for explanation of the destruction.

"This is Ranji Village. Or was. You see, this is what happens when oil companies are not challenged, not made responsible for their actions." Jigs' pompous tone masked a heartfelt response, a hatred for the irreversible damage.

David began to walk towards the ruined houses but found he had nowhere to go due to the separate slicks which lay randomly in isolated pockets and because of the size of the lake. "Trinex did this?" he asked, incredulous that such wanton negligence was possible.

"They allowed it to happen. Let me show you the pump." Jigs led them in a wide semi-circle around the village, through a small section of unaffected bush towards the pump. David found he was perspiring freely in the heat of the day; he considered it was a consequence of his illness or lack of acclimatisation due to his recent arrival. He was unable to remove his eyes from the oil lake in which everything was dead. Desiccated sticks, once shrubs or trees, protruded from the dark swamp like vertical driftwood. Dead birds floated on the surface. Around the edge of the lake, narrow beaches of spongy, oil-soaked soil, soft and unmoving, separated the vulnerable ecosystem.

They stood next to the pump; the frame, motor and balance remained but nothing moved. All parts had merged into an ugly, rusted mass of connected metal. Someone had arrived one night some years ago, decided to disconnect the pipe line from the well head then left. The pump had spewed oil because the motor continued to run. Jigs considered the possibility of sabotage or an attempt to steal oil, which was more likely; in any event, the residents had shut off the motor only after the stream of oil ran down the slope into the village square, polluting water wells along the way and rendering the community uninhabitable.

Trinex had moved all residents to Fyzabad where they remained five years later. The well had never been properly capped; it leaked intermittently to the present day. A promise to clean up the village had evaporated into the mists of time.

Jigs saw David's appalled expression. "About six years ago, I came here with my father to collect a body. It was a village of about ten houses and a small store. After the oil spill, Trinex promised to restore it, then forgot about it."

"What was the reason for leaving it like this?"

"Cost of clean up. Cheaper to relocate residents to where they are now. But a village has died." Jigs faced David directly. "This community was about the same size as Ramdass Trace. You see my point." He searched for and found the dilemma in David's eyes; this was the time to press home an advantage. "What has Wendell Soames asked you to do exactly with Ramdass Trace?" Jigs already knew the answer.

"It's not just Ramdass Trace. There are several other sites. Are there any other disasters like this?"

Jigs thought before replying. "Not that I know of directly, but this has been hidden behind a wall of lies and misinformation." He waved a hand at the abandoned village. "You saw how time has covered the evidence. There is no proper road into here now and no signs. Ranji Village doesn't remain in the memory of too many people. There are hundreds of disused pumps all around the country, many in the south. I expect most of the well heads have been capped off properly, but how would we know? There is the growing problem of oil theft from pumps like this when they are actually producing, and Trinex is not too careful about security."

David exhaled noisily between his teeth; he lifted his shirt from a damp shoulder. The sun pounded through gaps in the overhead tree crowns, casting green light on the oil ponds around their feet.

Jigs began to walk back to the car; sucking sounds emanated from his oil covered boots. As David followed him, he remarked: "I know you've been with Trinex a short time, but you have to understand that the company is just a gigantic machine which needs constant lubrication. There is never enough oil, it's never satisfied."

"Yes but for the island to thrive, it has to exploit its best resource. Oil is progress, isn't that so?"

Jigs felt the hand of Wendell Soames in the weight of David's words. David had probably heard this mantra many times already. Jigs let it pass. Twenty minutes later, after a journey passed in silence, they arrived back at the Trinex centre in Santa Flora.

"I know you have to see Wendell Soames. He thinks I'll be helping him with Ramdass Trace." Jigs smoothed his trimmed moustache with thumb and forefinger. "I want this process stopped. I realise that as an employee there's not much you can do, but if you could talk to Soames about the possibility of moving extraction away from residential areas, it would be a start."

David opened the car door. "It's hard to believe the company could destroy a village and leave it to die like that." He shook his head at the memory of the oil lake. "But it's not that simple is it? The company didn't actually cause the spill. You know about line tappers who steal oil from the pipelines? Wendell Soames knows it's an increasing problem and Trinex can't police every well. The wells are actually more secure nearer to residential areas." David lifted himself out of the car. He hesitated briefly. "I've got one or two ideas about cleaning up oil spills and I'll talk to him about Ramdass Trace. Leave it to me."

Jigs saw the bright, open smile and accepted the parody. They parted with friendly nods. As Jigs watched David walk away, he reflected on his plan and asked himself if there was any prospect of receiving help from David with Ramdass Trace specifically. He was not convinced whenever David gave the standard Trinex response to criticism; Jigs thought he could be malleable, pressed into using his natural sympathy for Ramdass Trace residents to assist Jigs in some way. David's parting words regarding his intention to talk to Wendell Soames sounded less vague than Jigs would have thought. There was an assurance and calm authority about him that inspired some confidence. If only Jigs could see the way forward, he might encourage David to use the Ranji Village disaster to help Ramdass Trace.

Jigs was rather troubled by the last hour in a way he could not have imagined. The only common bond between him and David was their shared history in Ramdass Trace. This might be enough to enable Jigs to use him gainfully in a good cause, but while his focus had been on Trinex, he now realised there was an uncomfortable feeling of empathy with David due to his difficult, contradictory position as an employee of the oil company on one side and sympathiser with friends and acquaintances in Ramdass Trace on the other. More than this, Jigs also found there was nothing to dislike in David, nothing that would reinforce his natural aversion to someone who might adversely affect his sister's future. However, one lasting belief bit at him in the midst of his sudden realisation that David might not be an enemy: he could never be a friend unless Girly let him go.

***

David crossed the car park and entered the Trinex administration building via a side door, avoiding the main entrance; a staircase gave him access to the first floor offices. He stopped outside the closed door of Wendell Soames' room; muffled voices crept through the panelled wood indicating that the local director of exploration was busy. David passed further along the sunlit corridor to a large open office on the opposite side of the building. This was the room he briefly shared with three experienced engineers before his sojourn in London. Ribald comments accompanied him to the desk he had left; it seemed like half a lifetime ago. He was not sure if he still had a position here until he was able to gain access to Wendell Soames. The satrap was a powerful local figure and David was not sure, despite the periodic contact when he was in London, whether his employer still required his services.

Meanwhile, David decided to make use of his short period of grace; he searched through files to find seismology reports on Ramdass Trace. Exact locations of the proposed drilling sites might be important to the residents and something to bargain with when the time came for site preparation. The files also contained details of legal issues, all of which were sketchy, probably lacking in complete legality but relying heavily on the 1962 Petrochemical Industry Act. The company would probably field any legal objections whilst moving onto hurriedly leased sites to commence operations; clarifying the law might take a long period, during which time the wells would be producing.

The earlier meeting and conversation with Jigs were playing on his mind. Although Ranji Village had been a shock in its utter desolation, David was aware that this was not rare in other oil producing countries, and he knew that the Trinex history in capping and cleaning up abandoned wells throughout the island was not good but was improving. Nevertheless, it was extremely unlikely that the process could be stopped in Ramdass Trace or anywhere else that Wendell Soames and his engineers had identified as promising locations.

His thoughts drifted towards Jigs as a person rather than the mission he was undertaking. It would have been very easy during the car journey to Ranji Village, when Jigs was effectively cornered, to press home his views on Girly's right to independence without interference. Despite the fact he was unsure of how much influence Jigs held over his sister, and whether it affected her attitude towards David, he somehow felt the need for Jigs' approval. Maybe it was because he saw Jigs as a parent to Girly instead of a brother that he hesitated.

Although David was sympathetic to the cause for Ramdass Trace, he was also aware that Jigs would use him in any way possible. He realised he did not mind because their objective was the same, but he could not envisage a time when they would become close friends. The withholding of his letter to Girly could not be forgotten.

David refocused; he was contemplating one or two potential areas for negotiation when he heard Wendell Soames out in the corridor saying farewell to his visitor. David walked to the director's office just in time to see his employer return to the room. As he followed, Wendell Soames turned on his heels at the sound of footsteps behind him.

"Ha! Finally...you return," he bellowed, eyes bulging, hands on hips. "Where have you been hiding?"

David ignored the thrust of the question. "Today, you mean?"

"No, not today," Soames thundered. "For the last three months!"

Again, David steered clear of the bigger picture; he wanted to focus on the matter in hand. He did not want to hold a prolonged discussion about his long absence.

"Compassionate leave, as you know."

"Three months?"

"It was difficult...to get away."

Wendell Soames stepped closer to David, fixing him with a piercing eye. He sensed a deceit which was nothing to do with

David's absence. "So where were you today? You knew I was waiting here."

"Ranji Village."

"Oh yes! And I expect you were taken there by that body snatcher!"

Wendell Soames felt a rage grow inside him which might have transferred to his hands and precipitated violence if he was a person so inclined. But he was not and David knew it despite the fact that they had not been colleagues for long. David had spent some time with Wendell Soames when he first started with Trinex; as a junior on the company's graduate scheme he had been immediately seconded to exploration at Santa Flora. Soames remembered well his own early days with the company when there was much to learn and, prompted by a liking for the boy which he could not define, set out to make an ally for the future. He would need close colleagues in the difficult times ahead now that onshore drilling was back on the company's agenda.

David knew that despite the bluster and probing eyes, Soames was not intimidating. One day during his first week with Trinex, David had been taken by Wendell Soames to several sites around the south as an introduction to how oil was extracted on a daily basis. He wanted David to see beyond the text book learning to the actual nuts and bolts of how the industry operated. On their travels, they passed through Princes Town; Soames stopped the car next to a field on the west suburban side. The shack that was his first home was long gone, the field now contained no sugar cane. He spoke wistfully of his early, poverty stricken life, the long walks to school in worn, handed-down sandals . He was clearly proud of his achievements with Trinex and more than grateful for the chances he had been given. This gratitude manifested itself in a determination to meet the obligations of a local director; head office in Port of Spain needed more oil to sell. He would provide.

Despite his fierce loyalty, Wendell Soames was not immune to the dangers posed by onshore drilling and its impact on human life and nature. Ranji Village had been a constant weight on his mind – he was haunted by his first visit to the site several years before, although the disaster had not happened during his time in office at Santa Flora.

David did not answer his accusation. They stood face to face in the spartan office. Soames subsided as the reality of Ranji Village overpowered his ire.

"You know, I asked Port of Spain several times to clean up that place. Reinstate everything. You know what they said?" he asked quietly, as if confiding a secret. He did not wait for David's answer. "They said it should stay as a permanent reminder of what oil theft can do." He gave a short laugh. "Except nobody sees it, nobody remembers now." The momentary shadow of sadness in his eyes was banished by resolve.

Soames surfaced from the depth of a sore memory. "So, you're back. I'm reinstating you, but I want results in the areas on this list which include Ramdass Trace." He retrieved a single sheet of paper with typed locations from his desk and handed it to David. "You have to check the seismology reports, legal agreements and liaise with the production section."

Wendell Soames saw the expression of doubt on David's face. "Legal agreements? I suspect the legality will be challenged, especially in Ramdass Trace."

Soames walked across to an open window; he wiped his forehead with a white handkerchief. "What is it about Ramdass Trace? Why is everyone so concerned about overgrown bush? Nothing happens there!" He projected an intentional look of incomprehension, then immediately rearranged it to one of suspicion. "It's that undertaker, isn't it? He has family there but what's your special interest?" He forestalled a response. "I merely propose two or three wells there for which land rent will be paid. Besides, isn't there already a long-established well at one end of the road?"

David sat without being asked on the guest chair which groaned. "We both know that if there is a legal challenge, it will take forever, during which time drilling will begin. I just don't want to see another Ranji Village anywhere. I know the people in Ramdass Trace – that's my special interest but the principle remains for any new site."

"What do you propose?"

"We could place the drilling rigs nearer to the main road, away from the houses as far as possible. The whole area should be an oil reservoir so we don't need to start too far from the road and it's a shorter distance to pump the oil to storage. Also, start with one rig to confirm that the well will be viable. No point in setting up more than one rig at vast expense if the seismology is not accurate."

"There's always oil in that area," countered Wendell Soames.

David knew that seismology in terms of accuracy in locating oil was less than perfect but it was a good indicator and the region around Ramdass Trace had produced since the early days of exploration on the island.

"We both know that a well can produce one day then run dry in a short period. We shouldn't invest too much at once. I would also propose that security should be stepped up around the pump when it is operating. Fence it off, regular inspections."

"We do that anyway."

"Not always – I've seen most of the current sites."

Soames had to concede that the budget for security in preventing pipeline tapping was tight. It involved employing too many people to make the production viable. The whole premise of land drilling was that relatively small quantities of oil were produced by individual pumps and therefore many pumps were needed to make the process profitable over a long period of time. This stretched investment resources; security was one of the aspects that was not a high priority unless oil theft became a constant problem.

Wendell Soames changed the direction of the conversation. "What I want to know is this: now that you're back, are you staying and can I rely on you?" He subjected his junior to an uncomfortable stare which was unrewarded as David focused on the sharp light emanating from the window. The room perspired through its walls. David decided that although he had not resolved his long term future, he would be in a better position to affect local Trinex policy from within the company. For now.

"Yes, I'm staying. But I want to ensure the new licences for drilling are properly managed and supervised. We can't have any more failures."

"Ranji Village was a long time ago. I can see you are as affected by what happened there as I was. However, we seek to improve. You have to report on progress to me regularly."

David nodded. "And if the drilling at Ramdass Trace or anywhere else is abandoned because of low yield, we cap the wells and reinstate the sites." It was a question rather than a statement.

Wendell Soames smiled the smile of a beatific angel. "Of course."

David threw one more thought at his employer as he left the room. "You know, there's so much oil just lying on the ground at Ranji Village. The valves are leaking and it's killing everything that still lives. If it ignites at any time...." He left the complaint unfinished.

***

The journey to Galeota Point was long and not straightforward. Situated on the south eastern tip of the island, it was not easily accessible by road from Santa Flora. David drove the hire car back towards Penal where he negotiated a loop on Rock Road to Cats

Hill Road, travelling due east. Past the wildlife sanctuary containing deep redwood forests, streams and clear waterfalls, he turned south onto the Rio Claro Road towards Guayaguayare on the coast. Galeota was a short distance away along the coast road and situated on a high- security, peninsula site.

Just before the oil terminal, a side road led to a small residential area running parallel to the beach. After one or two enquiries in roadside stores, David found the address of his parents' temporary home. He approached a small two storey house next to an ivory coloured sand beach; a side path led into the rear garden comprising a worn, under-watered lawn and a short row of wind swept palm trees at the end. A narrow gap between the trees framed a damaged gate giving access directly to the beach. Far off to the right, an extensive oil terminal sat on the tip of the peninsula; David could make out several oil or gas storage tanks, a long jetty out onto the sea and a helicopter pad, currently occupied. David knew that this was an important terminal; crude oil was periodically loaded onto visiting tankers for export to Europe. Gas was produced and stored. Between the beach and the terminal, sandstone rocks and low cliffs dominated but were constantly eroded by the Atlantic surf.

David walked along the side of the cream coloured house into the garden; he had no idea whether his parents would be at home but was unsurprised to find them sitting on the edge of the lawn in multi-coloured deck chairs, talking in low voices as they looked out to sea through spaces between the palms. The ocean breeze teased the fronds into an uneven rhythm, masking the sound of his approach until he stood next to them in black shadow.

They reacted together, rose as one, pulled aside the chairs. His mother stepped forward then retreated a pace, driven back by shame and the notion that her growing guilt was given impetus by the knowledge of a long-standing, negligent act she hoped to explain but could not begin to articulate. His father stood next to his wife in a show of shared culpability, not of defiance. They were late-forties, normally vibrant, upright examples of expatriates who have embraced their adopted home. Outwardly, there was no sign in their physiques, bearing or attitudes that they could not be his parents. David looked at the two people closest to him in his life - physically recognisable from three months ago but changed in every other way by a secret now uncovered. He withdrew Ronny's letter from his shirt pocket; he did not trust himself to be coherent or reasonable at this point. Handing the letter to his father, David passed through the gate onto the beach. He allowed ten minutes to drift by before walking back.

"Yes, it's true. Everything Veronica writes. But she can't know the whole story so it's incomplete." In his absence, David's father had placed a third chair to form a small circle in the garden . He sat with the letter hanging from a limp hand at the side of the deck chair. David sat down reluctantly.

"What's missing?" he asked evenly. "What is there to add that would make everything right after twenty or more years?" His father sighed and slumped deeper into the canvas. David thought both parents wore the signs of a mental burden that would not be lifted even though they must have prepared for this day over many years, as if the passing of time made the task more difficult. But he should not be denied a full, truthful explanation of why he had been sent away to find out his real identity. Had it not been possible to reveal the truth before he left for London? To leave it to chance that all might surface in London smacked of a cowardice he had never before thought possible in the two people before him.

His father suddenly appeared to throw off the loss of confidence settling over him. "Your real father was a bad person, a criminal who became wealthy as a young adult, not through petty, minor acts but the sort of crime which ruins those he preyed upon. He stole fortunes from unsuspecting investors in a fraudulent scheme.

I'm convinced my sister knew nothing about it at first, but she was infatuated by him so she possibly ignored any misgivings she might have had. Whether Veronica is aware of this, I can't say."

David looked at his surrogate mother; she seemed frozen by indecision, afraid of saying the wrong thing. His surrogate father continued: "I met him once or twice – there was a darkness about him, a heartlessness that Christine couldn't see. Eventually, as Veronica mentioned, he left the three of you. I think Christine suspected she was living on the product of his criminal activities but she was trapped. How he managed to arrange for the Gallery Street property to be transferred to her, I don't know. I suppose the authorities could not prove that it was the proceeds of crime. Anyway, it was all done from abroad and he never returned."

David interrupted the sequence of events to approach the area he felt had most meaning. "I can understand why you would take me away at a difficult time for Christine – it's in Veronica's letter. But all I really want to know is why you never told me this before. That's what counts really."

His mother rose and hurried into the house, not waiting to hear her husband's explanation.

"Because it became more difficult as time passed and, I suppose, like any lie, you build up a story, a background until it becomes real and you can't tear it down, even if you know it's wrong. When you were the right age to know, we were already here. Christine wanted you back but we just couldn't let you go. We convinced ourselves that this was the right place for you because...who could say? Maybe your real father would return to London and we didn't want you to go through that. So we kept Christine at bay – I didn't travel to London at any time, even when she told me she was seriously ill."

"I can't believe you didn't even travel for her funeral...your sister! And why send me *after* the funeral? Did you know about the content of the will?"

"Yes, I knew. She wrote to me regularly. I didn't tell her you were in London as a student for three years. And if we had attended the funeral, I would have had to explain to you, at some point, that you had an aunt who was not really your aunt but your mother...it was just too difficult after so long. I suppose also I hoped you would come back now without knowing but there was always a chance that Veronica would tell you."

David searched around the quiet garden for a sense of reality not currently inside his mind. Why had they needed him so much? "What about children? Of your own."

"Wasn't possible." His father looked away, towards the house, then towards the beach, not willing to elaborate. Then, in an effort to lift the strain that the conversation heaped upon him, he remarked: "We move back to the compound tomorrow. The water problem has been solved. It was the well drilling, you know. Contamination – all sorted out now." An attempted lightness in his tone died on his lips.

Although there were further aspects of the explanation that should have been clarified, David had just one final question. "When Christine wanted me back, how did you keep her away? If you would not go to London, did she not try to come here?"

As his father began to speak, his voice lowered so that the sound of the surf on the beach almost filtered out his words. "We...I threatened to tell you that you were abandoned by her, given up in favour of Veronica. I also persuaded her that you would have a better life here and you should never know about your real father. I think it was this that kept her away. Of course, my regret *should* be that you didn't have the chance to meet her – but I don't regret it at all."

David discerned the first sign of defiance and self-righteousness in the appalling admission. There was no advantage in staying, no more facts to learn, only opinion, justification. For some reason he couldn't explain to himself, he felt an overwhelming need to be with his sister. He walked away from the garden, back along the side of the house. Inside, the woman who could never tell him he was not her own, who loved him more than anything in her life, listened to his receding footsteps. And when they died, the pain inside her forced a cry; she had seen the hurt in his eyes, the look of betrayal. The cry opened her mouth into a silent yell.

PART TWO

1 MOONFLOWER

Sixteen days after Sumatee Dhanraj passed away at Santa Flora, in accordance with tradition and with a nod towards religion, Mr. Dhanraj opened his house to visitors. By this time, the deceased was now considered an ancestor and the house was no longer impure. The gloom that had settled over Ramdass Trace was lifted, not only by the re-entry of Mr. Dhanraj into the fold, but also by the lack of activity by Trinex: the expected arrival of drilling equipment in the bush had not materialised and those potentially affected dared to hope that Jigs Boodoosingh had exerted an influence they suspected he possessed, turning Trinex on its heels, forcing the giant to retreat.

The truth was somewhat different. In accordance with normal procedure, a lull ensued, a period not of contemplation or reassessment, for the intention was clear, but a time of consolidation during which the oil company made preparations for oil prospecting in Ramdass Trace. Although the term 'prospecting' might indicate that something of a risk was involved, the company was always loathe to invest in chance. Therefore, Trinex's expert employees did their work and concluded that there should be a decent return on investment, as far as could be predicted. These things were never certain – an oil well could run dry after one day, but as far as Ramdass Trace was concerned, the intention had now been upgraded: three oil wells and pumps were proposed, one each on the lands owned by Ravi Bishoo, Sagar Narsingh and the Jaggernauth cousins. This did not take account of any verbal agreement between David and Wendell Soames that a single trial well should precede the full plan.

Meanwhile, Mr. Dhanraj was desperate for comfort and contact; his period of mourning, deep distress and isolation had pushed him into a darkness that would not be dispelled until his neighbours considered he was cleansed of the lingering pall of death. Sixteen days were generally considered adequate, although forty was common in some small communities. In the intervening period, he underwent a gradual reintegration as the time passed ranging from almost complete loneliness in the early days to this day when many visitors helped with his open house gathering. During the sixteen days of ostracism, Mr. Dhanraj only received immediate family; this was not of his own volition. Jigs and Girly spent time at the house, fussing and reassuring; the widow Dookie risked the condemnation of her neighbours by stepping across her rear garden before dawn, through pockets of dark mist and avoiding tepid rain pools, to place small parcels of vegetarian food outside the side door of number twelve.

Then, on the sixteenth day, after the house had been thoroughly cleaned, a small army of neighbours and relatives arrived to prepare for a grand reception: an awning was erected in front of the basement room, cooking equipment was set up, hired chairs and temporary tables unstacked and placed around the perimeter of the yard. A pundit stopped by the house but no *Puja* was performed. Prayers would not be appropriate for a year when deities could be re-invited to the house. The pundit fed heartily then left. Specific notices and invitations had been issued but it was acknowledged that during the day a number of non-invited guests would attend as the word spread in the district that a feast was in progress. In fact, between midday and midnight, a hundred people drifted in and out of the trace to stop at number twelve, many staying for hours, some leaving when the cooking was over. Women arrived in their best saris, hair drawn back and plaited like black ropes; men were more casual in loose shirts to lessen the effects of the sweltering heat. It was an occasion. Laughter grew as time passed, new acquaintances were introduced, names immediately forgotten. There were familiar faces from places not remembered. Those who knew Mr. Dhanraj whispered words of condolence, hoped he was coping; some passed on their confident predictions that all would be well, his days would pass surrounded by family and God's blessings. Mr. Dhanraj spent much time next to the chennet tree shaking hands with his many guests; he was comfortable standing in the same place his wife had occupied so often. Adjacent to the tree, he had long ago planted a moonflower for Sumatee which could be seen from the veranda. The sweet-fragranced, trumpet shaped flowers opened at dusk and closed the following day. She told him she liked to watch it 'climbing for the moon'.

Twilight fell. The solid surfaces beyond number twelve, the houses and the bush melted away below a lavender sky leaving only the front yard in clear, artificial light. Candles were lit outside the house. The weight of the approaching night rested on the trace; it was humid, perfumed by the moonflower and beautiful. Small voices, lilting and amused, decorated the air.

Then music came from inside the house, loud, inviting, reaching out of the front window in a long arm of jumbled notes. Sunil Jaggernauth stood in the centre of the yard, arms outstretched holding a half-full glass in each hand. He stood on one leg swivelling his slim hips, not spilling a drop. Amit Jaggernauth shimmied over to join his cousin face to face, mimicking his dance. Soon, Jaggernauth daughters, sons and second cousins emerged from the awning leaving their excited chatter floating behind them. They formed lines in which they swayed and bobbed; the *Bhangra chutney* beat, compelling and irresistible, drove them on. They were joined by strangers and family until the yard was a sea of movement and a joy lifted above Ramdass Trace inspired by the memory of Sumatee Dhanraj and a faith in Jigs Boodoosingh.

Mr. Dhanraj stood on the side steps of the house, beaming benevolently; the widow Dookie, still for the first time that day, watched the Jaggernauth girls with vicarious pride. The beat bounced over the yard forcing the Pump Man to join the end of a dance line and exhibit a sympathy for the music and a nimbleness of foot that belied his bulk.

Girly Boodoosingh, radiant and magnificent in a shimmering blue sari, stayed close to her uncle all day. She greeted guests with him, held his arm from time to time, followed him in and out of the house. Occasionally, she allowed her eye to wander in David's direction. Apart from a brief, smiled touching of cheeks at midday, they maintained a distance.

Now, in a dark corner of the yard close to the chennet tree, David and Jigs dropped into a casual conversation. In the days since they had last spoken at the Trinex compound, Jigs had been busy with funeral parlour business both in Penal and in San Fernando where he had started negotiations with a small undertaking chain for a reciprocal arrangement in which the San Fernando parlours, wishing to extend their area of operation further north, would relinquish business in scattered parts of the south, and Jigs would give up some unprofitable work north of Debe and Princes Town to scoop up more in the south. In addition to this load on his mind, Jigs had given much thought to the Trinex problem, and was about to admit defeat when an idea occurred to him that forced a slight smile to his lips. He was sitting with Angie and a rum punch on her veranda one evening during the previous week when she remarked that she had seen the Reverend Sproule from the Presbyterian Church with 'that Trinex man' outside the church near Penal. Jigs had stepped off the veranda towards the teak copse, black and impenetrable in the darkness, lost in deep concentration.

David gave Jigs a resumé of his last meeting with Wendell Soames.

Jigs was dubious. "Do you accept that only one well will be set up initially? Will he keep to your agreement? And what about security?"

David did not hesitate. "Arrangements are in progress for one well on Mr. Narsingh's land. Work starts very soon, but I have to say that I can't promise the other two wells will not follow on. It depends on results. Security can't be guaranteed but I've been assured the sites will be fenced off. "

Jigs experienced a sinking feeling. He had been putting off for some time a decision on how best to update the Ramdass Trace residents on progress. His initial idea of arranging a meeting in conjunction with Mr. Dhanraj's open day was now out of the question; he couldn't dampen the day with the news that so far he had failed in his mission with Trinex. Also, the indication that the Pump Man's land would be affected first was a bitter pill to swallow. The man was in a fragile mental state and this would increase his anxiety further.

Jigs left David with a recommendation that he should look for Girly inside the house; ten minutes earlier, after seeing the widow Dookie escorting old Mr. Roopnarine to his house, he had said the same thing to Devendra Roopnarine.

David had no intention of entering the house in search of Girly; he waited for her by the chennet tree. And waited. Inside, Devendra Roopnarine restarted a conversation with Girly interrupted many days ago at Mosquito Creek. He was again encouraged by her generous smile. "I now have a house in Penal," he began, "and it have gates." He had her full attention. "Will you come to see the house?"

"Who lives in the house?" she asked, in full knowledge of the answer.

Devendra spread his arms and laughed, as if the question was unnecessary. "It is empty!"

"Then I'll come." Girly felt Mr. Dhanraj's hand on her arm, easing her away with a half apology to Devendra as departing guests required her attention. Devendra left the house, crossing the yard where David stood alone. There was no need to speak to David about Girly; the agreement had been made, it was just a question of spending time with her so that he could express his wishes for the future. Half way along the trace on his way home, Devendra realised that he had made no arrangement, no date to show Girly his house. He stopped, leaned forward with hands on his knees, exasperated, disappointed. He looked back at number twelve; the yard and house were still in bright light but the music had stopped, car doors banged shut as guests went home. He couldn't face going back.

Girly stepped out of the house onto the side steps. It had been a long day – she wanted to go home. She would wait for Devendra to contact her about the house visit; despite her best efforts, she had not been able to think of Devendra recently without David's voice and face impinging upon her thoughts. She found it unsettling, even mentally tiring. Yet whenever she was with David, it required an effort to be indifferent; there was so much to think about – his life was complicated, interesting.

She descended the side steps looking past him next to the tree. He intercepted her. "Walk with me? Along the trace?" Girly hesitated, looked at her car standing at the end of the trace, thought of home. But she found herself treading slowly along the blistered tarmac, no street lights, just the dim lamps in the widow Dookie and Pump Man's houses to supplement the mottled moon. They were level with the vacant house just past number eleven before they spoke; Girly would not look at the numberless house. It had been owned by Sumatee Dhanraj, unoccupied for several years but maintained. Sumatee had offered it to her niece earlier that year to occupy whenever she wanted to get away from the funeral parlour. The same open invitation was available to Jigs but he would never leave the apartment above the parlour, apart from the occasional visit to Angie in Quinam Road.

Girly couldn't look at the house – too many painful memories, a feeling of shame. It stood ten metres back from the road, dark and unused, sheltering the secret of several months ago when she had taken David there, just once, because it was the right time in their relationship. And because she loved the truth, her subsequent loss was a true sign that she had taken things too far, stepped beyond all that she felt was right and possible in her small world. His world was much bigger, there was more scope for casual friendships which, now that she had crossed an intimate line with him, she could not tolerate. A few months before she had believed in him, accepted him, taken him to the house. Now, she wanted to pass the house without looking, without comment. If he mentioned the house, she would turn and walk back to her car.

David was expecting gentle questions concerning his parents, his new found wealth. She steered away onto more neutral ground. "What's happening here with Trinex? Jigs won't talk about it."

"Oh, drilling starts soon over there." He pointed to his left, into the distance between the houses of the Jaggernauth cousins and the Pump Man. "I can't stop it but it won't be as intrusive as people think. I hope it will be just one pump and for a short time."

They had reached the end of the trace; Girly had quickened her pace as they passed Devendra Roopnarine's house. She thought about David's words as they stood close to the oil pump on widow Dookie's land; the thing was barely visible in the night but its noise was incessant, producing day after day. It was screened by a thin line of bush on three sides and not in direct view from the trace; the ugliness of the beast was assuaged in Girly's mind by the knowledge that until now it had maintained a comfortable life style for Indira Dookie. They reached the company road and turned back.

"The thing is..." David began, as though he had finally ordered his thoughts along the way and now reached the crux of what he wanted to say. "I have to make a decision soon. Stay here, with or without Trinex, or go back to London. If I go, it might be long term." He avoided the word' permanently'. "You know everything that's happened to me recently. What do you think?"

She thought it sounded a lame question. "Why do you ask me? You have a straight choice. Have you seen your parents to ask them?"

He avoided the question. "They moved back to the Trinex compound. I haven't been there. I'm staying in San Fernando." David stopped at the point outside Indira Dookie's house. Hot pipes gurgled and sang along the road; the sounds from number twelve had dissipated in their brief absence. Lights were dimmed, the trace was quiet. "The thing is..." he began again. He gave up attempting to formulate a good enough reason and with a sigh which might have anticipated rejection he asked: "Come with me. Three months, or six months. I have a sister now who needs help with a business. This time, I'm not leaving a note. I'm asking you directly."

Girly looked at Indira Dookie's house; Indira and the garden beyond would always keep the secret of her lost child. But should she tell him now? Was there any purpose? She looked at him closely, his familiar stance, steady eyes, his apparent calm confidence she suspected he did not always feel. He still looked so young. His question balanced between them on the fine edge of her decision. And she wanted to go with him, to explore his new life; she trusted him despite his long absence in the past, his failure to communicate. Maybe she saw something in him she had believed in since their earliest days together, or a connection with the spirit of a child she couldn't abandon. She had every reason to agree, to perpetuate a long-held vision of her future she had never quite been able to dismiss despite, at times, her best efforts.

"No. I don't feel a good reason to leave." She tried to emphasise that it was final. There had never been enough of a child to really count.

They walked back to number twelve in silence.

***

Two days after the open house gathering at Mr. Dhanraj's house, Mr. Sagar Narsingh went to work as usual in the early morning. An air of normality floated over the trace, the assimilation of Mr. Dhanraj had been completed; he could expect a sedate retirement on his veranda waiting for neighbours to pass, to share an old man's memories. There were some who had attended the open house day who were appalled at the break with tradition: the day had descended into a lively party, inappropriate as a memorial for a much loved friend. Those who held this view were from outside the trace; within the trace it was considered a wholly acceptable way to celebrate a life.

The Pump Man had set off early so that he could enjoy a leisurely breakfast at Donna's on Clarke Road in Penal. His pump examinations today were in and around the Penal district; he carried many copies of a pre-printed form on which his readings were to be recorded. The map of the local area was superfluous - the Pump Man knew the exact location of all working oil wells.

Donna had just opened for business when the Pump Man settled at a corner table close to the counter. She was always careful when engaging him in conversation; he was a regular visitor in whom she recognised a fragile spirit without knowing his personal circumstances, although she knew something of his work. One day recently, the Pump Man had walked into Donna's, flustered, sweating and dizzy; he had been to Fong's yard to look at building materials —he saw galvanised sheets, some coated in red, others a sharp silver in the sun; there were door frames and doors, grey tiles for floors, windows of wood, buckets, forks and spades. Within store sheds he saw timber and boards, paint tins jostling for space with piles of pipes. He touched a pipe and drew back sharply as if shocked by an unexpected current; his head was spinning, he reeled away from the yard gasping for air, his feet taking him towards the sanctuary of Donna's where he could calm himself, banish the images of hammers and nails, drills and screws, a nightmarish compendium that set his pulse racing, forcing small sobs from his lips as building materials translated to dilapidation in the frayed edges of his mind.

The Pump Man once went to a doctor in San Fernando on the recommendation of Doctor Naidu in Penal who could do nothing to help his patient with a non-physical complaint. The San Fernando doctor was a psychiatrist who found Sagar Narsingh an interesting case. When he heard the symptoms, he initially diagnosed domatophobia, a rare anxiety based around the fear of houses, but he then decided this would not necessarily cover the complaint. Although the phobia could encompass the fear of a specific, deteriorating house, or a dread that the house might be in bad condition, which was true, the doctor struggled to find a cause in the Pump Man's background. Also, the patient found it difficult to describe the effect his house had on him; he did not dare to mention the 'voice of the house' which hurt him, tormented him on occasions. The Pump Man was a difficult patient. The doctor decided that behavioural therapy might help to instil in him the idea that his fear was irrational, but the house deterioration was real. Alternatively, as the poor condition was apparently a fact and the fear was only felt in this one building, perhaps there should be a recommendation to pull the house down to remove the source of the pain and start again. But the thought of rebuilding, of actually buying materials to rebuild, also prompted extreme symptoms such as the sweating, breathlessness, depression. The doctor believed the fear was so well entrenched that a new house would make no difference; also, contrary to the preliminary diagnosis, the Pump Man actually loved his house and land but the weight of responsibility imposed on him was a possible trigger for his illness, a fear based in the past, not of the present. He asked the Pump Man to envisage a happy event or situation in his life whenever he entered the house in future. This would provide a basis for regarding the house in a different, more pleasant way. It was decided he would think of the occasions he spent in Tobago with his sisters at their bar, a beach side establishment where he was cosseted and treasured. The Pump Man also tried to look back into the past, that most useless of friends, to find the point when there was no pain or sadness. But the images were blurred; he found the doctor's probing questions intimidating and went back to Ramdass Trace unable to conjure up the visions, aromas and sense of Tobago inside number sixteen. He abandoned his visits to San Fernando.

"How your pumps goin'?" Donna asked.

"Catchin' my backside. Trinex have me drivin', drivin'." The Pump Man examined a laminated menu, thinly coated with thumb-printed grease. He asked for *buljol* - flaked fish with tomato, peppers and lime, and chocolate tea. Donna disappeared into the kitchen just as Jigs Boodoosingh walked in. Jigs might have backed straight out again but the Pump Man had seen him; Jigs sat down opposite a fat smile. It was too early for prevarication. Jigs went to the point. "Sagar, you have to expect some action very soon by Trinex. I'm hoping it will be for a short time and they'll give up. I have an idea to make them go away but it might take some time."

The Pump Man recognised the Jigs sign of sincerity: his hands were flat on the table. However, nothing was to be absorbed purporting to be an antidote to the shot of optimism that Jigs had injected into the Pump Man at their last meeting. The offer of help with his failing house had possibly been misconstrued to include a guarantee of non-intervention by Trinex in the part occupation of his land. If Trinex could not be prevented from entering the plots owned by Ravi Bishoo and the Jaggernauth cousins, well that was no longer the Pump Man's concern; Jigs had taken control.

"It real pressure on you but it safe. I happy to rely on you."

Jigs' heart sank. There was clearly no way of bringing Sagar Narsingh back to earth gently. Jigs watched him demolish the breakfast, rub his stomach then disappear with a pat on Jigs' back to seal their private agreement.

Donna brought more chocolate tea to the table; it was too early for rum. She stood next to Jigs with hands on hips, lips pouted. "Angie passed by me yesterday. Talkin' 'bout that husband of hers. He not comin' back, you know!"

Jigs sipped the tea and summoned up vague facial expressions to indicate that he was listening. Donna hissed in frustration. "So she waitin' for you! You movin' to that pink house of hers?"

Jigs was too polite to indicate that it was none of Donna's business. "I have responsibilities and people depending on me," he replied, folding his arms across his chest. "Now is not a good time," he added limply.

"Angie talkin' of startin' a bar."

Jigs lifted one curved eyebrow. "News to me."

"Because you never listen to her!" Donna stomped off to serve one of the yard workers from Fong's.

Jigs resumed a thought about Angie that Donna had interrupted, not in the sense that he was contemplating their future together, although she had been making further overtures in that direction, but in relation to the innocent comment she had made recently about the pastor at the local Presbyterian Church, Reverend Sproule, and Wendell Soames. Several months ago, Jigs had arranged a funeral for one of the Reverend Sproule's parishioners. It was a budget affair for which Jigs had donated a reinforced cardboard coffin and halved his usual fee for a poor family at the request of Reverend Sproule. The Reverend now owed Jigs a small favour. After the funeral, whilst in conversation about the deceased's family, Jigs ascertained that a certain parishioner was in a position to help needy families, those who owned undeveloped residential land, by means of purchase in order to assuage the effects of bereavement. The private ownership of large areas of unused land which produced no income was quite common in south Trinidad amongst poorer families. The benefactor was introduced by Reverend Sproule, who in turn received a donation to the church for his trouble.

Jigs thought no more about the conversation until Angie's casual report; then, for no apparent reason, he formed a mental picture of Wendell Soames with Reverend Sproule discussing property. The following Sunday morning, Jigs had passed by the Presbyterian Church then stopped and walked back to the site. The church occupied a narrow plot behind a pair of corroded metal gates; a short path led to an unusual building approximately twenty years old comprising exposed, non-ferrous metal supports from ground to top, arranged to form a ridge at the peak for a roof, and enclosing the timber-framed body of the church at ground level. The roof was covered with the ubiquitous galvanised metal sheets; the single floor church encompassed a central aisle, teak pews either side and a pulpit at the far end in front of a white painted wall adorned with Christian icons. A small area in one corner was partitioned and presumably used as the pastor's private room. At the entrance, a pair of white doors carried separate carved crosses beneath clerestory windows.

Jigs stood furtively and unseen just outside one of the open doors so that the congregation and pulpit were visible. The Reverend Adequate Sproule was in the middle of a fiery delivery which caused his smooth head to glisten with perspiration. He kept his first name to himself; his parents, committed Presbyterians, had wanted to give him a name he could surpass, not just live up to. It was intended as an incentive in his life. Jigs watched him glare at the front row of pews which were full, in contrast to the rest of the church which was only dotted with randomly filled spaces. The pulpit creaked slightly as the reverend place two hands squarely on its top; in this position, he became God's clarion and the front row would feel his displeasure. Oddly, Jigs noticed, the congregation seemed only too ready to recognise their own shortcomings; there were nods of agreement, even wringing of hands to reinforce the reverend's words. It was a devotion, a compulsion. Near the back of the small church, alone, Wendell Soames sat in casual repose, formal smart dress, attentive but not apparently exulted by the experience. Jigs withdrew – a half suspicion had been confirmed. He waited a short distance along Erin Road in the shade of a rum shop's overhanging roof until the service was complete, the congregation and Wendell Soames had departed. Then he cornered Reverend Sproule in the church entrance porch on the pretext of discussing an impending funeral service with which the reverend was not familiar because it was fallacious.

"I wanted to speak to you about a service this week but I've just realised it's not a Presbyterian funeral." Jigs touched his forehead to emphasise the point that his reasoning had temporarily left him.

"Always a pleasure to see you, nevertheless." The reverend became a different, courteous character as soon as he left the pulpit. The thunder, fire and passion receded to a safe place inside him, to be locked away until recalled for God's purpose.

"But while I'm here....there is another matter." Jigs projected a casual air. "I know of a deserving case and your acquaintance, the one you told me about, might be able to help. I'm afraid this is not a Presbyterian parishioner but I believe there is an area of land for disposal which would help with finances."

"Would you like my parishioner to contact you about it?"

"No!" Jigs retorted a little too firmly. "No," more quietly with an apologetic smile. "No, I really just need a name."

"Well, it's Mr Soames, he was here a short while ago..." Reverend Sproule looked around him at the vacant church.

"No matter, I know of Mr. Soames. I'll be able to track him down. Just one other thing – do you know how his land acquisitions are valued?"

Adequate Sproule looked bemused, as if the matter was entirely beyond his field of understanding. "I really have no idea." They shook hands and parted on the doorstep of the church. Jigs moved on, back towards his car parked in the shade of a pink blossomed *poui* tree by the side of the road. By the time he reached the car his casual, loose fitting shirt was clinging to him in an uncomfortable saturation caused by a broiling sun and draining humidity. Jigs removed one or two fallen blossoms from the car roof; he quickly turned the engine and switched on the air conditioning whilst thinking about Wendell Soames. So, the Trinex zealot was buying up land; was it for himself, or for Trinex to sink more oil wells? Surely not the latter, as the current thinking was that land should be rented temporarily, drained of oil then abandoned. What was Soames doing with the land and, more to the point, were the families selling the land receiving reasonable values? Jigs needed to probe further but if his suspicions were well founded, there might be a way of applying a lever to prise Trinex from their entrenched position on land prospecting through Wendell Soames. Or at the very least, Ramdass Trace might be removed from the company's current catalogue of excesses.

Donna's bar began to fill with breakfast seekers while Jigs had been mulling over events. Since the day he had realised Wendell Soames was the local 'benefactor' for poor families, Jigs had done nothing with the information; now, it might be relevant and of particular use. He remembered that the poor family in question several months ago lived at Quarry, a short distance away from Penal. He also remembered collecting the deceased from a plain, timber-boarded house at the beginning of a trace surrounded by open ground up to the edge of Erin Road. Five minutes later, he threw several dollars onto the table and a 'thank you' over his shoulder to Donna as he hurried out of the bar. He drove to Quarry, recollecting the exact trace on the way; he turned left off the main road past the Presbyterian School into Satnarine Trace which was similar in many respects to Ramdass Trace in size and number of houses but with virtually no surrounding bush. There was no need to look far for the relevant house – Jigs remembered it was the first house on his left. It had changed from how he remembered it; a new roof covering was almost complete and, of greater interest, a new building was being constructed a short distance from the house, leaving a margin of flat, fenced ground in between. A rectangular concrete foundation was visible on the new site, out of which sprung several reinforced concrete columns linked by ground beams and higher concrete beams to support first floor slabs. Although only a skeleton of the building was apparent, Jigs thought it might eventually be larger than an average house but the shape did not give the impression of a dwelling. He was confused. Was Wendell Soames building for profit? It was unlikely to be a Trinex project. At this stage the building was not important but he had to ascertain whether the land owner had received a reasonable sum for selling the land to Wendell Soames. Two builders were laying blocks in cement mortar between the columns, there was no sign of life in or around the house next to the new site. Jigs decided on a method of ascertaining the sale price of the land without alerting the previous owners.

One hour later, he was sitting opposite Basdeo Persad in the single-room office of Penal Realty, an estate office in the centre of a terrace of low rise retail and service outlets opposite the Penal Funeral Parlour at Penal Junction. As an advertisement for the professed customer satisfaction, strength and prosperity of the Penal Commerce Union, Penal Realty was a poor example. In fact, the union was moribund. Members were few: the Fong family had declined to join because the store did not need it. It was prosperous without having to advertise widely or seek promotion; it dealt fairly with customers because volume of business allowed. Jigs had signed up the funeral parlour because he liked Basdeo Persad, the union's creator, and he thought he should. Donna became a member in the hope that somehow the annual fee would improve the quality of her clientèle but there was no discernible difference.

Basdeo Persad came from a wealthy family of San Fernando doctors; he had not followed the family line. As the eldest son, he was indulged in his passion for all matters relating to property and land dealing. The office in Penal and Basdeo's own speculating in real estate were paid for by his parents who generally received no return on their investments due to Basdeo's incompetence; their love for their eldest son was undiminished. During the previous year, Basdeo had acquired a plot of land at San Francique upon which he arranged for two identical bungalows to be built by a local contractor. The bungalows were completed and finished to a good standard – smooth rendered block walls, painted in cinnamon; open, recessed front porches for shelter, proprietary roof systems which put the common galvanised roofs to shame, and attached car ports at the sides. The builder, a taciturn man, assumed that Basdeo knew all about low-lying San Francique and its propensity to flood in the wet season and therefore made no comment about the location of the houses close to a narrow waterway. It was beyond the scope of his employment. The houses, pristine and of little value, remained unsold.

Basdeo also acted as an agent from time to time in the sale of land and buildings in the Penal district. The office was not welcoming: in the large, single-pane window, gummed tape held details of properties for sale to the glass until the gum dried in the hot afternoon sun, the paper yellowed and fell to the floor where several examples remained. The furniture was sparse and basic quality, the whitewashed walls had long ago become patchy and ochre stained with dampness in several areas. In contrast to his surroundings, Basdeo Persad was always immaculately dressed in suit and tie; Jigs had never seen him without a jacket even on the warmest of days. The two businessmen were of a similar age but under normal circumstances had little interest in each other's private lives or careers. They met occasionally to discuss the commerce union but at the last meeting there was talk of winding it up due to lack of interest.

"You see, these people have small minds," Basdeo complained to Jigs, conveniently forgetting that those businesses outside the union were succeeding and only Jigs inside the union was making a good living. "Strength in numbers, that's my mantra."

After one or two preliminaries, Jigs now steered the conversation towards property. He found that a little flattery often made Basdeo expansive on any topic. "Bas, I need some information about a plot of land in Quarry. Your finger is always on the pulse – do you know about a new building in Satnarine Trace?"

Basdeo scratched his scalp through wet-look hair with the end of a ball point pen. "Satnarine Trace? I know some land sold a few months ago but I'm not aware of a new building. Where in the trace?"

"First plot on the left. There's a bereaved family I was able to help. The pastor at Erin Road Pres' says there's a local man buying the odd plot here and there to help poor families but I wondered if the correct value was being applied. Are you valuing land for anyone?" Jigs looked for signs of evasion on Basdeo's pleasant features but he was an open book. Besides, Jigs did not think that Basdeo would be confidently engaged by any right thinking developer.

"No, not for the longest while. I know of that land, however, and the previous owner came to me with an offer they had received, asking me if it was reasonable. I thought it was twenty per cent short because it's quite a big plot."

"What happened?"

"I heard that there was a sale but I never knew the buyer."

Jigs smoothed his moustache, deep in thought. "Twenty per cent?"

"Yes. It's good land."

A recommendation, a professional opinion from Basdeo Persad might not be totally reliable but Jigs had the feeling he might not be too far out on this occasion. However twenty per cent below value, although a substantial amount of money, especially to a poor family, was hardly theft and could be given credibility by market forces. What was Soames doing? It was, nevertheless, something to use against him personally if handled correctly.

Jigs thanked his fellow commerce union member and left, taking the direct route across Penal Junction to the funeral parlour.

2 ...'SLIGHT DARK SHADOW ON THE MOONLIT TURF'

Several days later, Mr. Sagar Narsingh awoke late from a troubled dream. It was one of those mornings in Ramdass Trace, a morning of clear air and stark colours, which frequently followed a dry season dawn. The air was already hot enough to discourage even minimal exercise unless such movement was necessary; to most residents of the trace, it was not.

The details of the Pump Man's dream disappeared with his growing consciousness leaving him not unduly discomfited. He sat up in bed, rubbed his face with both hands; it was mid-morning, there was no work today. As he lifted himself slowly from the bed, he was vaguely aware of external sounds which were unfamiliar in the trace but they did not register fully until he had showered and dressed in undersized tee shirt and voluminous shorts, at which point he ambled to the rear window of the kitchen overlooking a small portion of his land. There was nothing to see, but the sounds, hollow metallic scrapes and faint voices, penetrated the bush to arrive as a slight warning in the Pump Man's ears. He decided to take a look; he tested the side staircase with half his weight before stepping out, descending and turning behind the house at ground level. The morning appeared normal, except that everyday bird sounds had been replaced by a background noise of human activity not far away. The Pump Man strode on towards the unusual noise. A sensitive mimosa bush recoiled as he brushed past, a carnivorous sundew plant sensed new prey when jostled by a meaty leg. On he walked until the sounds became separate, more distinct to his alert ears.

Before the Erin Road boundary, the Pump Man stopped at the edge of a newly formed clearing which was growing in size by the minute as a result of bush cutting machinery and the removal of debris by low loading vehicles. A temporary track for vehicular access was already in place; fine and coarse gravel was being dumped, spread and compacted to form an approach from the main road to the clearing. The Pump Man walked to the open space and stopped, horrified, scandalised by the intrusion. He counted ten men engaged in the various operations on his land; he had seen it before, elsewhere, like an inexorable tide. He could not speak to them, protest, ask them to stop – they would ignore him. He turned and hurried back to the house, each step more difficult as the weight of realisation pressed down on him so heavily that by the time he reached home, he was almost crushed. He lifted the phone receiver in the living room and dialled the Penal Funeral Parlour in an attempt to raise Jigs Boodoosingh; Jigs was away for the day at an undertakers' convention in Port of Spain.

As the sounds from the clearing pounded in his head, Sagar Narsingh lay down on a battered sofa; small black clouds gathered above him. He covered himself with a thick blanket and faced the wall behind the sofa, pulling the blanket over his head. His mouth opened and closed rhythmically as if he were chewing on the fragments of his shattered luck.

***

Days and weeks passed in fast-paced activity at the clearing. A water well was dug nearby as water is required for drilling; excavation of a reserve pit was started for storing the waste products of drilling until David decided this was dangerous and insensitive. His experience of water contamination had sharpened his appreciation of the possible consequences of drilling. He falsified an order from Santa Flora for the spoil to be carried away by trucks. He would worry about any budgetary repercussions later. Further holes were dug for the drilling rig and the central opening. Much mobile machinery came and went during these days; there was a storage area for pipes and drill bits, one or two small huts constructed for the workers, and the clearing became larger.

The operation proceeded smoothly from Trinex's point of view; the Pump Man recognised the changes in site noise and sounds as different parts of the exploration were put into practice, but he never once approached the clearing after the first day, never looked out of his window towards the bush. He had reported to Jigs Boodoosingh on the second day, tried to pull himself together so that he left the house early every morning, trusting that one day soon Jigs would prevail and the sounds would disappear.

Meanwhile, drilling began through the main hole, initially by means of a mobile drilling rig on a truck; the hole was lined with a large diameter pipe. Full rig equipment was then brought forward by truck and a derrick, generator, platform and turntable were assembled and constructed. Drilling began and eventually reached a pre-set depth where oil was expected to be found. The constant clang of pipes being added to the rig as the hole deepened, the generator hum, the thrum of lorry engines all drifted over the top of the bush towards the trace where residents waited for salvation and Sagar Narsingh maintained his faith despite the demons in his head.

The Trinex crew knew their business; they were acutely aware, and had been reminded by their employers, that insertion and placing of the casing pipe in the correct position and with a proper cement seal, was vital. The recent disaster close to the Fyzabad staff compound where water contamination had followed a defective installation was still a very sore point. The casing was sealed, tested then tested again.

Drilling proceeded with new casings inserted in stages until a depth was attained where oil traces were detected in the waste material; there was a delay as core samples were taken, tested and reports sent to the Santa Flora office. Wendell Soames read the reports which brought a "Ha!" to his lips and a gleam to his prominent eyes. He called David into his office one morning:

"You've seen these?" he asked, holding the positive reports below David's chin. He did not wait for an answer. "Just as I thought – we'll be pumping oil in no time. Are arrangements in place for the other two rigs at Ramdass Trace?"

David assured him they were although in truth he was waiting for further information as to the likelihood of a prolonged supply of oil from the first well.

Meanwhile, with optimum depth reached, the crew at Ramdass Trace prepared to install a pump, which might well have given a sign of permanence and further distress to Sagar Narsingh if he had been inclined to look. Which he was not.

When the lower casing in the well was intentionally perforated, oil began to flow into an inner tubing. The outside of the tube was sealed and a valve fitted to the well head; when satisfied that oil had been induced to flow, the site engineer determined that a pump should be placed on the well head for production to begin.

From time to time, Jigs Boodoosingh visited the site without the Pump Man's knowledge. He stood on the perimeter of the clearing and although he had no understanding of the drilling procedure, he deduced that the works were unfortunately progressing towards oil production in the near future. On behalf of the Pump Man, Jigs dreaded the time when the pump would be installed.

Trinex wasted no time in erecting a pump: a new steel structure of frame, beam and horse head produced the familiar 'nodding donkey' type of pump, ubiquitous in south Trinidad; when a motor, gear box and counter balance were added, the pump was almost ready. At this point, other wells should have been drilled on adjacent land to exploit the anticipated oil reserve, but again David forced delays by a mixture of deliberate withholding of information and minor sabotage of the process, the link between the site and Santa Flora. He continually queried the conclusions of experienced engineers and seismology reports, using his position as a close but not entirely trusted colleague of Wendell Soames. He also ensured that there were no delays on other sites to offset the slower progress in Ramdass Trace.

*****

One afternoon, David was standing in the bush clearing on Sagar Narsingh's land when Jigs Boodoosingh appeared through the thick foliage. David wondered why he had not used the new site entrance on Erin road; perhaps, David speculated, Jigs did not acknowledge that it now existed. They watched as a connection was being made from the well head valve for a supply pipe to take extracted oil away from the site to Santa Flora for storage. Jigs puffed up his cheeks then exhaled softly; he wiped his damp brow with a small, yellow cloth whilst squinting towards the sun. David appeared unaffected.

"It seems you've made fast progress," Jigs observed sourly. His last visit was not recent; he was trying to avoid the Pump Man until he had positive news, but in truth he was treading water, waiting for a break such as a dry well to stop the Trinex process, but he found himself surprised at the speed with which the Trinex crew was operating. He had a vague notion that oil well drilling would take a long time, possibly months, but he now assumed that with this part of the country reputedly standing on oil reservoirs not too far down, the whole procedure was uncomfortably straightforward.

"I've delayed all I can for now," David replied. They walked towards the well head; a metal mesh perimeter fence now formed a rectangular protective barrier around the pumpjack with inside space for materials and a large personnel gate. "This is as secure as we can make the site. I've also argued that the waste from drilling should be taken away."

Jigs had to acknowledge that the immediate area, although devoid of natural vegetation, trees and bushes for many metres in any direction, was at least clean and tidy. The bush would grow back in time. Meanwhile, the final part of the pump assembly looked ominously close; Jigs feared that when it began to nod and produce, day after day, the Ramdass Trace residents would feel the full effect of 'progress'. Two more pumps would no doubt follow. It was time to take Wendell Soames to one side and offer a subtle threat, which was completely against Jigs' nature but he was in a corner, partly of his own making. He couldn't abandon his promise to the residents and he did not want to relinquish his exalted position. He left the site and by a circuitous route through the bush he regained his car at the end of the trace without having to pass the front of any houses.

***

David glanced at his wristwatch after Jigs had left. He decided not to return to Santa Flora – there was nothing he could usefully do for the remainder of the day, nothing that could not wait. He had already visited the other sites entrusted to him by Wendell Soames.

Since Mr. Dhanraj's open-house day at Ramdass Trace, David had been repairing his damaged reputation with Trinex; the memory of his long absence had faded with those who mattered. Although he had been stealthily impeding progress on Sagar Narsingh's land, he was also assiduous with all matters relating to the other sites in south Trinidad. His role was as a facilitator, progress chaser and envoy of Wendell Soames. Fortunately, the locations tended to be away from sensitive areas, remote from villages; where drilling rigs impacted on nature and the enjoyment of land, no-one seemed unduly bothered. Rents were accepted.

David looked at the pump installation on Sagar Narsingh's land and sighed. There was nothing more he could do to stop the imminent oil flow despite his best efforts. The crew was efficient and motivated, as if prodded to maximum efforts. It was not strange that he felt this way about Ramdass Trace, he thought. The pressure from Jigs was unnecessary: his ties to Mr. Dhanraj in particular conflicted with what should have been a professional approach but he could not help himself. This trace had formed such a prominent part of his life that he was embarrassed to be associated with anything that would so upset people he had known since he was a boy.

The time since his return from London had passed in a whirl of Wendell Soames inspired activity. If, originally, he had any thoughts that his presence and position at Trinex might be of help to engineer a satisfactory outcome at Ramdass Trace, he soon realised this was fanciful. He had been swept along with the unstoppable Soames tide so that his efforts to slow progress now seemed petty and, worst of all, ineffective. The business had moved on despite him and, in a similar way to Jigs, he would have to explain his position to someone in the trace.

He decided to seek out Mr. Dhanraj. He followed a course through the bush towards the side of the Pump Man's house, emerging eventually at the hot pipes running parallel to the road surface opposite the widow Dookie's house. He saw Mr. Dhanraj in his habitual position on the veranda as he stepped across the front yard and climbed the steps. Mr. Dhanraj welcomed him in the same way as when they first sat together in this same place. Nothing had changed except his loneliness: the chairs, dried out floorboards, cracked-paint balustrade, were exactly the same. Initially, they avoided talking of Trinex, but it was like a very large elephant standing next to them – it could not be ignored for long.

"No one here blame you for this," Mr. Dhanraj leaned forward offering a consoling pat on David's arm. "When Trinex make up its mind, nothing to stop it."

"I feel like giving it all up and going back to London." David slumped in his seat. "I don't know why I came back to Trinex. It's like fighting an unstoppable machine, even from the inside."

"You come back for Sumatee and because this is home."

David looked at his long time companion who had the ability to simplify the most complicated aspects of life into a single sentence, but south Trinidad did not feel like home at this time. He reflected on the period since he came back: rejected by Girly, estranged from his putative parents, hounded by Wendell Soames into representing the local face of Trinex, exposed as the man who stole land for commercial gain. Mr. Dhanraj's assurance that local people did not see it that way, that the company was to blame, hardly softened the feeling that he did not really belong here now.

Soon after reporting back to Trinex and resuming his duties under the Soames regime, David had tried to bring some temporary order to his itinerant life. He arranged a loan with a bank in Penal to refresh his depleted finances; the stay in London had drained his resources and the fruits of his inheritance would not be realised for some time. He returned his hire car, purchased a sensible, third hand, four-wheel drive from Bobby's dusty forecourt at Duncan Village with the proprietor's personal guarantee, and gave up his temporary accommodation in San Fernando. He called into Basdeo Persad's office in Penal where he was offered, and accepted after a cursory inspection, a small apartment in a reasonably well maintained block of four just past Penal Junction, set back from Erin Road. He did not bother to negotiate the rent.

Some time after the evening on which they last met in Ramdass Trace, David called in at the Penal Funeral Parlour and asked for Girly. Despite her refusal to accompany him to London at some unspecified future date, they had parted on reasonable terms that evening; he found her difficult to read but his hope was that she might still be open to persuasion and periodic visits to the parlour would do no harm. The parlour secretary, Mauva Tocks, had informed him that Miss Boodoosingh was out. Her blank expression made him feel he would have been more welcome as a corpse. A short time later, while in Basdeo Persad's office discussing a matter related to his apartment, he had seen Girly leaving the parlour on foot dressed for leisure rather than business. He had to assume Mauva Tocks was under instruction and therefore he made no further visits to the parlour.

Mr. Dhanraj nudged David gently away from his thoughts: "I think it time you go back to that place, you know. No sense to cut yourself off." He was referring to the Trinex compound where David's parents had returned. In recent weeks, David had confided in Mr. Dhanraj that his relationship with them had changed so completely that he doubted he could go back. He was still incensed that he had been deceived for so long, yet, with the passing of time, he missed them both. The old comforts and privileges of the compound did not interest him; he knew through Trinex that the damage caused to the development had been repaired and all former residents were back on the site. After such a long time away, he could not force himself to visit. There had been several telephone calls for him from the compound near Fyzabad to the Trinex office which he had decided not to take.

"I can't go to see them. I wouldn't know what to say this time."

"They just waitin' there for you. Desperate to hear. It have more than one way to settle, you know." Mr. Dhanraj went inside the house, returning several minutes later with drinking glasses and tins of beer. They sat quietly whilst sipping the cold brew. David focused on Ravi Bishoo across the road at number fifteen who returned his wave with what might have been a cool nod.

Ravi was unpacking a delivery from Fong's at Penal Junction; from David's slightly elevated position on the veranda, it looked like many metres of hose pipe and some accessories in cardboard boxes.

"You write to London yet?"

The last time they met, David had told Mr. Dhanraj everything that had happened to him in London, including the fact that he now had a sister who needed his help. "Yes, and I've promised to go back but I didn't say when. The thing is, I really want to stay here, maybe visit London occasionally, but there's not much to stay for. I don't believe in what Trinex are doing so my position with them will probably end soon, I can't see my parents and Girly..." His words trailed off. "Sumatee would know what to do..." He stopped again, looking at Mr. Dhanraj in case he had given offence.

Mr. Dhanraj smiled at the thought and looked at the chennet tree in the yard. "She would know," he agreed. "But now is up to you. First, go back to that place, talk to parents. You should go now, you know."

They looked across to Ravi Bishoo who was connecting a pipe to the large water storage tank at the side of his house and uncoiling a hose towards the rear garden.

"Ravi! What it have?" Mr. Dhanraj shouted to his neighbour.

"For grass. It goin' to be green, green, man!" Ravi smiled broadly at the prospect of the perfect lawn he was about to create.

David drained his beer glass and rose from the chair. He had always considered himself a person who would not avoid confrontation for the sake of an easy life, would not shy away from difficult decisions, and yet he had allowed this stand off with his parents to continue indefinitely. Mr. Dhanraj's words rang in his ears. It was time to settle the argument one way or another. He touched Mr. Dhanraj on the shoulder, crossed the front yard and made his way by car towards Fyzabad.

***

The days and weeks passed slowly for Girly Boodoosingh at Penal. There were occasional visits to bars with old friends, mostly reinforcing her view that you can outgrow the company of people you have known for a long time. Attitudes change, comments once taken as friendly advice now become personal slights, there is no longer the common thread of education or career, the things that put you in the same place with shared experiences.

At the exact time, weeks before, when she had been seen by David leaving the funeral parlour while he was in Basdeo Persad's office, she was on her way to meet Devendra Roopnarine at Penal Rock Road. She decided to walk the half mile to the house with gates; Devendra had made the arrangement in a hurried telephone call to the parlour, a brief exchange of words in case she changed her mind.

Girly's mood had darkened as she left the parlour when Mauva Tocks informed her of David's visit. She sometimes confided in Mauva to a limited extent, gave her vague accounts of her private life just as a daughter would vaguely inform her mother. If Jigs felt he was *in loco parentis,* then Mauva also saw herself as a substitute mother for certain duties, looking after the interests of her charge which, on this occasion, had been to shield her from the perceived unwelcome attentions of David when he passed by the parlour.

Girly was furious but concealed her ire behind unreadable facial features. "You sent him away? When?" She looked through the window of the reception area out onto the junction in case David was lurking outside, although she reminded herself he would not lurk. He would wait openly or leave. She left quickly without further words to Mauva, searching the street on both sides as she turned left towards Penal Rock Road. She saw no sign of him on her journey; she had no cell phone number to call.

By the time she had walked to the house with gates, it was late in the afternoon and the sun was low over the distant Gulf of Paria. Girly looked through the open gates towards the house. Since she had last passed by, the walls had been painted stark white but this was now softened by sunbeams through the royal palm trees on the western side of the plot. The roof covering was renewed with individual tiles, the windows and all joinery appeared to be recent. Gloss black metal gates hung on high brick walls either side; the walls ran for twenty metres before turning at right angles, forming a security screen around the house. Girly thought the cost of the external renovation alone must have amounted to a small fortune; the materials were not in common use locally and were of superior quality to anything readily available at Fong's.

She passed through the gates towards the front door; Devendra appeared with a builder who was leaving for the day. Devendra immediately became a solicitous host, anxious to show his house in its best light. He steered Girly comfortably through the vestibule which, with a section of the first floor removed, extended up to the top of the house where a roof window permitted natural light.

On the ground floor, they walked through living rooms with plain, newly plastered walls, a kitchen which was complete with new counter tops and cupboards, a fully glazed side room having clear views over a small garden containing, here and there, potted plants waiting to be inserted into newly tilled soil.

There was a wide central staircase rising from the vestibule with a gentle curve to the left; it supported an ornate balustrade comprising hand rail and separate balusters. The first floor landing gave access to several bedrooms, two bathrooms that Girly could remember, all with new fittings and plain decorations to new wall surfaces.

Devendra superfluously described the use of each room and any notable features which he thought would not be apparent to the casual observer; he also gave estimated costs wherever possible. Girly wondered at the effort and finance that had gone into the whole project. It was clear to any inspection that the house had been reduced to its original four walls and started again everywhere else. It was plain inside, currently unfurnished but expensive.

"House belong' to Fong," Devendra informed Girly, who was aware that the Fong family used to own the property before their prosperity allowed the purchase of a Rio Claro mansion.

"I have to start again because everythin' old, old." Devendra explained with pride. "How you see it?" he asked.

"I think it's fine," she smiled, looking at Devendra, seeing him framed by the house, imagining the future.

"You could live here?" he asked quietly, his voice betraying the moment that everything around him, the effort, cost and patience had been leading to and had now arrived. Before she answered, he suddenly felt an odd loneliness as if she had drawn back; he saw a shadow pass across her eyes that he failed to interpret.

Girly looked at the house around her and recognised the effort, cost and patience; she knew it was all for her. She loved the location, the house, the dream. But a small chill ran along her spine which told her it was not possible. She did not love Devendra.

Two days later Jigs Boodoosingh heard muffled sounds in the reception area outside his office. He strode to the door and flung it open. Girly stood next to Mauva Tocks in light conversation.

"I saw Devendra Roopnarine this morning!" Jigs broke in, immediately realising his error. He apologised for the interruption before leading Girly into his office. It was not in his nature to engage in what might be a heated debate in front of Mauva. "He said you went to his house then turned him down! The man is...is..."

"Yes?"

Jigs saw the set of her jaw. "He expected a different response," he retorted lamely.

Girly placed herself directly in front of her brother who was only slightly taller. "And what did *you* expect?"

Jigs noted the danger signs in her eyes which meant he should retreat, but he was determined. "Devendra is a good man. I thought you were...close." He assembled a hurt expression.

"You thought that if I go to the house with gates, I would never leave Penal. Is that so?" Girly smiled, taut and humourless.

Jigs swallowed. "I have nothing to say usually about your life outside the parlour." Girly raised her eyebrows, parted her lips in anticipation. "But since David came back, you have changed. Unhappy, discontent, it's not as if you even see him." He walked to the desk then straight back to his former position in front of her, a thought occurring to him. "I see more of him than you!" he almost shouted. "What is it you want?" Jigs suddenly felt weary. He had feigned annoyance but in truth he was concerned in the same way he had always been at the prospect of his sister leaving for London. He felt she was oblivious to his deep reservations, preferring to believe his only motive was to keep her tied to the funeral parlour. The reality was that the parlour would survive without her but his devotion to her would not allow him to disregard the potential for huge disappointment if she left Penal.

"As soon as I know, I'll tell you," she replied coldly.

***

David slowed his car at the entrance to the Trinex staff compound close to Fyzabad. The same guard, reinstated after the looting and closure of the site, stood at the barrier. He gave David a smile of recognition as though he had seen him only yesterday, as though the recent past had not happened. He lifted the red and white pole. David advanced slowly along the tree lined drive; the interruption of the barrier diverted his thoughts which he now refocused on the letter he had written, read through several times then sent to Veronica in London. He had considered typing an e.mail and dashing it off to her as a quick response, but it was not appropriate. She had clearly taken time and expended much emotional effort in composing her letter. She deserved the same from him.

He wondered whether he should have waited until after this visit today; the visit had been long postponed but he should have known it was inevitable. The letter was at least a proper response to the life changing information Veronica had presented him with in her own letter.

He recaptured salient passages of his response as he slowed the car next to a parking area:

...thank you for the candid written reply to what must have been irritating and difficult questions I posed in London. Yes, the truth was shocking, especially as I could not believe my parents (I have to refer to them as parents, even now, just as you recommended) were in any way capable of such a profound deceit. I'll overcome it, no doubt, but I can't find it in me to see them regularly. In fact, I've only visited them once in all the past weeks since I returned here....

David continued with a brief account of the scene at Galeota Point, not omitting the obvious effect he had created with his sense of outrage. Then,

...Now that they've returned to their old home, I might find it easier to go back, maybe try to resolve the issues that have hurt so much. At least it will be on familiar ground. Maybe I'll try soon....

He stopped the memory run to recognise how hurt he had really been, but there was a stark choice: nothing would change the past so in dealing with the future he had, in accordance with Mr. Dhanraj's advice, taken a first step on a long road. He had no idea where it might lead but the starting point was in the neat bungalow he could see in the distance. If only he could think of what he would say when they opened the door...

...You said in your letter that there is no need to write, just turn up. I will come back to London and the Oven House soon but life is both interesting and complicated here at the moment. I'm trying to help people who have been close to me for most of my life but it would appear to them I'm doing the opposite. As I say, it's complicated.

By the way, forget about the financial arrangement regarding the restaurant – I'm giving half of it to you now that I know the truth. I hope to be of practical help to you but I just don't know when....

David stepped out of the car and paced across the tarmac, past the fully repaired and restocked shop, towards three streets of bungalows, all familiar and showing no signs of damage. The contrast with his new home in chaotic Penal was stark. He could not dislike his old home in the way it offended Girly, but he knew even now he would never come back here permanently. Despite its perfectly maintained buildings, comforts and facilities, it was part of an old life which had faded away when he travelled to London.

As he neared the detached bungalow he knew so well, memories walked a scenic route through his mind, the very best of childhood moments passed with small friends, European exiles just like him, innocently finding no incongruity between their immediate environment and the world outside which was only occasionally glimpsed. Then, much later, the new world was discovered for him in Ramdass Trace, an unlikely setting in which to begin the change to adulthood, a place deep in his affections and affecting his life to this day.

The front door of the bungalow was slightly ajar; David hesitated before pushing gently and standing in the small lobby as a stranger would stand, reluctant to step forward. His mother heard the gentle sweep of the opening door. She stood alone in the centre of the bright living room; it was unchanged since David's last day there, same matching furniture and drab rug. She saw him framed by sharp daylight around the entrance; it jolted her in the same way as something assumed lost forever but now found, a glimmer of hope offered only by his presence before a word was spoken. It elicited a gesture from her: open hands on extended arms to indicate she was alone; she was at once anxious but filled with a sense of pride that he possessed it within himself to come back, if only to continue that which was unfinished at Galeota Point.

David looked at her more closely than he could ever remember. The fixed vision of his mother was of the past and no longer appropriate. She had changed: once slight greying of the fair hair was now more pronounced, sun lines slightly deeper. There was a narrowing of her frame which might have been related to age but possibly due to a burden of guilt taking its physical toll. Not until he walked into the room did he realise that he could not regard his mother as an aunt.

On her part, she had invested the best of her life in him, never required anything from him except to be who he was, a boy and young man raised in her care as if he were her own until the point when all reality, whilst not erased, was suppressed so that in effect he belonged to her; she had made him the best he could be, and now that he had discovered the truth, he was lost to her. She recognised this could be his final visit.

She saw David glance around the room. "He's away. Galeota Point."

"I won't be coming back to live here," he said.

"No." She brightened, falsely. "We're leaving. Back to London. No reason to stay now." She shrugged. "Are you?..."

"Yes. I'm going back soon."

If all that had been revealed to him recently weighed heavily on him and constantly occupied his thoughts, if all feelings towards the two people foremost in his life had become tainted and sullied, then the importance of these revelations was now diminished in a way that he could not fathom, could not comprehend until he saw the mute despair of his mother. She stood not two paces from him, heartbroken by her own failing and lack of honesty; yet, even in recognising the depths of her shared dishonour, he knew she had looked after him, never left him, shown him the way. Sumatee

Dhanraj had been a supplementary, not a substitute mother; the woman now moving to stand next to him was his ideal and that fact finally overcame all anguish accumulated since Veronica's letter.

He touched a hand hanging limply at her side, leaned towards her. "Will you tell me where you are in London?"

She recalled when he was a boy he had once told her he never wanted any other mother. That was a long time ago; now that he no longer needed her, she was free to reflect that despite her crime, her pride in what she had created was justified.

***

In what might be described as a 'now or never' frame of mind, Jigs Boodoosingh decided to show his hand. He was driving the hearse away from a particularly upsetting cremation at Mosquito Creek. A sudden rain shower drifted in from the Gulf to douse the burning pyre of a client's father; the process had to be restarted with dry timber on passing of the cloud, an action guaranteed to send mourners into even deeper paroxysms of grief. It occurred to Jigs that he needed to be proactive. Consequently, he awarded himself an afternoon away from the parlour; he left the hearse in Raj's care at Penal, changed into casual clothes in his apartment and set off for Santa Flora armed with evidence of what he believed to be, at the very least, sharp practice by Wendell Soames, and possibly fraud, dishonesty and misrepresentation, although he was rather hazy on the actual meaning of the legal terms.

He was also aware that his evidence was thin; he was relying to a certain extent on the opinion of Basdeo Persad, which was not generally a good idea, and he had failed to identify other recently purchased plots of land acquired by Wendell Soames. A further visit to the Reverend Sproule had not borne fruit; the Presbyterian was unable to remember the names of any other parishioners 'helped' by Wendell Soames and Jigs' offer of a donation to the church had been unrewarded. He relied therefore on the evidence of his eyes at Satnarine Trace.

Without delay or ceremony, he hustled into the Trinex building at Santa Flora, making his way to the office of Wendell Soames which he entered, uninvited and unimpeded, to stand in front of the local director of exploration.

"You look like you have something serious on your mind," Soames said, rising from his chair. His eyes bulged in reaction to the intrusion; he made a mental note to provide some security to the building.

"We need to speak about Ramdass Trace."

"Again? The subject is closed. We're producing oil - what is there to discuss?"

Jigs would not sit down. He walked to the window and looked out, assuming a slightly detached air whilst weighing his words. "I had a client some time ago – Satnarine Trace in Quarry." Wendell Soames said nothing. "I went back there recently and I noticed that part of the client's land has been sold for development." Jigs turned away from the window, shortening the distance to his foe and lowering his voice so that no-one in close proximity to the partitioned office would hear. "I think you bought that land. Are you sure you paid the correct price? This is a poor family we're discussing."

Wendell Soames was in the grip of a fury he was struggling manfully to control. "So now we come to the point. You're a blackmailing undertaker," he replied coldly. "An unlikely combination!" He focussed on the neck in front of him; he was close to grasping and squeezing it. But he was a local director of Trinex Oil and Gas; he had left such actions behind him long ago. Mental intimidation was his forte now. He was not going to be bullied by this funeral director. Self-righteous indignation spurred him. He pointed a finger and stopped it very close to Jigs' chest. "You're coming with me!" Soames picked up car keys from his desk and stomped out of the room, assuming Jigs was following behind him. Which he was.

The local director drove his car quickly and in silence out of Santa Flora to make the short journey to Quarry Village. As they arrived at Satnarine Trace, Soames got out of the car, not waiting for Jigs as he strode onto the building site Jigs had seen recently; the building works had proceeded rapidly in the intervening period to the point where the structure was taking on the shape of a residence but clearly not a single-family dwelling house.

Jigs caught up with Soames who stood in familiar pose, hands on hips, regarding the building in front of him. "This is your property, not so?" Jigs asked.

"Yes, it's mine," Soames replied quietly. "But not for long. Look at this." He walked to a carpenter's trestle on which an architect's drawing was flattened by small stones on each corner. "You see? Not a house, it will be deeper onto the plot but not out of scale in width or appearance."

Jigs looked at Wendell Soames and saw the anger he had provoked disappearing into the soothing balm of the project before him; he was impassioned, proud, even moved.

"What is it?" Jigs was feeling out of his depth.

"When I was very young, living in a shack near Princes Town, there were friends, neighbours who had nothing, even less than us. Sometimes, all we had to help us was the Presbyterian Church. In short, they looked after us and, more importantly, they helped orphaned children. I once saw an orphanage up at Tacarigua – a decent place but overcrowded. I can't build an orphanage but this will be a small contribution, a supervised hostel of several rooms for children and given to trustees of the Presbyterian Church. I won't be involved at all."

Jigs was staggered. "How do you....?" he trailed off.

"Finance it? I'm going to tell you so that, once and for all, you will leave it alone. I purchased this land below market value as you somehow found out." A cloud of irritation darkened his eyes. "The family in the next house needed money and no-one else wanted to buy the land, so the ah... discount is their contribution to the church and the project. Also, I acquired one or two other pieces of land which I have sold to Trinex for exploration. Naturally, these are good prospects for Trinex otherwise I could not do it. Let's say that it's the Trinex contribution to a worthy cause."

Jigs, abashed, could find no words of apology or contrition. He had been thwarted in a transparent blackmail attempt which, although he believed it to be a worthy cause, was always doomed to failure. His heart had never really been in the idea – it was born out of desperation and now he had made an enemy of Wendell Soames. He had misjudged him.

"So what were you going to do? Inform Trinex their local director was a criminal who preyed on poor families?"

"It would never have reached that point. Either you would have given up on Ramdass Trace or called my bluff, in which case I would not have pursued it. I don't have the stomach for it, you know." Jigs looked at the nascent building in front of them. "How did you get permission to build this in a residential trace? It's not the same as a house."

"And if I tell you...." Wendell Soames allowed his cheeks to sag into an expression which conveyed the message that he need not explain further.

Jigs was trumped, beaten and without any further cards to play. Somehow, he would have to explain to the residents of Ramdass Trace that he had let them down.

***

The madness attaching itself to Mr. Sagar Narsingh at number sixteen Ramdass Trace did not strike suddenly. It grew. It grew and festered daily, intensified by the activity on his land. He was visited by strange dreams in which oil taken from his land translated to his own life blood being sucked away and stored at some remote point, never to be retrieved; his strength ebbed away in his dreams, the monster was winning a slow battle.

Then, one night when the trace slept, the Pump Man gathered himself, summoned up a defiant mood that was powerful enough to inspire violence, and walked out of the house leaving his shredded sense behind. The words he spoke to himself under his breath would not be recalled later; they had no meaning at the time but they spurred him on.

He left the house carrying a key and a torch. At the side of the house below the staircase he opened a large tool box which contained, amongst other common items, a sledgehammer; the Pump Man had gathered this heavy tool on his travels one day, years before, from a location he no longer remembered but on the basis that it appeared to belong to no-one and would no doubt prove to be useful in the future.

The path to the pump site on his land was, at this time, well trodden by himself and, if he had known it, by Jigs and David, so that there was no difficulty in reaching the new oil pump by a delicate moonlight that gave the trace and its associated bush an ethereal quality. As the Pump Man drew near, the incessant slow sucking of the pump, its electric hum and metallic grind infuriated him beyond endurance; he used his pass key to open the padlock which was common to all Trinex security fences, and passed through the personnel gate. He stood in front of the leviathan, instantly overcome to the point when he cried out, shouted at it, berated it, held the sledgehammer in both hands above his head. And, with weeks of frustration guiding his arms, he aimed a crushing blow at the well head, believing in his madness that the beast would be slain, the pump would lay down and die.

The single random blow, guided to no particular part of the well head, had connected with the pipe which, running at a right angle to the pump, carried the flowing oil away to storage. The pipe fractured instantly producing a spurt of oil, spattering the Pump Man; he snorted to disperse the thick liquid from his face but it was as though he had received a slap to the cheek, a sobering blow to restore some of his stretched sanity. He looked at the result of his labours: oil that was extracted at approximately thirty litres every time the pump nodded was now flowing away from the open pipe across sloping ground, through trees, over foliage, low fronds and grasses. The initial thin line of oil became wider. It broadened into a small stream under the force of the pump, then as litre after litre followed, the stream became a steady flow away from the site. If the Pump Man had taken control of his senses, had recognised that turning off the electricity supply to the pump would have disengaged the process, he showed no sign of it. The oil-slap to his face merely awoke in him a question of what he had done:

"What I do? What I do?" he asked himself.

He looked at the flowing oil, the metal structure of the pump still nodding with its unbreakable rhythm and he fled, believing he had lost the battle. He scuttled out of the security gate carrying the sledgehammer and torch, telling himself he needed the sanctuary of his home. By now, his mind had cleared sufficiently to prompt him to put the hammer back into the tool box. But when he had regained the old sofa and buried his oily, distressed features in a threadbare cushion, the horror of his deed filtered through the pain of defeat.

And then, the final blow struck when he was at his lowest ebb: he heard laughter through the creaks and groans of the house. Cracks in the walls assumed parted lips, turned upwards into smiles. The voice of the house grew louder in his ears despite the cushion over his head. Sagar Narsingh was at the end of his tether.

***

The moon fell slowly on a gentle heavenly path above Ramdass Trace. At the same time the Pump Man was suffering in a catatonic state at number sixteen, Ravi Bishoo dined well at home courtesy of Safina's curried crab and dumplings. Ravi walked out into the warm-bath humidity of his veranda, belched pleasantly and settled down to consider the effects of his recently acquired lawn irrigation system. After only a few days, Ravi was delighted with progress; in the faint light, he could see the main connection to his water tank firmly in place and watertight. There was no seepage from the joint. A length of pipe snaked away from the tank to the rear of the house where it separated into several perforated hoses surrounding the lawn. In between the water tank connection and the final destination of the hoses, a pump and timer on an electrical connection controlled the irrigation so that the lawn was, as recommended by the manufacturer, watered at night and early morning before the sun could induce evaporation.

Ravi never tired of watching the watering of his lawn. He loved the mechanical whir when the timer kicked in as programmed, smiled at the sudden spurting of the hoses as water was forced through the angled perforations onto the grass in a fine, even mist, soaking the greening blades and filtering through to the roots. Ravi assumed the habit of rising early around dawn just so that he could check the system had responded on cue to the timer's calling.

There was no doubt that the lawn was thriving: the success was evident in the upright, broad grass blades and the colour which, if not exactly resembling the picture of mown perfection on the irrigation system's packaging, was now at least far removed from its normal brown hue.

Ravi decided to go to bed; he went in the happy knowledge that he would rise early again to inspect his grass and to contemplate whether he should sow a better quality seed recommended by the horticultural adviser at Fong's store.

Just before dawn, Ravi stirred himself from a refreshing sleep; he slipped on his sandals, collected a torch as he made his way to the back of the house. He heard the satisfying rotation of the water pump, heard the hiss of water through a hundred pipe perforations and saw, in the waning light of the moon, a slight dark shadow on his lawn.....

Something was wrong, out of place. Ravi stepped across the irrigation hoses into the shadow which became a glutinous mess covering his sandals, causing him to emit a short, involuntary shout of surprise, disgust and panic. He turned the torch onto his feet, then about him to find the source of the outrage. He hurried off the ruined lawn in the direction of the oil stream, hardly noticing that his underwear, his habitual night wear, was soaked through by the water sprays he had forgotten to turn off. He almost ran through the bush to follow the trail; he barked his shin on an unyielding stump, splashed through small tributaries of the oil stream until he came upon the source; the gateway to the pump was open. If Ravi had taken a moment to consider, he might have realised that closing off the pump's electrical supply would have disabled the machine and prevented further damage. Instead, he saw the oil spurting from the broken supply pipe and panic drove him out of the clearing, into the bush to the back of the Pump Man's house.

He shouted his usual call: "Pump Man! Pump Man!" There was no response. Ravi was desperate. He hurried to the front of the building then along the trace to Amit Jaggernauth's house, dark and dozing, as the lemon streaked sky sent a faint glow from the east.

Ravi rapped on the front door, instigating a loud yawn and shuffling of feet within. Amit Jaggernauth – wild haired, unkempt and drunk with sleep – opened the door, eyeing Ravi with disgruntlement.

"Early, man!" Amit rubbed his hair and both eyes.

"Come, come!" Ravi was by now beyond coherent explanation. "Oil all over!" He pulled Amit through the door and set off into the bush. Amit followed against his better judgement, but intrigued nevertheless by the unlikelihood of an emergency in Ramdass Trace at that time of day.

By the time Amit caught up with Ravi, who had never before moved at such a pace, they were both at the clearing. They saw the pump still grinding on, pushing oil through the open pipe. With the clear headedness available to those who have passed through the slow state of awakening into the sharp reality of day, when the brain has entered the 'live' phase of uncluttered thinking, Amit summed up the situation. He passed through the security gate, searched for and found a small rock nearby with which he battered the metal cover of the electricity isolating switch on the motor. The cover yielded after three blows, Amit flicked a large switch and the pump slowed to a standstill.

Ravi and Amit stood side by side in the silence, Amit barefoot and wearing only dark blue shorts, Ravi in wet, off-white underwear, his feet and ankles streaked black. Daylight gathered beneath the great lever of the pump. They watched the flow of oil subside from the open pipe; there was a lull in time until the bush began to sweat with the rising of the sun. A pair of house wrens sang from the eaves of Sagar Narsingh's house in the distance. Ramdass Trace awoke.

3 OLEANDER

Mr. Sagar Narsingh lifted himself from the sofa some time just after dawn. He had heard voices shouting in the bush earlier but ignored them; there was a numbness to his senses that would not permit him to respond. But the effect of the previous night's disaster had provided him with one path, one course of action he could not ignore. The idea of it sprang from his thoughts about himself, his belief in the abject failure of his existence, the inevitable disappointment of his sisters in Tobago when they heard, as they eventually would, of his aberration and, worst of all, the realisation that he was a poor representative of his family. He was mentally unable to cope with life's setbacks and this created a burden of shame his broad shoulders could not carry.

There was, however, one thing he could do. He pulled himself together sufficiently to stride through the side door, down the staircase to the tool box underneath. He pulled out a length of thick cord. The Pump Man spoke to himself quietly for encouragement; he clambered onto the top of the tool box where he stood one metre from the ground. He threw the cord end over a timber support below the first floor platform, tied it to a post within reach, formed a rough loop and knot with the other end and slipped it over his neck. The Pump Man's last thoughts before he stepped off the tool box were confused: he conflated the silence of the bush with the peace of mind he was about to achieve.

The widow Dookie knew that the local taxi service sent many vehicles up and down Erin Road at that time of day; she only had to stand at the end of the trace to wave down a car. It would take her to Siparia where she could walk to the cemetery. It was a Wednesday morning.

As she walked stiffly past Mr. Dhanraj's house, the crash startled her. She was beyond the Pump Man's house, the source of the noise, and too far past the gable end to see what was happening. She turned to her right, crossed the road and descended the front steps; she found the Pump Man prostrate, beached, next to the complete timber staircase structure which lay on its side. The Pump Man's walk off the tool box had not been entirely hands free; at the last split second when he found himself unsupported, his hand grabbed the cord above his neck as a chink of clarity passed through his clouded mind and he realised with desperation that he did not want this to be a final gesture. He would never know why the moment of self preservation had hit him so late, but in due course he was grateful that he had never completed the necessary repair to the staircase; the tug on the cord allied to the Pump Man's weight had finally caused the securing screws to yield, to fly from their holes. It was the sound of the collapse, timber hitting the ground from a height, along with the Pump Man's groans, that had alarmed Indira Dookie. Remarkably, the staircase was almost undamaged on its side flat on the ground; it still held the Pump Man, although loosely, by his neck.

Indira went to his aid; she freed him from the noose, examined his rope- burned neck then led him slowly into the house via the front veranda. She left him while she went to her own house to collect some medication. When she returned, she rubbed a healing salve into his neck, and gave him a home made sedative from her mother's recipe.

The Pump Man coughed intermittently. He sat in the wreckage of his kitchen trying to make sense of his change of mind. He realised he had been unable to go through with the final act; he could only speculate on what would have happened if the staircase had not collapsed. He would have been hanging grimly onto the cord, suspended until help arrived or his strength ebbed away.

He looked at Indira with grateful eyes.

"They put me behind bars, you know!" He was resigned to wait for the police to arrive and take him away for his crime.

Indira looked at him closely, recognised the need for her to stay. "Rest, Pump Man. I stay." She ushered him to his bed. "Rest or you get a next attack." Indira wasn't really sure what had pushed him into his desperate act but she did not want to be present when whatever demons visited him decided to make a return. She had to get him to sleep while she sought assistance.

An hour later, while the Pump Man dozed, Indira crossed the trace to Mr. Dhanraj's house. She told him excitedly in language no outsider would have understood about the situation she found herself in from the moment she heard the crash of the staircase up to the point at which she left the Pump Man becalmed on his bed. Mr. Dhanraj asked her to return to number sixteen while he telephoned Jigs Boodoosingh and Trinex to report the damage to their pumping equipment; he also decided to contact the Pump Man's sisters in Tobago. It was Mr. Dhanraj's opinion that they needed to take him to Pigeon Point for recuperation.

⁂

Two days later, Sagar Narsingh was taken away, not by the police in Siparia but by his sisters, recently arrived in response to Mr. Dhanraj's prompting. They knew Mr. Dhanraj well from their early years in Ramdass Trace; they knew he would not have called unless the situation was urgent. The sisters had not returned to the trace for some years, preferring to invite their brother for holidays in Tobago. Consequently, they were shocked and appalled by the dilapidation they found at their childhood home.

Jigs Boodoosingh met the sisters at the house. After some time speaking to them outside about the Pump Man's condition and the parlous state of the building, he had the uncomfortable feeling that they were attaching a degree of blame to him. They knew Jigs often spent time with their brother and he had therefore been remiss in reporting to them his mental difficulties and house deterioration.

Jigs decided to reduce the feeling of guilt imposed by the sisters; he told them that if they would take their brother for a long rest in Tobago, he would make good on a promise he had made to repair the house, bring it to a habitable standard and arrest any further decline. He reluctantly waved away a tentative enquiry as to the likely cost, feeling that he was backed into a corner. He wondered whether, in any case, a financial offer to defray the expense would have been forthcoming. He also wanted the Pump Man out of the trace as soon as possible. When Trinex decided to investigate the damage to their equipment, they would no doubt inform the police of sabotage, if they had not done so already, and an investigation would follow.

"You will take the plane from Piarco?" Jigs asked the sisters. He did not feel the Pump Man would be able to tolerate the five or six hour boat journey from Port of Spain; the small aircraft, which Jigs would never contemplate boarding himself, only took twenty minutes in a direct flight from Piarco to Crown Point Airport on Tobago.

"But the plane cost dear, you know!" wailed Chandra, the eldest sister.

Jigs knew that the aeroplane tickets were not expensive but he handed over several banknotes.

"How we get him to Piarco?" Chandra asked.

Jigs looked at her. She dressed well, appeared to be groomed; neither sister gave the impression of being impoverished and Jigs knew all about their business at Pigeon Point.

"How did you get down here?" he asked.

"Maxi taxi cost dear, boy!"

Jigs sighed. "I'll take you as soon as he's ready."

Chandra gave her sister a slight nudge. "We not travellin' in no hearse."

Jigs sighed for the second time and walked into the house.

Some time later, Sagar Narsingh was led from the house, a sister on each arm, soothing cream glinting on his neck, his face a picture of abject misery. Indira Dookie had packed a suitcase for him; Jigs placed it in the back of his shiny Ford. He pocketed the key for the secured house then drove out of the trace after discussing the situation with his uncle. Mr. Dhanraj would contact Trinex to inform them that their employee was ill and convalescing in Tobago.

***

When Wendell Soames heard about the damage to the pumpjack at Ramdass Trace and the subsequent oil spill, he fought down his fury with difficulty, hovering between calm deliberation and promises of brutal retribution, then called his secretary into the office. He asked her to contact Jigs Boodoosingh with a request that he travel to Santa Flora without delay. Soames also wanted David to be available at the same time.

In the meantime, the local director of exploration busied himself with reports of oil yields on land in the working wells of south Trinidad and updated seismology data, especially relating to the Fyzabad area. The reality was that whilst most new wells were producing steadily, Ramdass Trace was likely to prove a long or even medium term disappointment; although repairs to the supply pipe had been made without difficulty and the pump itself was undamaged, the prospects did not look good. The reservoir may have been substantially depleted by the pump on Indira Dookie's land over many years. After all his insistence, his dogmatic approach, Wendell Soames found himself in a difficulty that could be exploited by others if he was not careful. There also remained the question of sabotage of the pump, his pump as he saw it, which surely could not be unrelated to the antipathy towards Trinex in Ramdass Trace. On the one hand, he could hand the problem over to the police to root out the culprit, but he had a theory that led him directly to a Ramdass Trace resident: there was no damage to the security gate around the pump. There was much to ponder.

Later, Jigs Boodoosingh joined him in the office with David. The room gave off transmitted heat from every plaster-covered brick in an unbearable, relentless assault on the flesh and brain. Wendell Soames sat at the desk, Jigs and David stood beside the open windows. At any other time, the local director might have enjoyed their discomfort and seen it as an advantage but this was a serious matter, not to be trivialised.

Jigs was happy to be summoned once again to Santa Flora; it was likely to be the last time he would be here. One way or another, his awkward relationship with Wendell Soames, and possibly with David, could end now. He had to be on his mettle. There had been no time outside the office to discuss the latest situation with David but Jigs saw him point to his own chest as they entered the room, presumably in a sign that he would take the lead and Jigs should trust him.

David looked at his employer and construed a short nod as permission to outline recent events from the Trinex point of view.

"The pump in Ramdass Trace is back in operation, the damage was not significant but there is an oil spill. It would have been worse if the pump had not been disabled early that morning. The spill runs across Mr. Narsingh's land through to Ravi Bishoo's..."

Jigs interrupted. He decided Wendell Soames was about to pounce and that attack would be his best way forward. "I did warn you about this. I've seen the damage and I can tell you the residents are extremely upset."

"Are you suggesting that we did not take adequate security precautions?" Wendell Soames' tone was icy despite the heat.

"A gate in a chain link fence is not difficult to overcome."

"Especially when a company key is used!" Soames got to his feet in one fluid movement which cost him dearly. Perspiring freely, he cursed the uselessness of the ceiling fan, as he did every day.

"There's no evidence of that," Jigs retorted in a conciliatory tone. "Maybe the gate was left open."

Soames decided to cut across the argument. He knew there was no direct evidence to pinpoint an individual for the damage. He moved out of the sunlit area of the room into a shady corner.

"This is the point." He looked at Jigs. "I would like you to consult with your friends in Ramdass Trace."

"What is there to talk about? The pump site is clearly not secure, and the spill means you can't carry on pumping. It's too vulnerable and the bad publicity will hurt Trinex."

Wendell Soames held up a hand. "We can and we are pumping oil. However, this is what I propose: we continue to pump for three months, then close down. No new pumps in Ramdass Trace, the existing pump will be removed along with the old pump at the end of the trace." He did not feel the need to explain that oil reserves were dwindling and possibly near exhaustion in the immediate area. He also did not feel the need to explain that he would have to justify the considerable expenditure already incurred in the exploration to his masters in Port of Spain. He would try to hide it in the more encouraging returns elsewhere in the south; these things happened in a business unable to depend on exact science. LaBrea in the west was also looking a better prospect for the exploration budget. However, he made a mental note to haul his seismologists into the room later to explain the sudden collapse in projected yields at Ramdass Trace. He continued: "If you accept the Trinex proposal and there are no further...accidents, the recent interruption in supply will be set aside."

Jigs was thinking furiously, trying to analyse the offer. On the one hand, the inference was that the Pump Man would be free from the threat of prosecution and losing his position with Trinex, but on the other hand there would be three more months of production. Effectively, however, this was a statement by Wendell Soames, not an offer. Jigs had to secure the best terms possible. He also had a feeling of disquiet regarding the removal of the pump on the widow Dookie's land. It had been in place for many years, effectively screened, causing no problems and accepted by everyone because it gave her an income. It was evident Wendell Soames could guess who the culprit was for the pipe damage on the Pump Man's land but he was prepared to overlook it for three further months on the site. Why would this be? Unless there was a problem in pumping oil out of the ground. It was useless to speculate.

"And the oil spill? There's a lot of oil lying around and not only in the bush."

David received a second nod. Earlier, there had been a heated discussion with Wendell Soames in private; David maintained that the oil spill was not extensive and could be cleaned up quickly. Soames, still seething, initially refused to see the advantage to Trinex of more expenditure on a problem that was not of the company's making. David asserted that closing down completely in Ramdass Trace and providing a clean site would be good publicity for the company; it had been agreed reluctantly – the calculation was that another three months of oil would more than cover costs.

"We can start cleaning the land very soon by bioremediation..."

"Bio..?" Jigs asked.

"It's an effective, harmless way of clearing surface oil. No chemicals are used, it's just microbes which consume the oil then die themselves. The site can be water hosed after a few weeks. It's perfectly safe." David was about to go into detail about the advantages of bacteria and fungi treatment when Jigs asked: "You mean the land will be good as new after a few weeks?"

"Yes."

"So why hasn't it been used at Ranji Village?"

Wendell Soames cut in: "Because it's damned expensive!" He did not add that Port of Spain had declined to authorise the contract.

Jigs decided he would not be able to wring any further concessions out of the discussion. "So, you want me to go to Ramdass Trace and tell everyone you will be gone in three months."

"More or less." Wendell Soames saw the look of doubt in Jigs' eyes. "Yes, three months," he said irritably. "And no more damage!"

Jigs saw the possibilities with regard to his own reputation; it had received something of a dent in the trace. "I'll do it, and I'm relying on your word."

Wendell Soames nodded curtly to both men then left the room.

***

During the early part of the morning several days later, gusts of hot wind like blasts of hell's breath swept along Ramdass Trace threatening to singe palm trees and low level bush. But it did not last; by noon, the air had settled, the sky became a low grey cover and rain began to fall, initially in large, individual drops then in vertical sheets until it ran in torrents along the road surface, spilling over at the sides into front yards and threatening to flood basements.

By the time David arrived at Mr. Dhanraj's house in the afternoon, the downpour had eased. He ran lightly from the road to climb the side steps, shook himself before knocking on the side door and entering the living room. Within five minutes, he was settled in a comfortable chair next to the front veranda doors gazing at the houses opposite while Mr. Dhanraj prepared two cups of strong tea. As he sat alone for several minutes, David's thoughts focused on the previous days; it had taken a lot of effort and persuasion to bring Wendell Soames to the conclusion that Ramdass Trace should be abandoned. In fact, the local director had initially pushed his heels firmly into the ground. It was only David's own, biased interpretation of seismology data and the way he presented it that finally sealed an agreement. David could not have known that Wendell Soames, by this time, had become thoroughly tired of the subject of Ramdass Trace – enough oil had and would be extracted to cover the costs of exploiting a fading asset. He was ready to concentrate elsewhere on richer, constant rewards to satisfy Port of Spain and its demands.

"You ready to travel?" asked Mr. Dhanraj, sitting opposite David and setting two cups down onto a small teak table.

David nodded. "Yes, any day now. I've told Trinex." In fact, this was partially true; he had tried to follow Wendell Soames out of his office after the meeting with Jigs Boodoosingh to explain his intention, knowing it might lead to an eruption of bad temper, but it had to be faced. Unfortunately, Wendell Soames had disappeared and David did not feel like pursuing him all over the complex. Instead, he drafted a letter of resignation, explained the reasons and left it on Wendell Soames' desk.

Mr. Dhanraj looked at David thoughtfully. "I expec' you'll be back one day. Have to see to that restaurant first."

"I'll come back. Have to see how you are." David smiled, studied his friend's eyes for a moment, then added: "And how are you?" It was the first time for a while he had felt able to ask.

"Survivin'. Indira Dookie lookin' after me."

A car drew up outside on the road. Girly Boodoosingh stepped out, splashed up to the house and entered via the side. She saw David instantly; without any outward sign of surprise, she said: "Sweet boy! I track you down."

She seemed very relaxed, assumed a casual manner and used an expression, an endearment David had not heard from her before.

Mr. Dhanraj greeted his niece warmly then left the room.

"You were looking for me?" David asked.

"Not really," she replied. "I saw your car and I was coming in here anyway." In reality, she had been hoping to see David recently without making it obvious she was searching for him. He looked slightly deflated after what she fancied was a hopeful edge to his voice.

"I'm leaving in the next few days. Remember I mentioned I have to go back to London?"

"Finished with Trinex? Permanently?"

"Yes. But I'll be back here." He was careful to add: "To see your uncle."

Girly sat down into her uncle's vacated chair. A brief awkward silence was broken. David frowned: "Sweet boy? I've heard that before somewhere. Doesn't it mean....?"

"Yes. I didn't mean it that way." Girly laughed at her mistake. Locally the expression could refer to a man kept by a woman, which she had not intended. David, defensively, wondered if it was an oblique reference to his impending return to London to be reunited with his sister who, he had informed Girly, managed the Oven House restaurant successfully. She may have seen a fleeting irritation as he looked away through the doors towards Ravi Bishoo's house almost opposite.

"I'm pleased to see you before you go, anyway. I was thinking about your...invitation. For London. As I said before, there is no good reason for me to go and I haven't changed. But thank you because I know you really want me to travel. It's just that...." she trailed off seriously.

David realised she needed to explain but, as before when they walked along the trace in the darkness, she was finding it difficult to tell him that heart and mind would not converge to allow her to take the final step. The trust and confidence were not quite there.

"I know why," he said kindly. "There's no need for you to worry about it. I'll come back some time and then maybe something will have changed."

She brightened visibly because he understood. "You would only have me on my feet as a waitress, anyway."

They laughed simultaneously. Then a thought occurred to him which, at first, he thought might be cruel if voiced but then his curiosity forced out the words in a genuine question that would not hurt, not spoil their understanding.

"How was the house with gates?" There was no mocking tone; he assembled a visage he knew she would associate with a light hearted enquiry but he was nevertheless on dangerous ground.

If she was shocked at his knowledge of Devendra Roopnarine's offer, she did not show it. She aimed her reply directly at the green eyes, returned his curiosity succinctly: "Beautiful. But there's nothing inside for me."

Later that afternoon when the sun emerged to steam away the pools and puddles, a small group gathered in Mr. Dhanraj's front yard, returning memories of his open house day some weeks before.

On this occasion, it was strictly Ramdass Trace residents present, except Indira Dookie who, unusually, had not returned from her Wednesday visit at Siparia Cemetery, and Sagar Narsingh who was still recovering in the warm embrace of his sisters in Tobago. The Jaggernauth cousins had brought all their children; Devendra Roopnarine escorted his father to one of the plastic chairs arranged in short rows facing the road; Ravi Bishoo, Safina and son ambled across the road. Mr. Dhanraj had cooked earlier; he served *roti* while his guests waited. David and Girly departed before the guests arrived, Girly to avoid Devendra and David to avoid everyone who might consider he represented the foe that was Trinex.

Jigs Boodoosingh was the last to arrive. He was a hero in Ramdass Trace; there was no doubt about it, no dissenting voices, although Indira Dookie was understandably silent on the matter. Jigs had called the meeting to spell out the new Trinex policy but word had already reached the trace. Jigs arrived with much hand shaking and complementary comment to merely confirm what was known. The meeting was inevitably short, Jigs received his plaudits graciously. There had been only one question: could Jigs be sure that, in a few months' time, Trinex would no longer be a presence in the trace and the oil spill would be eradicated? Jigs was happy to confirm this was the position.

When Mr. Dhanraj's food had been consumed, the meeting broke up, people went home, Ramdass Trace settled quietly in the comfort of rural Trinidad, satisfied and relaxed by its imminent reversion to the way it had existed for so long. Jigs sat with his uncle inside number twelve, occasionally glancing out at the road until a builder's lorry arrived outside number sixteen. He excused himself then trotted across the yard and road to greet the builder recommended by Basdeo Persad.

The builder spoke little, followed Jigs into the Pump Man's house and listened patiently to his new client's requirements. Jigs had already decided how far he would take the repair and maintenance of the house – there would be no open cheque but the house would have to be secure for the long term. Despite the parsimony of Sagar Narsingh's sisters, Jigs knew the Pump Man would contribute on his return but there had to be adequate evidence of a full resurrection of the house to lift his spirits. Jigs had visited the two houses built by this same man for Basdeo Persad in San Francique and admired their quality, style and finish; it was a shame about the location.

In compiling a list for the builder, Jigs included basic structural repairs and eradication of wood boring insects, dampness and pests; bats were to be encouraged to leave and their access points sealed. Internal partitions and wall linings should be strengthened and renewed where necessary, kitchen cupboards and surfaces repaired and painted. Overall, there would have to be a contingency for unexpected defects uncovered as work proceeded.

The financial outlay was unlikely to hurt Jigs excessively; he saw it partly as an act of compensation for failing to stop the anguish heaped upon the Pump Man when he, Jigs Boodoosingh, had been expected to deflect Trinex completely. There was one other matter to arrange with his uncle: the Pump Man's possessions would be moved temporarily into the vacant, numberless house once owned by Sumatee Dhanraj, now by her husband. If the Pump Man returned during the maintenance works, he would have to camp in the same house.

Jigs shook hands on his arrangement with the builder who promised to let him have a detailed estimate by the end of the week with a view to starting work within days.

As he drove away from Ramdass Trace, Jigs saw Indira Dookie climbing slowly out of a taxi on Erin Road. He was later to reflect deeply on that fleeting moment in time.

***

The widow Dookie was tired; it had been a long day and she felt unwell. Her physical aches and pains normally increased each afternoon after a morning's activity usually beginning at sunrise. On this day, there was the morning trip to Siparia Cemetery; fresh flowers cradled in thin arms were later placed carefully on a grave maintained in perfect condition, the plot smaller than those around her. The plot next to her daughter was untouched, vacant; Indira rested there while she arranged the flowers in a vase that had long ago been secured at the head of the grave. After a long pause, longer than usual, she collected a container of rainwater from a water butt nearby, filled the vase then left without a backward glance.

It was afternoon by the time she walked into a lawyer's office in the centre of Siparia, the second of such visits she had made recently. She emerged almost an hour later carrying documents in an envelope. She would not know where she spent the rest of the afternoon, no recollection of where she passed the time in deep thought before taking a taxi back to Ramdass Trace. Her thoughts were dark, despondent but touched with a sense of indefinable relief. Her plan was clear, several factors clung together to become an unbreakable decision. At the same time that she was tiring of her ailments, Trinex informed her initially that the rent from leased land would be substantially reduced, then she heard that the pumpjack at the end of the trace would be decommissioned, the land no longer required after so many years. There would be no more clothes purchased from San Fernando, less taxi visits to Siparia cemetery.

By the time she descended from the taxi and made the short walk to number eleven, she could hardly support her meagre weight; the thought that something was seriously wrong occurred to her briefly but was then dismissed as being of no consequence. It no longer mattered. She went into the garden at the rear of her house carrying the envelope, a medicine bottle and a small box of matches. The garden was still and warm in the very late afternoon with just the occasional flutter of palm fronds brushing the air.

Indira walked slowly into the bush, stopping along the way to collect leaves and twigs from a white flowered oleander; she searched for the place in the bush where she had begun to mourn her daughter so many years ago, where she had passed a day asking herself whether she was to blame, whether she had in some way mismanaged Caroline's brief existence, and received no answers. Any proof of her own negligence would have given her a future of self-hatred, preferable to no reason other than a medical explanation she did not understand.

She gathered the oleander leaves and fresh twigs in to a small pile, mixed them with dry grasses and sat down. A gentle breeze collected the scent of oleander flowers from the nearby shrub then passed by. Sweet oleander, a deadly beauty. She struck a match to ignite the pile; instantly, thick and bitter smoke lifted to her head, entering her frail body, drying her kindness to a husk, choking the heart of gold. Indira lifted the medicine bottle to her lips; she consumed a preparation of liquidized oleander leaves. If she hoped to recall her daughter with renewed clarity through the drug's power, it was fleeting. She saw the baby, the imagined adolescent and the young woman whose features were indistinct until they cleared and became Girly, sharp and perfect. Then there was only intoxication, dizziness and poisonous pain tearing through her gut, slicing like a hot knife, until, after a long time, she slipped away, her heart slowing to a stop.

When Mr. Dhanraj passed by number eleven early the next morning, he was surprised to receive no answer to his persistent call through a half open side window. He walked into the garden, then, for no obvious reason that he could later recall, he followed the narrow, foot-trodden path into the bush. He found Indira immediately, damp with dew, long ago beyond help. As if the trauma of his own recent loss was not enough, Mr. Dhanraj felt a stab of anguish as he slipped slowly onto his knees beside the body of his dear neighbour. Without touching Indira, he carefully removed the envelope from her fingers, walked home and telephoned Jigs, as he always did when overwhelmed by events. Jigs arrived within the hour; he assumed control by telephoning the police station in Siparia and standing over Indira until an officer arrived. He handed over the envelope unopened and returned to his uncle's house. They sat together for a long time without saying a word.

**

The faint, dark smudge of Venezuela, when viewed from the sands of Quinam Beach, might have been a low cloud above the horizon but it was unmoving, solid and, to Jigs Boodoosingh, reassuring. Not that Jigs would have ever contemplated visiting the smudge. One or two people he had met told him about Caracas – busy, fast paced, different tongue. Even Port of Spain could bring on a headache if he stayed too long. No, looking at it from the beach was enough. He was happy to know it was always there, always keeping its distance.

Jigs looked along the sands. There were no Hindu groups today but several Baptists were erecting flags to form a square prior to a prayer meeting. Further along, the same white fishing boat he saw regularly was beached, unattended. He sipped a cold drink purchased from the vendor at the entrance to the sands; the man was normally only there at weekends, a time Jigs avoided because he liked to have the beach to himself. Today, he counted ten Baptists and no-one else. This was almost an uncomfortable crowd.

Of all the funerals Jigs had attended, directed and arranged in the past, the burial of Indira Dookie had affected him more than any, with the exception of his aunt's cremation. He believed as an undertaker you could become inured to the fate of the deceased you had never met, but repetition, professional procedure did not make it easier to deal with the death of those close to you. He found burial especially hard to take.

On the day after Indira Dookie was found, Jigs was summoned to Siparia Police Station; although an autopsy would confirm, self-inflicted poisoning was the assumed cause of death. The local police had seen the result of oleander's work before. He was handed the envelope Mr. Dhanraj had found in Indira's hand; it had been opened, examined and declared to be of no official interest but Jigs was entrusted with its contents. He later read the documents at his desk in the funeral parlour with an enervating sense of sadness.

The first paper was a funeral instruction addressed to Jigs personally: Indira was to be buried next to her daughter in the adjacent vacant plot. A receipt for purchase of the plot was attached to the instruction; Jigs noticed that the receipt was dated many years before. All writing was in the hand of Indira's lawyer in Siparia.

Secondly, there was a note to the effect that funeral costs were to be collected from the same lawyer. Indira had made provision.

Finally, there was a legally signed and witnessed will in which Indira left everything she had to Girly. There was no-one else.

Jigs preferred not to dwell on the funeral and the small grave-side service performed by a pundit; he assumed Indira had lost all faith in religion long ago, but he remembered the re-numbering of her house on the advice of a pundit and thought there should be some recognition that she came from a Hindu family. The lasting impression for Jigs was of many Jaggernauth children, normally so vibrant, stunned into silence as Rishi and Raj lowered Indira carefully into the exact place she had intended to be so long ago.

Jigs pushed his arms above his head, looked at the calm sea and began to relax. Recent pressures were beginning to lift with the satisfactory conclusion to events relating to Trinex in Ramdass Trace. He trusted Wendell Soames, although in fact there was no alternative. Not so long ago, the trace was a different place; now, Sumatee Dhanraj and Indira Dookie were gone, Devendra Roopnarine would probably soon depart for the house with gates. On the plus side, the Pump Man would return, hopefully rejuvenated and relieved of the worry of his declining house.

Away from Ramdass Trace, there were other issues for Jigs to ponder. Girly was not only keeping her distance from him, she was also deeply affected by Indira Dookie's death. When Jigs broached the subject of the will, Girly refused to engage; she had not been inside Indira's house but Jigs knew she had visited Siparia cemetery several times. After the funeral, he suggested a sabbatical and was hopeful she would accept the offer; it would give both of them time to ease the tension that had grown slowly but relentlessly.

On a personal level, his relationship with Angie was at a critical point. Donna's assertion that Angie was thinking of opening a bar had proved correct. Angie had found premises along Quinam Road between her house and the beach – a basic shack which required demolition but sitting on a good plot a few metres back from the road. She was currently working on Jigs, appealing to his business sense, to invest with her. He was mulling over the proposition and any misgivings he had with regard to the possible return of Angie's husband were being soothed away by the sunshine and hypnotic music of the sea surf.

He stretched luxuriously. Some time later, the vendor at the entrance to the beach packed up his goods and left, just as a brief gust of wind lifted a torn poster from its nail on a tree and sent it spinning through the clean air to rest at Jigs' side on the sand. Jigs looked at the grainy portrait of Mr. P.W. Ramday, split almost in half but maintaining a persuasive smile. So, Mr. Ramday had eased past Michael Nelson in the recent election; there was an Indian prime minister now but it was all so far from Quinam Beach. Politics were for Port of Spain and even if the government should endure, Jigs was not excited. The deep south was unlikely to command the attention of any government for long.

The Baptist prayer meeting was ending, flags removed. Jigs would be on his own in a few minutes. In celebration, he waded out into the warm waters until he could float on his back and listen to the sea.

EPILOGUE

Six months later, David was travelling to Ramdass Trace to visit Mr. Dhanraj when he decided to make a short stop in Penal. He walked from the junction to Penal Rock Road. The heat was suffocating – any year in London would bring four distinct seasons. Now there was a fifth season, Trinidad's dry season, to make him suffer in a way that never affected him when he lived here.

He stopped after a while at the house with gates. Although he had never been to the house before, he knew where it was located. He looked through the gates into the front open area, at the same time staying out of sight from the house. Beneath a green and white awning close to a boundary wall, old Mr. Roopnarine sat with his son in conversation. David saw Devendra lightly patting his father's knee, emphasising something that was either not understood or clearly heard, perhaps a reassuring gesture to signify that it did not really matter. They looked comfortable but dwarfed by the house and its enclosure. David saw no-one else.

After the walk back to Penal Junction, David hesitated. He looked at the funeral parlour; the façade was unchanged, not just from the last time he had seen it but from his earliest memories of Penal: the sign above the entrance, mottled wall finish, flaking paint on the windows of the apartment above. Soon after he left Trinex, he had sent a letter to Girly from London. There was no reply and he had not tried again. Now, in a spirit of curiosity tinged with hope, he entered the cool reception area which was vacant. He stood for two or three minutes in a state of indecision until Mauva Tocks appeared from a back room. He could see immediately that after an initial jolt of surprise, her attitude towards him was different from his last visit.

He smiled. "Is Miss Boodoosingh here?"

Mauva frowned, as if wondering why he would ask, as if he should know. Then she realised it had been a long time since his last visit.

"No...she went away."

"Away?"

"Yes," Mauva lowered her voice to project a tone of sympathy. "She went away."

***

On his return from Tobago, refreshed and optimistic, Sagar Narsingh had occupied, at Mr. Dhanraj's invitation, the numberless house in Ramdass Trace for a short period while the renovation of his own property was being completed. The basic repairs had been more extensive than anticipated and from his temporary home he was able to see the daily progress; his smile grew exponentially.

He resumed work with Trinex gradually, never hearing one word from his employer regarding damage to their now redundant, capped off oil well. From time to time, the Pump Man wandered across the road into his own house or the bush at the rear. His perambulations led him on one occasion to the edge of the former drilling site where he hesitated before pushing aside thick foliage for a clearer view. He found a calmness within himself promoted partly by his convalescence but also from the knowledge that his land, all of it, had been returned to him. The sight of the deserted Trinex-free clearing made him hum a tune.

On another occasion he let himself into his house when the builders were temporarily absent and works were almost complete; he ran his hand lovingly over new surfaces, smiled at the lack of cracks and distorted frames, drank in the aromas of new joinery and paint. He saw several small handles on a kitchen counter top. Some time later, the taciturn builder returned to find the Pump Man screwing handles on to kitchen cupboard doors with a confident dexterity appropriate to his new home.

He made a substantial contribution towards the costs of renovation and when he finally re-occupied number sixteen, the Pump Man found his mood never darkened, the feeling of hopelessness had gone, the voice of the house retreated into a place where it was imprisoned with no release.

The only sadness in his life was the loss of Indira Dookie as a close friend. He often sat on his front veranda with Ravi Bishoo looking at the house across the road discussing the years they had known her in hushed tones.

***

Ravi Bishoo seldom visited the site of his ruined lawn. Whenever he walked to the back of his house, he deliberately avoided looking at the rectangular patch of ground that once held his attention and dominated his aspirations. Although the soil had been effectively cleaned and decontaminated by Trinex, Ravi had lost the will to start again. He missed the early morning rising from bed to witness the miracle of his watering system, but the spark had gone. The pursuit of a perfect lawn no longer inspired him despite the occasional cajoling by Fong's garden department; he received glossy pamphlets advertising the latest techniques and equipment to produce a tropical carpet of grass, but the disappointment he felt could no longer be soothed by the prospect of starting again.

Trinex had dug and turned over the soil as part of the cleaning process, then replaced the scarecrow in the centre of the garden plot. At first, Ravi looked for signs that blades of grass would push through the uneven clods but as time passed there were only ugly weeds to be seen on the crusty, pale surface. The irrigation system was stored away in its original packaging, gathering dust.

Ravi's reluctance to visit the land at the rear of the house meant that he spent more time on his veranda. He contemplated a future of indolence and it began to worry him. He regularly sought out Sagar Narsingh and Mr. Dhanraj to discuss local affairs but avoided talk of land and gardens. There had to be more, however. One afternoon some time after the destruction of his lawn, whilst leafing uninterestedly through Fong's latest brochure, it came to him. He considered his qualifications; this did not tax him unduly but in the slow-moving river of his mind, the subject eventually lapped over memories of conversations held at Fong's with their affable garden expert, an elderly man from Siparia who was on the cusp of retirement. Ravi looked ahead and saw an opening for his horticultural skills.

***

David went straight to Ramdass Trace from Penal Junction, but before calling on Mr. Dhanraj, he decided to walk the length of the trace. He strolled slowly past Indira Dookie's house, empty, locked up, never visited except by Mr. Dhanraj who entered from time to time, dusted surfaces then left. The new owner had never been inside since Indira died.

Walking on past number eleven, David stopped outside two more vacant properties. Sumatee Dhanraj's numberless house, now her husband's, shone a bright yellow with newly painted wall surfaces. There was no particular reason why Mr. Dhanraj should have brightened up the exterior; he had no purchaser in mind. His intention was to keep it maintained in memory of his wife. David did not dwell on the one time he had been inside the house. It was all too long ago.

The vacant house of Devendra Roopnarine and his father was boarded up at the windows. Clearly Devendra had no need of the property now; there was evidence of minor repair works which were not recent but no major renovations. The house looked abandoned with no future.

At the end of the trace, David stepped onto the Company Road next to the plot formerly owned by Indira Dookie and occupied by an oil pump. There was silence; Trinex had removed the pump and screen, cleaned the soiled ground and capped the well. The road was maintained in perfect condition, largely unused. The hot pipes that for years ran the length of the trace were gone.

On his return along the trace, David looked to his right: three houses owned by two Jaggernauth families. He had often wondered why three houses were needed but it was a substantial, expanding family colonising that end of the trace. Oddly, there was no sign of life in any house or garden. He passed on.

At number sixteen, David stopped to admire the change in Mr. Narsingh's house. The exterior was unrecognisable from the previous year, and many years before. Later, Mr. Dhanraj would describe to David the metamorphosis he had witnessed as the builder engaged by Jigs went to work.

Following a well-remembered path at the side of number sixteen, David trod through the bush, enjoying the scents and small sounds he had missed during the last six months. The clearing formed by Trinex close to Erin road was discernible but vacant and all evidence of oil exploration removed. Low level scrub was starting to cover the ground; in time, there would be no reason to suspect the land had been touched.

It was clear that the oil pollution affecting much ground behind Ravi Bishoo's house had also been cleaned; David had seen the process before and was not surprised. He pushed through heavy foliage to the back of Ravi's house. David was vaguely aware of

Ravi's attempt to cultivate a lawn, but he saw no signs now. The ground was weed covered, lumpy; a basic wooden cross draped with a faded black jacket stood in the centre of the plot in isolation.

Mr. Dhanraj greeted David with a barrage of questions concerning his last six months in London. He queried the finer points of information in David's regular letters, to which Mr. Dhanraj never replied, requesting clarification of events loosely described in writing and now, to David, of no consequence. But he indulged his friend as they occupied their habitual positions on the veranda until dusk fell with refreshing whispers of wind audible above the quiet trace. There was no singing from hot pipes, no metallic or motor sounds from oil pumps. The trace rested.

The time spent in London had not offered the stability David expected in his life. He worked almost non-stop in the Oven House restaurant, shared in its success, but found that his relative wealth did not bring the satisfaction he expected.

His relationship with his sister grew to an easy mutual trust but he felt it was a pity that their only common bond was the restaurant. They had no shared parents now and she was ambivalent towards an uncle and aunt now returned to England in a south London suburb. The best of both worlds for him would be periodic trips back to south Trinidad; apart from his regular letters, he kept in touch with Mr. Dhanraj by telephone and would always have a place to stay in Ramdass Trace. He just wished there was a greater incentive to travel via Penal Junction. He did not ask his friend about Girly and Mr. Dhanraj offered no explanation of her absence.

David looked across the road to Ravi Bishoo's house, almost obscured by the fading light but the soft glow of a lamp in the rear kitchen confirmed the family was at home. The sky above the house was peach and blue behind small puffs of grey cloud.

"Ravi not starting a new lawn?" David asked.

"He give it up," Mr. Dhanraj confirmed. "He take water system back to Fong but they refuse it. They say it used and not refund cost." Mr. Dhanraj thought for a moment. "Ravi talkin' 'bout gettin' a job."

They looked at each other across the veranda and their loud, simultaneous laughter drowned the sounds of crickets and roosting birds.

***

A taxi brought Girly Boodoosingh back to Ramdass Trace and the yellow numberless house. It was almost dark. The last two months for Girly had been lonely: one month of self-imposed isolation in a beach-front cottage on Tobago's Caribbean coast followed by one month at her parents' house in Arima tending to her dyspeptic mother who missed her daughter and exaggerated the seriousness of her condition in order to regain a companion. Girly saw through the pretence but complied; a month in Arima away from Penal was no hardship.

On the journey south from Arima, Girly reflected on how she had left her brother to cope at the funeral parlour, knowing also of his commitment to Angie's bar. But she left on good terms, partly she assumed because Jigs knew she was not travelling to London.

When long hot days staring at the slow Caribbean swell had begun to pall, Girly gathered her thoughts and packed them away with her luggage to set off for Arima. Despite the change of scenery, her sense of loss in rejecting David would not recede. She believed her decision at the time was correct but now the chance had gone, doubts previously suppressed would surface and wash over her like the tide. Normally, she had no inclination to worry about the past but a quiet sadness occupied a small corner of the heart.

The taxi driver set a suitcase and small bag down on the road side and drove away. Girly looked at the yellow house: dark inside and unwelcoming. After Indira Dookie died, Girly would not think about her inheritance. She pushed the process and detail of the will out of her mind, preferring to occupy the yellow house when realising she no longer wanted to share the funeral parlour apartment with her brother. She had left for Tobago from the yellow house. Now it stared back at her. She barely glanced at the widow Dookie's property, now her own. She fumbled for a key in the darkness.

When the laughter on Mr. Dhanraj's veranda subsided, the friends were distracted by the arrival of a taxi in the trace; they saw it stop outside Mr. Dhanraj's yellow house, saw Girly step out. David immediately looked at Mr. Dhanraj; the pale light from inside the house failed to illuminate the space between them but David felt and heard the movement towards him. Mr. Dhanraj lifted David's arm until he stood.

"Go see her," he said. "Maybe last chance."

David's initial thought that his friend should have told him about Girly's new residence was overtaken by indecision, then realisation that Mr. Dhanraj seemed surprised to see her standing by the front steps. Perhaps he thought her move to the trace to be of no consequence or it was a temporary measure. David accepted his cue; he descended to the yard, stepped quickly across to the road then hurried to where Girly stood, still delving for a key in her bag.

The sound of footsteps made her suspend her search; David's familiar form registered immediately in her mind as he emerged from darkness to moonlight but was nevertheless a shock. Her surprise was, however, so short lived, so temporary it was extinguished by a joy that propelled her forward to meet him. At last, her soul entered her eyes.

"The key. I can't find..."

"You're living here now? Permanently?"

He seemed happy at the idea. He smiled, and every doubt she harboured, every misgiving fell away for no apparent reason other than he was here in the trace standing next to her and this time it was different. In the cooling night air, she believed the time was now right; her fear of the future melted away, hopes hung in the air ready to be collected if only she would reach out a hand.

She had always wanted someone to fall for her completely, but when she recognised it in Devendra, it was hollow, based on the ability to acquire someone he could now afford, rather than years of acquaintance and commitment. It was not enough.

She knew David had a second life available to him far away, but she made herself believe, in this brief moment, that he would always come back or insist on taking her with him. After years of uncertainty, the recent time away from Penal and Ramdass Trace convinced her there was no impediment to a different life, a life her brother would not contemplate for her or himself. And now was also the time to share her personal tragedy with David; she would tell him inside the yellow house.

David picked up the bags, Girly found a key in her pocket. She held his arm as they walked slowly across the yard to the house.

***

On the day before Girly came back to the yellow, numberless house, it was mid morning when Jigs Boodoosingh finally decided he could not face it, could not even countenance the prospect of travelling to Tobago. He reclined gracefully in the shade of a samaan tree's spreading branches; suffocating heat beyond the shadow cast by horizontal boughs was edging towards him as the sun moved towards its zenith. He stirred himself and came to the only possible conclusion: he would send one of his pallbearers, Rishi or Raj, to accompany the deceased's body from Tobago's capital, Scarborough, in spite of the express written instruction from the deceased's daughter that he, Jagdeo Boodoosingh, should carry out the mission personally.

Jigs thought about the journey once more, as he had many times since receiving the letter from Scarborough the previous day, but the result was always the same: several hours on a ferry from Port of Spain and several hours back; it was enough to make him feel queasy even in the current tranquillity of the bower. The twenty five or thirty minute flight from Piarco Airport, whilst on the face of it more attractive, was out of the question. He had seen the small, island-hopping aeroplanes from the perimeter fence at Piarco: fragile looking, prone to buffeting no doubt in high winds and, in Jigs' opinion, unsafe. And could the coffin be accommodated on one of those tiny craft? No, the only decision to make was who he should send.

On the one hand, Rishi was the more senior in years and service at the funeral parlour, but prone to lapses during his off-duty periods. There were few rum shops in the Penal district unfamiliar with his custom; his coffin-carrying the morning after a long evening at Donna's Bar on Clarke Road was often erratic and lacked the solemnity a funeral required.

Raj, by contrast, was a steady, undemonstrative character although not as worldly as Rishi. Jigs would need an experienced hand to see this through if he was unprepared to travel himself.

A welcome breeze ruffled the samaan tree's parasol shape. Jigs looked across the space between the tree and the back of Angie's new bar, of which Jigs was fifty per cent owner; he was taking a break from helping with the preparations for the opening. The building was finished: pink painted, cement rendered walls, just like Angie's house further along Quinam Road, beneath a pitched roof with front and rear gables. Angie had deliberately left a large open space at the side of the single storey building for car parking; the bar was situated close to the beach and Angie expected plenty of weekend passing trade.

The setting was perfect. The road to Quinam Beach was long and, in parts, fringed by thick teak forests, cocoa and citrus groves, along with haphazard planting of cashew, calabash and mango trees. Within the forests, purple jacaranda existed happily with chaconia and bougainvillea in red and white, unseen from the road. The display was accidental, rarely noticed.

Jigs was unperturbed by potential competition from the weekend beach vendors; he did not intend to target the market for snacks such as *baigani*, sliced aubergine in batter, and *saheena,* split pea and dasheen fritters, aimed at bathers and beach sitters. There were no tourists in this isolated, idyllic place. He wanted the local hungry hordes to stop on their way to and from the beach.

Inside Angie's bar, the installation of the kitchen and bar fittings was almost complete. Jigs was beginning to feel the financial burden: the cost of constructing a new building, as well as demolishing the original ramshackle structure, was taxing his personal resources. The speed of the construction had been impressive if expensive. Nevertheless, he was committed to the project, if not to Angie on a personal level. He was still reluctant to vacate his small apartment above the Room of Rest in favour of Angie's pink house; her marital status, despite repeated assurances that her husband would not return from his ex-wife's warm embrace in New York, was not sufficiently clear for him to take the risk.

The clamour inside the bar died as Jigs walked slowly through the back door. Builders, delivery men and installers left through the front. Jigs locked up and drove his polished Ford back to Penal Junction. South Trinidad dozed in the draining heat.

Later that day, Jigs shivered in the newly-installed air conditioning of his office at the funeral parlour. He was unable to master the controls of the cooling unit that left him alternately perspiring or uncomfortably chilled. He issued instructions to Rishi for the following day:

"It's an early start. You take the hearse to the terminal at Port of Spain, drive onto the Tobago ferry. When you get to Tobago, Devi

Seepersad, the deceased's daughter, will meet you and you go to the Williams' parlour in Scarborough to collect the body."

Jigs considered the reason for the instruction he had received. The client was adamant that the funeral should be in south Trinidad and not Tobago; it was to be a burial, vehemently confirmed in a return letter when Jigs assumed a cremation. The stipulation that Jigs should conduct the transfer of the coffin himself remained a mystery he was not anxious to solve. He wanted the business but no further contact with the client until the coffin was safely displayed in the Room of Rest.

A smile had formed on Rishi's lips. Jigs raised both trimmed eyebrows in expectation of a question.

"Devi Seepersad?" Rishi asked. His smile was partly a response to hearing a familiar name and also a reflex to his employer's precise language and almost complete lack of local accent which always amused him. He usually modified his own extremes of dialect in Jigs' presence in deference to his employer and as a matter of professional pride, although this did not prevail when he stepped outside the funeral parlour in his free time.

"Yes. She's from Tobago."

"Nah," Rishi corrected him. "She have a house in Rock Road."

Jigs sat back in his well worn chair. He was surprised by Rishi's knowledge of anything beyond local places of entertainment.

"You know this Devi?" He rose and walked to stand in front of a small wall mirror behind his desk. The lack of silvering here and there gave his reflection a mottled appearance. He peered at Rishi in the mirror's background; in Jigs' opinion, Rishi's moustache was a disgrace, an abomination of unkempt growth above the lip that offered no acknowledgement of the history of facial decoration but existed as an untrained example of Rishi's general attitude to life. Jigs made a mental note for later to trim one or two of his own almost unnoticeable but, to his mind, unacceptably long hairs edging past the otherwise perfectly maintained strip. He would normally have been too polite to mention Rishi's appearance in any derogatory sense, but now that he was representing the parlour on official business, Jigs felt it was time to call his employee to order.

"By the way," he said, forestalling an answer to his previous question. "You need to pull up on yourself."

Rishi smiled again at the local expression spoken in what, to him, was a foreign accent.

"Yes," Jigs continued, slightly irritated by Rishi's casual manner. He also thought there was a sense of mockery in the tongue momentarily flicking Rishi's top lip. "You should be in full uniform tomorrow, smart and with that thing under control." He waved a hand at Rishi's moustache. "Devi Seepersad is paying a lot for this service. I want to give a good impression."

Jigs thought it prudent not to mention that the client had asked for Jigs himself to fulfil the mission; he did not want Rishi to wonder why he was not travelling. Jigs remembered his earlier enquiry: "Devi Seepersad is local?"

Rishi thought for a moment, cataloguing the disparate pieces of information gleaned from casual conversations during his nocturnal bar visits.

"She born here and have a house and business here."

"Business?" Jigs asked casually.

Rishi had a moment of playful inspiration. He recalled something heard recently at Krishna's grill, something that made him smile inside. He also knew about his employer's latest venture.

"Devi have a coffee shop in San Fernando. An' she buyin' a plot nex' to Quinam Beach. She startin' a bar an' grill."

Jigs sat down heavily, placed his hands on the desk and closed his eyes. The air conditioning unit whirred and clicked. The room suddenly became very cold.

END

EXTRACT FROM A SILENCE IN THE SHADOWS

1

Jigs Boodoosingh stepped out of the Penal Funeral Parlour and hesitated. It was a hot, dusty afternoon; through a haze of heat and fine particles, he saw the small parade of shops and offices opposite: Penal Realty owned by Basdeo Persad, Doctor Naidu's surgery, various food stalls and the reason for his hesitation: Sanjay's barber shop at the end of the block. Jigs checked his wristwatch. It was after 3 o'clock.

His intention was to walk to Donna's Bar on Clarke Road where he could sit quietly with refreshments to mull over his latest problem. But the time made all the difference. He also needed a hair cut; between 3 and 5 o'clock daily Sanjay provided a complimentary beer with each trim. Jigs walked across Penal Junction as the sun pounded the pavement around his feet.

Earlier, a woman had entered the funeral parlour and upset the smooth running of the efficient machine that was part of the Boodoosingh service for bereaved clients. Jigs was assiduous in his maintenance of office records. The card index system so favoured by his father had been consigned to a large box in the embalming room where it lay silently along with transitory cadavers. As soon as his father had handed over the funeral business several years before and set off for retirement in Arima, Jigs had called in a computer and software specialist from San Fernando on the recommendation of Basdeo Persad of Penal Realty. This was a mistake because no recommendation by Basdeo Persad should have been taken seriously. His own property records were a disaster, mainly due to slipshod data inputting but also as a result of software defects that were bound to appear when used by any computer ever manufactured. But Basdeo was a friend so Jigs suffered frustration, undue expense and the ire of his secretary, Mauva Tocks, until the system was rectified by a company from Port of Spain whose employees really were experts.

Therefore when, earlier in the day, Jigs found himself at a loss to explain the absence of a particular record of cremation on his computer screen, his visitor was unsympathetic and Jigs himself discommoded.

"You burn him at the Creek long time since!" wailed the woman, referring to the cremation of her husband at Mosquito Creek.

"What exactly do you want to know?" Jigs asked mildly. He focused on the name, tried to recall the occasion of the cremation but it would not come.

The woman sucked her bottom lip in exasperation. "In his trouser, he have a package."

"But all personal effects in the deceased's clothes and on the body would have been returned to you," Jigs answered reasonably. "There was no package?"

"No! Man come to the house and ask for it!" The woman suddenly became sheepish. "I frighten' this man."

She appeared to shrink in front of Jigs' eyes. She was clearly uncomfortable recalling an apparently aggressive character.

"Leave it to me. I'll look into it and get back to you." He noted her address.

The woman looked at Jigs dubiously, then made a decision. She left without further discussion. Jigs tapped on the computer keyboard; he was concerned about the woman's fear and his inability to solve the mystery of a missing record. He would think about it and check with Mauva who would normally remember the parlour's clients even without recourse to the computer records.

Sanjay was removing a cape from his only customer as Jigs entered the barber shop. As one crossed the threshold of the front door, a complex mix of after-shave, pomades and brilliantine aromas hovered in the stale air; there was no air conditioning, the only window was fixed shut, the open door afforded little relief from the heat. Jigs was a regular customer and as such was now oblivious to the finer detail of the room: frayed electric cables ran down walls and along the floor perimeter, a 'No Credit' sign in black print hung on a hook above the only cracked white china sink. There was a bench by the window; a boy, who was not a customer, sat with his body angled to take in the view of Penal Junction whilst tapping out a beat with a forefinger on the bench and nodding to a private rhythm in his head. A radio sat on a teak shelf next to the door; low level *Soca* music with periodic spoken advertisements for local products and services faded in and out. Sanjay never bothered to adjust the tuning.

Jigs watched the customer leave then settled into the faux leather chair in front of the sink. Sanjay handed him a can of beer; Jigs noticed the small bin on the floor next to the sink was nearly full with empty cans. As it was not long after 3 o'clock, he calculated that Sanjay would be responsible for almost all of them, his intake not being constrained by the starting time for customers. After an approximate assessment of the number of cans, he looked at Sanjay and decided against a shave.

"Just a trim," Jigs confirmed, waving a hand over his head. Jigs was not bibulous but he enjoyed an occasional rum or beer; he believed the alcohol helped him to think, and at this moment he needed to think. Since early morning, his thoughts had been dominated by one subject, in fact one name: Devi Seepersad. As Sanjay wrapped him in a cape, sipped his beer and wiped a comb on a handy cloth, Jigs allowed a portion of his mind to slip onto the perplexing subject of Devi whilst partially focusing on Sanjay's cutting scissors.

Several weeks ago, Jigs had sent his pall-bearer, Rishi, to meet Devi Seepersad in Tobago to bring back her deceased father for burial in Trinidad. But when Devi, from whom Jigs had received a formal letter to confirm the arrangements, had seen Rishi emerge from the funeral parlour's vehicle at the Scarborough ferry terminal, she had been personally affronted that he, Jagdeo Boodoosingh, had not made the journey himself as specified. Rishi returned to Penal empty handed with the words: "She give a real boof, man!" which adequately illustrated Devi's displeasure.

Despite pondering the incident periodically over the last few weeks, and one or two failed attempts to contact Devi, Jigs was no nearer discovering why she was so insistent that he should have travelled himself, and why she had aborted the task at the Scarborough terminal. Something about the details of the arrangements and the outcome intrigued him; the problem would not leave him alone.

"How your dou dou?" Sanjay asked, using the back of a free hand to remove beer froth from his top lip. It was well known in Penal that Jigs was a part-time cohabiter of the pink house in Quinam Road with its owner, Angie, in the absence of her estranged husband.

"Angie is fine," Jigs intoned defensively. Sanjay was familiar with the lack of local accent but he nevertheless found it amusing. The accent was a result of hours in front of a transistor radio listening to the BBC World Service as a youth. Jigs thought it was appropriate for his profession.

An idea struck him. "Do you know Devi Seepersad?" Jigs asked casually.

"Ah, that Devi!" Sanjay's eyes momentarily lost focus, then sharpened as though the vision of an ideal had been tarnished by reality. "I know her since small. Devi have too much o' style, too much limin'. She have a business, you know!"

Jigs gathered that, in Sanjay's opinion, Devi spent a lot of time socialising and polishing her image.

"What business?" The question was disingenuous; Jigs had

already been informed by Rishi that Devi had a coffee shop in San Fernando.

Sanjay scratched the back of his head with the teeth of a comb then used it to form a parting in his client's hair. "Coffee shop. But she ambitious. Word is she have other property."

There was nothing further to be gained by questioning Sanjay, whose dexterity was becoming noticeably less professional and reliable. Jigs breathed a sigh of relief when Sanjay finally put down his scissors and released him from the chair with a final flourish of the cape.

Jigs paid his fee, including a generous tip, before pacing to the outside door where he stopped in order to adjust to the bright daylight. Penal Junction was busy: Fong's general store was holding another of its many discount sales, street vendors sold street food in large quantities, there was a queue of traffic along Erin road due to emergency road works. Jigs looked across the road to the funeral parlour. A well-dressed woman holding the hand of a young girl was about to cross the entrance threshold but she hesitated. She stepped back a pace, looked up and down the pavement, said something to the girl. Jigs saw a familiarity in the woman, something in her bearing, her gait when she finally decided to enter the parlour.

Two minutes later, his curiosity piqued, Jigs stood in front of Mauva Tocks in the reception area.

"Devi Seepersad is here to see you. She's in your office." Jigs was unable to discern any opinion from Mauva's gaze, no indication of what she thought of the mysterious client, but something was wrong. Mauva looked discomfited, as if she was suffering embarrassment on his behalf. As soon as he opened the office door and walked towards the desk, his two visitors turned away from the window to face him. There were no chairs for guests.

Jigs stopped suddenly, his jaw dropped involuntarily as ten years of living fell away in a second. "Devi?...."

The woman Jigs remembered as Devi Maharaj smiled and looked at the young girl by her side. Jigs also looked at the girl: a young version of her mother, for the likeness was stunning. But there was something else - he recognised her bright eyes, even features and formed an immediate impression, a realisation that hit him physically, prompting a grab for the desk top as a temporary support. Without any doubt, the nine or ten year old girl was his daughter.

Devi placed a hand on the girl's shoulder. "This is Jill," she said.

Jigs Boodoosingh blinked.

2

A fine mist hung over the narrow river tributary at San Francique, deep in the south of Trinidad. The surrounding land was partly under shallow water, a normal feature after heavy rain in this low-lying area; the sun was no more than a pale splash of cream as it sought a hole in the slow-moving clouds. There was no breeze; the air was hot and damp.

In the centre of the channel, a man paddled a white-painted skiff past wet pastures, abandoned shacks and occupied houses of rough timber with metal roofs. The man wore a pale blue singlet, here and there perforated by moth attack, and brown shorts. The water was calm but the minimum effort required to propel the boat forward still induced a grimace to the man's face, exposing damaged teeth below a full, unkempt moustache. His hair was slicked back, his dark skin dull in the mist.

The skiff eventually turned away from the centre to the right hand side of the tributary as soon as it passed a dying tree, as if this was a landmark the man had been looking for; he manoeuvred the craft up to a set of broken concrete steps and produced a frayed rope to secure it to a corroded, vertical metal bar protruding from the bank.

A short walk from the steps, a house stood at the end of a well-trodden dirt path; it stood in silence, away from the water's mist, fringed by scrub and rough grass. It was a house out of character with its rural surroundings, more like a town house of substance in design, although now dilapidated and vacant.

The man gathered a package from the bottom of the skiff, a package securely wrapped and taped. When he arrived at the rear entrance of the house, he slid back a bolt on a boarded door and walked into a spacious ground floor room devoid of furniture or belongings. He followed his instructions: place the package in the centre of the floor then leave.

Within one hour of the skiff passing back along the tributary, a slim figure dressed in an off-white singlet and grey trousers walked through a rice field opposite the house. He passed a tethered cow in an adjoining pasture; there were no labourers in the field, no people outside the few dwellings that stood on the waterside. The man walked unhurriedly across a rough road in front of the house, entering via the back door, moving like his predecessor to the middle of the room where he collected the package; he stopped, listened for movement. When satisfied he was alone and unobserved he left the house, making his way back along the same route.

Just after dawn on the following day, two lorries containing four men in work clothes stopped outside the house. Beginning with the roof, they methodically dismantled the house, carefully removing sections which were placed on the vehicles. Where demolition was necessary, this was handled without undue haste; electrical, water and drainage services were terminated correctly. The workmen left the site in a tidy condition five days later.

At Penal Junction, Basdeo Persad of Penal Realty received a telephone call on the sixth day requesting that he should find a suitable buyer for the now vacant plot of land. Details of the vendor would be provided in due course; all communication was to be conducted by letter, all correspondence to be left for collection.

Basdeo did not find it necessary to make enquiries as to the land's title or why the client expressed no interest in Basdeo assessing the land's value.

3

If Devi Seepersad had feared a hostile reaction from Jigs, against which eventuality she ensured her daughter was standing close by, then she was surprised and relieved. She saw him lean against the desk, realised the desired effect had been achieved - he looked at Jill and the shock of incomprehensible but undeniable fatherhood was almost too much for him.

After two attempts at formulating an introduction, a greeting, Jigs shrank into silence.

Devi watched him begin to turn away, to approach the worn desk chair, but even in the turmoil of his thoughts, she saw he immediately recognized he could not sit while they stood. As he paused uncertainly, she rehearsed her approach; she had allowed him a look at his future, now she led Jill out of the room into the temporary care of Mauva Tocks.

Devi Maharaj had met Jigs ten years before in Penal. Their lives touched when they stood next to each other at the bar of an open air arena close to Duncan Village. It was late; the staged *Bhangra* music entertained the flower of south Trinidad youth but the volume almost precluded conversation. Jigs invited Devi to walk away to a low-decibel nook far away from the stage; she discerned a business mind in his euphemistic description of a career in 'end of life service' even if she did not fully grasp the nature of the enterprise. In any event, it sounded like he was in life insurance or something similar. She approved of his smart, casual clothes and the faint beginnings of a moustache only confirmed this was a man of worth and self confidence.

Devi usually regarded the world through cynical eyes that reflected her impoverished upbringing but nevertheless outwardly shone with health; she hid a capacity for deception and ruthless exploitation. Her existence in a wrecked Rock Road shack with a useless father had also not erased her ambition. Devi sometimes walked up the staircase of her ideals and settled on the top landing, looking down on her past. But she was never sad for yesterday, there was always tomorrow when she would excel, climb higher and touch the topmost, sweetest fruit. Despite rudimentary schooling, she learned enough to hold a conversation on a variety of subjects; her trick was to open with "I really have no opinion on that, but..." then express just enough of a rehearsed understanding to attract interest and respect from men and women alike. Devi never failed to transport old dreams into the present, but never allowed past failures to diminish her expectations.

Their time together was brief. At first, when she became aware of the real nature of his career, she saw his business as an opportunity; she knew his parents would leave the parlour to Jigs and his sister. But when she gained access to his life, she was appalled by the funeral parlour itself, the claustrophobic apartment above, and the grim process that haunted the building's walls, covered its inner surfaces in layers of illness and causes of death. By the time she decided Jigs was not to be her passport to a life of comfort and wealth, it was as easy to leave him as she expected.

Ironically, he unwittingly provided her with the means to leave: just enough money for a ticket out of the Caribbean or to a distant island; she told him the money was to be spent on fees for a college course down at Bonasse in the deep south. In fact, she did not travel far: she fled to Tobago in the early stages of carrying their daughter but determined he should not know and pursue her. She soon met an older man, Virat Seepersad, exploiting his wealth which was founded on a narrow but lucrative field of crime.

The south coast of Trinidad has many quiet bays and beaches on the Columbus Channel; this waterway was a route from South America to the Atlantic Ocean for drug smugglers. When Virat Seepersad, who hailed from Moruga, found himself on the local beach one day some years before watching a chase out at sea between a speedy coastguard launch and a slower smuggler's fishing boat, he was fascinated by the outcome - several bags dumped into the water before the Trinidad authority could board the boat. Virat was even more fascinated when three of the bags washed up next to his feet some time later. A life hitherto spent on the extreme edge of the law, occasionally stepping over the line with petty theft, now irrevocably entered the world of serious crime when he opened the bags, uncovered wrapped packages of cocaine and decided they were his way out of Moruga.

Virat convinced himself the market was in Tobago selling his goods in small packages to tourists; there were few tourists in south Trinidad. He also calculated the safest route was the shortest crossing by fast boat from the north of Trinidad to Tobago's Caribbean coast. Despite the exhibition of maritime law enforcement he had witnessed out on the Channel, Virat was not deterred; he used almost every dollar he owned to buy a smart set of clothes and tourist luggage from a San Fernando mall on his way north. He travelled cheaply by bus with his merchandise evenly distributed in innocent looking navy blue cases on wheels; when he arrived in Port of Spain, he rented a room in a low-budget guest house with his remaining money, left the cases locked in the room's teak armoire, then stole further funds at knife point from local women using cash machines outside banks in the St. James district.

Virat had a good feeling about the whole enterprise. This was a different world from Moruga where, as a big, wide-shouldered youth, he had been forced to work daily on a few acres of land planted with sugar cane and various crops, for which there was a rapidly decreasing market and a consequential poor wage. Virat had occasionally used his size to enforce his opinions on others until one day in his late teens, an opponent in imminent danger of being battered had produced a cutlass from the rear waist band of his trousers and taken a rasher from Virat's upper arm; from that point onward Virat decided that his intellect, sharp if misguided, would be a better weapon. Nevertheless, his occasional use of a short blade to intimidate was seen as a useful adjunct to his brain power.

On the morning after his arrival in Port of Spain, Virat found his way to the port in search of a passage to Tobago but without using the services of a charter company. He fretted about the goods stored back at the guest house and the cash thefts of the previous day, causing him to maintain a vigilance during his perambulations with frequent glances over his right shoulder.

He had no luck at the port; it was vast, full of containers and several large ships including a cruise liner. Virat walked to the water's edge, paused and looked around him at the incongruous mix of sand coloured, colonial waterside buildings and straight fingers of modern high rise blocks against a back drop of the Northern Range.

This would not do. Virat needed a marina. Following casual enquiries at the port office, he boarded public transport which conveyed him along the coast to Clandon Cove, a private marina comprising pontoons, landing stages and a club house on pellucid water, a world away from the capital's port in style and opulence if not in distance. There, Virat surveyed the rows and rows of yachts and small cruise boats; he was looking for something slightly out of keeping with the rest, maybe a less expensive looking craft with a captain amenable to payment for passage that did not include cash. After half an hour of walking back and forth along the pontoons casually inspecting the array of boats, he realised he was drawing attention to himself. He pushed at the door of the club house; he needed somewhere to sit and think out of the midday heat, but a steward in club uniform shook a raised finger at him from the bar area. Virat held his gaze whilst allowing the door to close in front of him. On another occasion, he would have approached the steward, inflicted facial damage then left without a thought for the consequences. But not now. He swallowed deeply, feeling the jagged edges of anger and humiliation scrape his throat, and left.

In the welcoming shade cast by a side wall of the club house, Virat contemplated his position. He could not, would not return to Moruga; the assets in the guest house armoire had to be moved imminently – they were earning no income and his cash would soon dwindle. He was not keen on committing further robbery as his luck was bound to expire sooner or later.

He watched a small cabin cruiser manoeuvre into a vacant berth at the end of the line of moorings away from the club house; the shabby appearance of the boat would not normally be to his liking but he acknowledged that the handling by the pilot appeared competent to his inexpert eye, and the unclean, worn look of the craft might be to his advantage.

The cruiser was off-white with a faded blue perimeter stripe beneath an integral cabin; a clip-on awning covered the cabin entrance. There was no name that he could discern but Virat noted a registration number in black paint on the port side. The paintwork was generally dull and worn, the engine sounded tired. Virat assumed the pilot was used to mooring here but the question was whether the boat coasted around the marina and immediate shore line or whether it was seaworthy. He had no idea.

Virat decided to approach the captain. He did not lack courage, but he was socially awkward. There was no easy way for him to open a conversation based on small talk, a friendly enquiry or relaxed body language. He did not have the experience. Virat found knowledge disturbing; experience was the sum of what happened to you every day but knowledge was thrust upon you and Virat found it hard to take. It worried him that small pieces of information would always be part of a bigger picture he could not see. As a result, he was wary, occasionally indecisive and gauche, failings which sometimes prompted frustration and violent reaction.

When the boat's engine was cut and the starboard side bumped quietly against the landing, Virat stepped forward and, without a word, held out his hand indicating he would take the slack mooring rope and hold it while the captain climbed up on to dry land.

Virat saw a wary expression on the captain's face, a momentary glance into Virat's eyes then the rope was taken and the boat secured. The captain returned to the cabin to collect a holdall; when he re-emerged, his manner was different as if the intervening minute had given him time to assess the stranger. He smiled confidently. "You're not passing by," he said smoothly, waving a hand at the pontoon as if to indicate no-one would find themselves there by accident. "You need transportation and it has to be soon."

Virat tensed. His dilemma had been assessed correctly, clearly not the first time the captain had been in this position. The accent was American, the face weathered, reddish-brown beneath a flat cap.

"Tobago. Tomorrow," was all Virat could summon up. His throat was dry.

"Walk with me." The captain set off towards the marina's entrance. Half way along the deck he stopped, seemingly hesitant, as if several thoughts had collided to place him in the centre of a dilemma.

"Say. You're from Trinidad or Tobago? A citizen?"

Virat failed to see any relevance but confirmed: "Moruga. In sout'."

The captain nodded. "I can't take anyone who is not a national." He put down the holdall and faced Virat squarely. "I have to go to the chandler's for supplies. Fishing equipment. I run tourists out to sea from hotels in Tobago. Sea fishing, you know," he added as if he had quickly assessed Virat and decided detailed explanation would be required. "Look. I'm staying on the boat tonight but sailing early. You have to be here because I won't wait. Don't bring too much with you and be alone."

Virat decided one might take offence at the captain's brusque manner but he did not find it offensive; the instruction was clear, his passage was almost agreed and somehow he found the captain's words reassuring in their directness. He quickly examined the potential of the sea fishing story. He glanced back at the boat to confirm his earlier impression of its rather dilapidated condition. It was surely unlikely that tourists would board such a craft and set out to sea on fishing expeditions. Not that he had seen any such services in south Trinidad for him to compare. There was just something about the captain that made Virat sense he needed the fare - yet to be agreed - as much as Virat needed to travel.

The captain named a figure which Virat accepted without any thought. It was a detail that had no bearing at this stage. They parted with a brief wave rather than a handshake. The captain walked towards the marina entrance, passing the club house, exiting next to a small taxi rank from where he was conveyed to Port of Spain. He did not look back at Virat or his boat.

Virat returned to the hostel satisfied with his arrangements but apprehensive about his ability to raise funds for his passage to Tobago. He needed cash; he thought about offering the captain a reasonable sample of his booty with the promise of a pre-agreed portion on reaching Tobago. He dismissed the idea immediately; there was no indication from their meeting that Virat would be able to trust his transporter, especially with the goods on the boat during the voyage. No, there would be another way and Virat's thoughts immediately and inevitably turned to a different criminal solution.

The hostel in Port of Spain now holding Virat's worldly goods was a converted single-family house close to St. James district. The building was two storeys of white painted stucco on brick with a flat roof and low front boundary wall incorporating a metal access gate for pedestrians. Above the ground floor windows and external doors, sun blinds of candy stripe canvas were fixed to the walls and held over the openings on slim brackets. It was a house superior in construction quality (despite the flat roof) and design to its immediate neighbours and the owner's desire for security was displayed in uncoiled lengths of barbed wire fixed to side and rear boundary walls which were of greater height than the front structure. The vestibule inside the front entrance door served as a reception: smooth tiled floor, white walls and ceiling, polished wood counter top doubling as a desk.

Virat's only interest was the counter, or more precisely what lay behind the counter. On returning to the hostel he trudged up to his first floor room to rest and plan ahead; he thought about leaving the room before dawn, robbing the cash register he had noted on a shelf then making his way to the marina. But it was unlikely that cash would be left in the register overnight. No, it would have to be now. He collected his luggage, ensuring nothing was left behind in the room. As he had paid in advance for the room, there would be no problem in reception if he was seen leaving, but he parked his cases by the front entrance and moved back to the desk on the pretext of ordering a taxi just as the proprietor was placing a receipt into the cash register. Virat's plan melted away as he noted the money available would be totally inadequate and not worth his effort. He ordered the taxi while his blood boiled and his anger rose like lava from deep within him. By the time a taxi had returned him to the marina, Virat's ire became an energy directed at retribution and necessity.

ACKNOWLEDGMENTS

My most grateful thanks to Laura and Catherine for editing, proof reading and encouragement.

The heading for Chapter 2, Part Two is taken from 'Sohrab and Rustum' by Matthew Arnold.

About the Author

S R Christie has travelled extensively in the Caribbean. He loves the sounds of the islands. He lives in the south of England where he writes and walks every day.

The second novel in the Jigs Boodoosingh series, *A Silence in the Shadows,* is forthcoming in 2019.

You can contact the author by email at: srchristie3@gmail.com

As you arrive at the end of this book, please consider writing a review for Amazon Books.

Printed in Great Britain
by Amazon